THE FIFTH SCRIPT

ROSS H. SPENCER

DIVERSIONBOOKS

Also by Ross H. Spencer

Kirby's Last Circus
Death Wore Gloves

The Lacey Lockington Series
The Devereaux File
The Fedorovich File

The Chance Purdue Series
The Dada Caper
The Reggis Arms Caper
The Stranger City Caper
The Abu Wahab Caper
The Radish River Caper

Diversion Books
A Division of Diversion Publishing Corp.
443 Park Avenue South, Suite 1008
New York, New York 10016
www.DiversionBooks.com

For more information, email info@diversionbooks.com

First Diversion Books edition March 2015.
Print ISBN: 978-1-62681-958-0
eBook ISBN: 978-1-62681-647-3

The Fifth Script is dedicated to Vic Zileski, who brightened
my murky past — and to Shirley Spencer, who
brightens my murky present.

When all things were just as they seemed,
Man didn't lie, he never schemed,
But, being man, he always dreamed
Of wealth, a kingdom on a hill,
Of power great, then greater still,
Of nations bowing to his will.
Man's want must rapidly exceed
The limits of his honest need
And want, unbridled, turns to greed.
So, man, who plays the role of saint,
Has forged a world of stain and taint
Where all things seem just as they ain't.

—*Monroe D. Underwood*

1

When Lacey Lockington interrupted certain suspicious-appearing negotiations being conducted near the corners of Belmont and Kimball Avenues, a pair of alarmed potential buyers lit out for the Wyoming timberline. Not so in the case of the potential seller, who whipped out a Beretta automatic pistol. Interpreting this as a hostile and threatening act, Lacey Lockington shot the potential seller between the eyes. The .38 slug romped merrily into the twisted recesses of Sapphire Joe Solano's dark little brain, and he toppled from the curb squarely into the path of an overdue Federal Express truck. Sapphire Joe Solano had been an enterprising young heroin hustler, Lacey Lockington was a middle-aging Chicago plainclothes cop.

The incident, being routine as Chicago incidents go, drew minor mention from the news community, the Chicago *Chronicle* ignored it completely, and the Chicago *Morning Sentinel* jumped over it. The Chicago *Morning Sentinel* had spent the better part of three decades fashioning mountains from dung heaps, supporting left-wing political candidates, championing controversial causes, and insisting that the majority is always wrong, an editorial policy that had borne scant harvest in Chicago because Chicago's majority subscribed to the *Chronicle* and Chicago's minority had never learned to read. Nevertheless, the Chicago *Morning Sentinel* made money, *big* money, with its antagonistic, sensationalist marketing of such news as it chose to market, rarely in keeping with public moods, playing the role of devil's advocate to the hilt.

In the instance of Sapphire Joe Solano, the *Sentinel* August 10 edition was quick to admit that "sales of mind-altering chemicals constituted a mushrooming problem within the city;" agreeing that it deserved "immediate and diligent attention;" "*but*", it went on, "an even more insidious and deadly plague was prowling the midnight streets of Chicago." That plague was wanton police violence.

The guidon bearer for the Chicago *Morning Sentinel's* tubthumping safaris was a newspaper woman named Stella Starbright whose five times weekly column, *Stella on State Street*, declared that "some scant measure of human compassion might have been exercised here"—surely a police officer of Lacey Lockington's experience should have been capable of disarming Sapphire Joe Solano, or shooting him in the knee, or doing *some*thing, "Oh, Dear God in Heaven," *anything* short of blasting the back of Solano's head into the middle of North Kimball Avenue. Stella reasoned that Joe Solano had been a product of troubled times, a kid from the wrong side of the tracks who'd never gotten a fair shake at the hands of society; that he'd been a delinquent before he'd left the cradle, and that there was absolutely no record of his having been counselled in *any* fashion by any*body*—aside from an occasional wallop in the mouth with a patrolman's nightstick. The lad could have been turned around, Stella said, but no one had tried because no one had given "two whoops in hell." Then Stella got down to brass tacks. She stated that Detective Sergeant Lacey Lockington might very well be another of those hair-trigger personalities all too often encountered in the ranks of Chicago's law enforcement agencies, one more member of the self-appointed judge, jury, and executioner school.

The term "snakebitten" isn't necessarily confined to the poor bastard who's been nailed in the ankle by a water moccasin. It also applies to the baseball team that can't win for losing; to the housewife who spills the coffee after she's scorched the oatmeal; to the quail hunter whose first shot of the season blows a game warden's balls off. It refers to an inexplicable span of time during which nothing goes right. It's a condition known to all, but there are those among us who seem more vulnerable to the affliction, those with whom it lingers longer, with whom it would appear to be almost chronic. Lacey Lockington was one of these. He was on familiar terms with the malady, knew its early symptoms, and recognized the Sapphire Joe Solano business as a likely beginning for another stretch of snakebite.

Lockington wasn't a prophet, nor was he a fatalist by any stretch of the imagination, but he was fully cognizant of the fact that we are set on an unalterable course for tomorrow, and that most of us get there most of the time. So it was then that Lacey Lockington edged warily into each new day until he came to the tomorrow that saw him kill young Timothy Gozzen.

2

It came about on a sunny Wednesday afternoon in an alley, a few doors south of Diversey Avenue. Timothy Gozzen had snatched a six-year-old girl by the halter of her sunsuit from the seat of her tricycle and dragged the bewildered, screaming tyke into the dilapidated garage of an abandoned dwelling. Lockington, heading back to his West Barry Avenue apartment after a long and fruitless stakeout on Division Street, had taken notice of this burst of activity. He'd braked his aging blue Pontiac Catalina to a tire-smoking halt, unlimbering his .38 police special to sprint down the alley and into the garage. He'd covered Gozzen, Gozzen had dropped the youngster and made a break for it, and Lockington had shot him through the throat, severing the jugular vein.

By and large, the affair drew yawns from the media, but the ever-testy Chicago *Morning Sentinel* was Johnny-at-the-rathole with Stella Starbright waxing tearfully eloquent. She argued that although Timothy Gozzen's intentions had probably added up to something a few degrees south of honorable, *still* it was a matter of irrefutable record that Gozzen had been a mentally disturbed boy, neglected and abused in an impoverished foster home, shunned by classmates, ignored by teachers to whom he'd turned for help. There wasn't a single "smidgen" of doubt—poor nineteen-year-old Timothy Gozzen had been the warped creation, the utterly hapless victim of an apathetic society that had chosen to bury its blunders rather than face up to them.

The entire "barbaric incident" could have been avoided, Stella Starbright opined, had Detective Sergeant Lacey Lockington maintained presence of mind to pursue the unarmed stripling, catch him, overpower him, and turn him over to an appropriate agency for rehabilitation. True, she said, this had been Timothy Gozzen's sixth presumably sexually-slanted brush with the law, but no criminal charges had ever been filed against the lad, and half-a-dozen presumptions do not a conviction make.

It was a lengthy column, taking up nearly half of the *Sentinel's* third page. It pointed out that Lockington had probably been well within the boundaries of his extensive authority, and therein lay the fault—his authority was *too* extensive, virtually limitless, he was in a position to play God, and turning a man of Lockington's obvious leanings loose in such a preserve was closely akin to turning a hungry saber-toothed tiger loose in the corner meat market.

Having checked police records, Stella stated they revealed that Lacey Lockington had killed before, more than once, and he was very good at it. Ah, yes, there was a great deal more to this than met the undiscerning eye. Another criminal lurked in the trash-strewn alleys of America's great cities, one infinitely more dangerous than a regiment of small-time drug peddlers and addled childmolesters. He was the kill-crazy police officer who blew somebody's brains out and asked questions afterward, if indeed he bothered to ask questions at all. There was an overabundance of these rogue cops. Their number was legion, and this unchecked vigilante horde was epitomized in the person of one Chicago Detective Sergeant Lacey Lockington!

Stella Starbright dragged out her crystal ball and made a prediction—a calloused Chicago populace would give Lockington an approving nod for his cold-blooded slaying of the disoriented Timothy Gozzen. And why not, Stella asked, after all, the color line hadn't been violated, a white hadn't murdered a black, nor a black a white, and so long as whites shot whites and blacks shot blacks, and just about everybody shot Puerto Ricans, what did it matter anyway? "Well, Dear God in Heaven," it *did* matter, Stella fumed, it just wasn't all that darned simple. This was a close call, much too close to be glossed over by a perfunctory stamp of public acceptance. She called for immediate civil action against a rabid wolf in the fold and the rapacious jungle element he symbolized.

Her case presented, Stella Starbright popped with her second prophecy of the day—Lacey Lockington would kill again, and again, and probably again. He would kill repeatedly and without just cause; he would kill for the hell of it, for the sheer joy of killing. He would continue to terrorize the City of Chicago until he was brought under control. And when, oh, Dear God in Heaven, *when* would that *be*?

3

Lockington awakened to a cloudy Thursday morning, the taste of the Timothy Gozzen killing still bitter in his mouth. Determined to dwell on the episode as little as possible, he spat it out and phoned the South State Street desk to take two days of his annual leave and spent the early hours of his holiday with the Cider Press Federation.

The Cider Press Federation had been designed to occupy the vast void left by Julie. It had fallen considerably short of its intended purpose but it'd helped just a bit, providing Lockington with a flimsy buffer between himself and reality, and he'd spent innumerable hours immersed in the activities of the six-team baseball circuit. Its play was complicated, controlled by an intricate combination of cards, dice and highly detailed charts, and Lockington had made a policy of turning to the game when memories of Julie swamped his lonely hours.

Of the half-dozen entries in the Cider Press Federation pennant race, Lockington had become attached to the

Pepper Valley Crickets, without knowing why. Certainly, the Crickets didn't have pennant potential—they possessed excellent speed, but their pitching was mediocre at best, they lacked a consistent long ball hitter, and their fielding left much to be desired. Currently mired in fourth place, they trailed the league-leading Delta River Weevils by a dozen games. Bad fortune notwithstanding, Lockington played the Cider Press Federation's season one game at a time, hoping for a Pepper Valley turn-around, exulting in its victories and lamenting its losses. His picking of the Crickets had been a great deal like getting married, he thought—a man just hauls off and does it, then spends the remainder of his days making the best of it. Which was one reason Lockington had never married. There were others, probably, but he'd never looked for them. One was all he'd needed.

He always saved the Pepper Valley games for last, like dessert, and he sat at his kitchen table, rolling dice, flipping cards, checking charts, watching anxiously as the Crickets hung on to win a 6–5 nailbiter over the last place Hades Gulf Freighters, pleased with the triumph and particularly impressed by the performance of Nick Noonan, who'd busted a homer and a brace of doubles to chase in four of Pepper Valley's six runs. Nick Noonan wasn't a great baseball player, he was mediocre at best but he possessed a curious knack for rising to a difficult situation and playing over his head. Lockington could identify with that type of individual, sensing in Noonan a kindred spirit—they were birds of a feather, the paper Pepper Valley shortstop and the flesh and blood Chicago police detective.

He put on his second pot of coffee, bringing the league statistics up to date while it perked, noting with a frown that Nick Noonan led Cider Press Federation shortstops in errors. Well, what the hell, nobody's perfect and he liked Nick Noonan. Whatever Lockington's flaws, there was an indelible streak of loyalty in the man.

The doorbell rang and Lockington left the kitchen table, slouching in response to the summons. Duke Denny stood in the vestibule, sharply dressed as usual—crisp white shirt, beige golf cardigan, fawn slacks, highly-polished two hundred dollar alligator skin loafers—a walking Lucky Strike advertisement if Lockington had ever seen one. Nodding to Lockington, Denny eased into the apartment without invitation. He was a big man, standing better than six-three and weighing 210. He was from someplace in Ohio, thirty-two years old, redheaded, bright green eyed, ruggedly handsome with a quick, white-toothed smile. Single, ambitious, and a devil with the ladies, he'd bitten into Chicago as he'd have bitten into an oversize jelly doughnut—he flat-out *loved* it.

A few years earlier, Denny had been Lockington's partner on the force. Lockington had shown the greenhorn from Ohio the ins and outs of their trade, and if they hadn't shared the entire filthy tapestry, they hadn't missed many threads. They'd waded through street gangs, gambling, juice loans, extortion, whores, narcotics, rapes, murders and the assorted ingredients that made Chicago rotten to the depths of its incurably diseased soul. Denny had saved Lockington's life once and Lockington had returned the favor on a couple of occasions. They'd learned to anticipate each other's moves, and proved a brilliantly effective tandem until Denny quit the force to open his small private investigations agency on West Randolph Street.

Denny had been an exuberantly enthusiastic cop,

believing that the end usually justified the means no matter how drastic, and he'd cut a few fancy corners, quite a few, in fact. But Lockington had swept his partner's minor transgressions under the rug, not wishing to endanger their excellent working relationship by splitting hairs. They'd maintained their connection since the separation—small talk over beer at the Sherwood Tap, reminiscences over dinner at Berghoff's—that *alte kameraden* thing shared by old soldiers, old sewer workers, old whatevers who'd served under the same banners. As a rule, memories hardly matter until men begin to grow old, but Duke Denny was an exception, a young man to whom memories were already precious. He'd dredge up faded experiences from their days together, things that would bring a furtive tear, like the time Lockington had been forced to shoot an old lady's bull terrier when the beast had attacked him without provocation, and Lockington had taken a day off to buy her another. And there'd be chuckles—the night a good-looking North Clark Street whore had bet Duke Denny five dollars that she could rape him, and Denny had lost without putting up so much as a token struggle because her going rate was fifty, and he'd come down with a major league case of gonorrhea which had cost him nearly two hundred.

"I'm off today, Duke," Lockington said as they shook hands.

Denny said, "Yeah, I checked downtown. I got time for a cuppa coffee."

Lockington led the way into the kitchen. He said, "Black?", knowing the answer before he'd asked the question. Denny nodded Yes.

Denny eyed the chaos of Lockington's kitchen table, cluttered with Cider Press Federation paraphernalia, before flopping onto a chair and lighting a cigarette. "How's Pepper Valley doing?" he asked. Since the birth of the Cider Press Federation, Denny had displayed an amused interest in the fortunes of Lockington's favorite make-believe baseball team.

Lockington poured coffee, shrugging. "We're 29 and 31, but we'll come around—we still got a shot at third, maybe even second."

"Delta River's running wild?"

"Yeah, can't miss." He seated himself across from Denny, staring inquisitively at his ex-partner over the chipped rim of his coffee cup. He said, "All right, Duke, what's the shake? You aren't here to run a check on Pepper Valley."

Denny took a noisy slurp of his coffee, making a face. "God Almighty, that's *abominable* stuff—no, I wondered if you'd seen this." He dragged a folded section of the Chicago *Morning Sentinel* from a hip pocket, shoving it to Lockington between the sugar bowl and the salt shaker. "Hot item."

Lockington glanced down at the newspaper. "The *Sentinel?* I don't read that sleazy rag."

"Well, maybe you oughta start—the *Sentinel's* making you a celebrity! Sneak a peek at *Stella on State Street*—Page Three—Stella's always on Page Three, left-hand side."

Lockington unfolded the paper, found the column, skipped hurriedly through it, smothered a yawn, and said, "So what?"

"So *what?* Holy Christ, Lacey, this is her *second* barrage! She got all over your case when you blew Solano away! None of the guys told you about that?"

"Aw, c'mon, Duke—how many cops can read?"

"Maybe you know the tomato—this Stella Starbright."

"I wouldn't know Stella Starbright from a busted bass fiddle, but I know her *type*—she's forty-seven, fat, frumpy, bleached-blonde, watery gray-eyed with capped teeth, an incurable romantic, a born liar, a quick-weeper, and she needs a whole bunch of psychiatric help."

"Well, whatever she is, she sure got a roaring hard-on for *you*!"

"Stella Starbright got a roaring hard-on for the whole damned human race! Just last month she teed off on Johann Gutenberg, then she did a number on Jesus Christ—in the same column, yet!"

"Johann Gutenberg—who's Johann Gutenberg?"

"He invented the printing press."

"That's right—they should have lynched the sonofabitch! Hey, didn't you just tell me that you never read the *Sentinel*?"

"I don't. Gus Markowski was telling me."

"All right, who's Gus Markowski?"

"My barber. He knew all about Johann Gutenberg but he'd never heard of the other guy."

Denny maintained a straight face, shaking his head slowly. He said, "Lacey, you just ain't never gonna change, are you?"

Lockington scowled. "Call it involuntary resistance—I don't cotton to change."

Denny nodded. "Well, neither do I, but a man has to look it in the eye when it shows up. Take me, for example—I stand a damned good chance of losing Moose Katzenbach."

"Moose? Haven't seen him in months. What's with him?"

"He's talking about quitting."

"What for? Don't you two hit it off?"

"Sure, we hit it off, but he keeps yakking about moving

to Brooklyn; something about his brother-in-law buying a gin mill and needing a bartender."

"That isn't Moose talking—that's Helen. You know Helen Katzenbach?"

"No."

"Fine lady. Helen has a bum ticker. She's been talking Brooklyn ever since she got to Chicago. She's a sick woman, Duke—sick people suffer from attacks of nostalgia."

"What*ever*. But if I lose Moose Katzenbach, my ass is in a sling!"

"Run yourself an ad in the *Chronicle*—Chicago's crawling with busted-down gumshoes."

"How about you, Lacey? If Moose checks out would *you* be interested?"

"You can't teach an old dog new tricks."

"You don't need *new* tricks. Hell, you invented all the *old* tricks! I'd sure as hell beat what the City of Chicago's paying you!"

"Naw, Duke. I'm a has-been, stuck with what I got. But thanks, anyway."

"Okay, partner, I figured as much. Well, keep it in mind, just in case."

"I'll do that. More coffee?"

"More coffee and I'll piss from here to Randolph Street." Denny got up, retrieved his hat from the sinkboard, jammed it onto his head at a rakish angle, gave Lockington an affectionate wallop on the shoulder, and went out whistling a bit of "Musetta's Waltz," or a bit of what Lockington *thought* was "Musetta's Waltz." Lockington wasn't much on opera. He preferred ragtime.

He walked to his living room window to watch Denny

pull away in a sparkling black Caddy convertible, peeling rubber. Denny was a big spender, a little man in a large hurry; streetwise but far from all-knowing. And, Lockington had heard stories—Denny was in over his head; Denny was accepting big bucks to handle shabby cases; Denny was cooking his books to stay a jump in front of the IRS. Lockington had shrugged these off as sour grapes from Chicago's unreliable vine. So far as Lockington knew, Duke Denny was doing just dandy. Beyond that, it wasn't what a man *was* that mattered to Lockington, it was what a man was to *Lockington* that mattered, and Denny had always been straight-up with Lockington. About Moose Katzenbach, Lockington remembered him fondly. He'd been Lockington's first partner, a fat, good-natured guy with a heart bigger than all outdoors. He'd blown his physical exam a half dozen times and they'd drummed him out of service. Out of sight, out of mind. He'd have to drop in on Moose one of these days.

Lockington checked the Cider Press Federation schedule, wincing. Pepper Valley would be departing Hades Gulf to move into Bannerville and it'd be tough sledding in Bannerville. The Crickets would be running into Dayton McClure in the series opener, and Dayton McClure was 11–2 with three shutouts and over a hundred strikeouts.

Well, that game would have to wait.

He showered, shaved, slipped into a blue shirt, blue slacks and gray sports coat. He drove to the Shamrock Pub on Grand Avenue where he drank Martell's cognac until he went to bed with Edna Garson, the part-time cashier at Evasheski's Liquor Emporium, a block west on the south side of Grand Avenue. That was where Lockington had met Edna Garson—at Evasheski's Liquor Emporium, back in April.

4

It'd been a bitterly cold and gusty-gray early April afternoon when he'd stopped at Evasheski's Liquor Emporium to pick up a bottle of Martell's cognac. Prowling around for ten minutes, he hadn't been able to locate Martell's, so he'd settled for a quart of Flemish Pride and headed for the checkout counter, narrowly beating a fat woman to the cashier's chute. The fat woman had been carrying a six-pack of Hickory Barrel Ale and she'd tapped Lockington brusquely on the shoulder. She'd said, "Let me go first."

If she'd been a skinny woman, or even a pleasantly plump woman, he'd have said, "Yes, ma'am," and stepped aside, but she'd been fat and since he'd never gotten along with fat women, he'd said, "Why?"

The fat woman's eyes had glinted dangerously. Over the years, Lockington had noticed that fat women's eyes usually glint dangerously. She'd said, "On account of I only got one item."

Lockington had glanced at her six-pack of Hickory

Barrel Ale. He'd said, "Excuse me, but *you* got *six* items—*I* got *one* item."

The fat woman had been joined in line by another fat woman, this one lugging a gallon jug of Old Roma chianti wine. The first fat woman had turned to the second fat woman. She'd said, "There are no more gentlemen!"

The second fat woman's eyes had glinted dangerously. She'd said, "Oh, goddam, ain't it the goddam truth?"

Edna Garson had been perched on a rickety wooden stool at Evasheski's cash register, her buttocks bulging ever so slightly over the seating surface. She'd been reading a paperback copy of *Nine Loves Have I* by Carolyn Bliss, whose real name was probably Ophelia Snodgrass, Lockington had figured. Edna had put her book to one side, ringing up Lockington's purchase, looking him over as she'd punched keys. It'd struck Lockington as being a rather thorough looking over. She'd said, "Haven't I seen you at the Shamrock?"

"I don't know—have you?" Lockington said, knowing that she probably had.

Edna had said, "Do you spend a great deal of time at the Shamrock?"

Lockington had nodded. He'd said, "And a great deal of my paycheck."

Edna had slipped the bottle of Flemish Pride carefully into a slender brown paper bag. She'd said, "You like cognac?"

Lockington had said, "Not really—I'm buying this for the Pope. The Pope likes cognac."

Edna had scratched her upper thigh. It'd been just one helluva upper thigh, in Lockington's estimation. She'd said, "Just where do you intend to gargle this turpentine?"

Lockington had said, "My place." He'd winked at Edna Garson. He'd said, "Unless I get a better offer, of course."

Edna had winked back, handing him his change and meeting his eyes. Edna had unblinking smoky-blue eyes, the kind that convey sincerity in huge gobs, or any number of things, also in huge gobs. She'd said, "I was coming to that. Why not my place?"

"Where's your place?"

Edna had peeked at her watch. She'd said, "I could show you—I get off in a little under twenty-five minutes."

Lockington had said, "I've seen it done in a little under twenty-five seconds."

Edna had nodded, her tongue bulging her cheek. "Possibly, but there's a difference between popguns and cannons, you see."

Lockington had said, "I see."

Edna had said, "Not yet, you don't." She'd run the tip of her tongue slowly across her lower lip. "But seeing is believing."

"Who was it said that?"

"I did."

"Yes, but haven't there been others—Bacon—Wordsworth—Johnson?"

"Well, certainly, but some you remember, and some you don't—there might have been a Johnson."

"Are we talking about the same thing?"

"Probably not, but we can get it straightened out at my place."

The first fat woman had heaved a martyr's sigh. Fat women are very good at heaving martyr's sighs. The second fat woman had shuffled impatiently. She'd said, "What are they doing up there, rewriting the goddam theory of goddam relativity?"

The first fat woman had said, "She mentioned a *cannon*—they could be *terrorists*!"

Sitting in his car in front of Evasheski's Liquor Emporium, waiting for Edna Garson, Lockington had watched the fat women come out. The first fat woman had said, "I *do* believe he was carrying a *gun*!"

The second fat woman had said, "I know goddam well he was, I *saw* the goddam thing!" She'd heaved a martyr's sigh. "Where are the goddam cops when we need them?"

5

Hitting the feathers with Edna Garson wouldn't have earned Lacey Lockington a great deal of space in the *Guinness Book of Records*—Edna Garson knew what mattresses were for. She was an upbeat woman possessed by an unflagging zest for life and all its trimmings. She wasn't beautiful, far from it—her ski-jump nose was slightly askew, her cheek bones were too high and too prominent, her mouth was too wide, her jaw too resolute, but she had those wonderful, fetching, smoky-blue eyes, she was damned attractive, and she knew it.

Edna's willowy contours belied her thirty-seven years, her dazzling shock of honey-blonde hair was identifiable from a quarter-mile's distance, her skin was whipped cream smooth and sun-stained to gold, her tailored slacks clung to the more important creases of her exquisite body with magnetic tenacity, and her free-striding saunter had been responsible for more traffic accidents than any six-inch snowfall in Chicago's history.

She had round heels, she made no secret of the fact,

and on a scale of ten, the bedroom Edna Garson had been awarded a multitude of fifteens. Edna was a thoroughly-educated, highly-skilled sexual technician—she savored men, she devoured them, and she discarded them with gleeful gusto. But she hadn't dropped Lockington, not yet. Since that March afternoon at Evasheski's Liquor Emporium, they'd spent considerable time together, not all of it in bed, their brief relationship blossoming into more than could have been stuffed between a set of Edna's discount-store sheets.

That she'd developed something for Lacey Lockington was readily apparent to the most casual of observers, if Edna Garson had any casual observers. When they'd sit talking in a Shamrock Pub back booth, she'd touch him constantly, her fingertips brushing the backs of his hands, her alert smoky-blue eyes growing dreamy, her knowing smile dissolving into a wispy thing bordering on the naïve, her saucy, Chicago-style banter fading to be replaced by the gentle tones of a sister of the church.

They'd discuss a variety of subjects, most of them inconsequential, their conversations amounting to irrelevancy stacked upon irrelevancy. They'd take turns at defending indefensible positions, arriving at no firm conclusions whatsoever, but enjoying the trip nonetheless. They'd tease as lovers sometimes do once firmly established as residents of that blindly blissful state—Lockington would remark that Edna's lipstick was smeared, demanding an immediate explanation, and she'd fake a yawn, responding that she'd taken the entire Pepper Valley baseball team to bed, and Lockington would ask if it'd been a rewarding experience and she'd say, Oh, yes, downright mindboggling despite the fact that Nick Noonan had been a lousy lay.

It'd continue along such lines until around midnight when, with the late workers pouring in and the juke box being turned up to ear-splitting volume, they'd walk the half-dozen doors east to Edna's second-story Grand Avenue apartment where Lockington would sit on Edna's sagging blue corduroy-covered living room couch, smoking, nursing a glass of Martell's, watching Edna peel to the skin, save for her open-toed spike-heeled pumps, because a naked woman in spike-heeled pumps has a helluva lot more appeal than a barefooted naked woman, and Edna was aware of this.

It was a leisurely business, Edna draping her clothing over the back of the couch, studying him as she stripped, measuring her effect with experienced smoky-blue eyes before sitting beside him to share his glass of Martell's.

It'd become a ritual, prefacing those moments when they'd chat about where they'd been and how they'd gotten to where they were, a treadmill colloquy that whiled away their cognac period. Lockington would glance at Edna's lithe, tawny body, biding his time, anticipating that which he knew would come, making no move until she'd pop to her feet, taking his hand to lead him into her bedroom, and shortly after the lights had gone out she'd observe that their doing this—"oh, God, Locky, *Locky!*—seemed such a—*there, that's* it!, that's it!—perfectly natural thing—do it, Locky, for Christ's sake, *do* it to me!—didn't he—now, Locky, now, *now, NOW!*—agree?"

And Lockington, who'd never dwelled on the subject at great length, would struggle to regain his breath because Edna Garson was eleven years his junior and she possessed a sexual master's degree plus the stamina of a race horse, and he'd mumble Yes, certainly he agreed, having only the foggiest conception of what he was agreeing to, doubting

Edna's veracity and his own because, after all, they were big city people and big city people rarely mean what they say, just their saying it tends to suffice. He'd put these fuzzy exchanges down as attempts to justify what they'd just done and, later, with his face buried in her sweet-smelling shaggy mop of yellow hair and her breath hot on his chest, he'd drift in the general direction of sleep, rationalizing that what they'd just done wasn't in dire need of justification—if it hadn't been completely moral it certainly hadn't been illegal, they hadn't hurt anybody. It'd happened before and it'd happen again, with each other and with God knew whom, and he'd wonder if these efforts to defend their lust didn't indicate something beyond the ordinary, since ordinary lust requires no flowery epilogues nor does it seek them.

It was an excellent affair, as affairs go, typical of its time and location, a thing of understanding that defied understanding, a substantive thing devoid of substance, a demanding thing that made no demands, and it would cross Lockington's mind that at sometime during the progress of their arrangement he *must* have lied to her, and he'd hope to Almighty God that he had, because if he *hadn't* it was twenty, ten and even that he'd fallen in love with Edna Garson, and that was a position Lockington wasn't anxious to occupy. He'd been in love, and he'd experienced the agonies of withdrawal.

During the dawn of Friday, August 17, Lockington sat on the edge of Edna Garson's bed, listening to her contented breathing, smoking his wake-up cigarette, considering his recent case of snakebite. It appeared to be healing, but there is no trusting appearances, as Richard Brinsley Sheridan said.

Unfortunately, Lacey Lockington had never heard of Richard Brinsley Sheridan.

6

There are thoughts that come unwanted and unannounced, they come like locusts, blackening the green fields of a man's mind, ripping, devouring. There is no putting them off, and no dealing with them. So it was with Detective Sergeant Lacey Lockington and his thoughts in a booth of a little Italian restaurant on Barry Avenue during a rainy Sunday evening in Chicago.

She'd slipped into his life some eight months earlier, a slender shaft of sunlight piercing the gloom of a darkened room. It'd been December, a week prior to Christmas, and Lockington had been coming home from the Shamrock Pub's Christmas party at twelve-fifteen in the morning in the middle of a driving snow storm, half lit-up, singing "Beautiful Dreamer" at the top of his lungs, "Beautiful Dreamer" having had nothing whatsoever to do with the Christmas season, but Lockington had felt like singing something at the top of his lungs, and "Beautiful Dreamer" had been the first thing to cross his mind, meshing with his sentimental mood.

The storm had been sweeping the city like a great white broom, visibility had been twenty feet at best, and Lockington had taken a side street, cutting north from Grand Avenue to Barry, an inadvisable move that he wouldn't have made had he been sober because any Chicagoan knows that you should stay the hell off the side streets when it's snowing. In Chicago the main thoroughfares get plowed when they get around to it, the side streets never, ever, ever.

And there she'd been, smack-dab in the middle of the street, trying to start a 1979 Mercury that wouldn't start, her lights growing dimmer with every unsuccessful attempt. There'd been no way to get around the Mercury, cars had lined both sides of the street, there'd been a parking place or two but nothing large enough to let him slip past, he'd have had to back up three-quarters of a block to avail himself of another street route, so he'd taken his flashlight and walked to the stricken Mercury to find her hunched over the steering wheel, her parka hood over her head, and above the weakening grind of the starter he could hear her cussing a long bright-blue streak, employing words that Lockington would have hesitated to use at a longshoremen's convention. He'd knocked on the Mercury's window, she'd spun to stare out at him and snarl, "Get the hell away from this automobile or I'll call the police!"

Lockington had said, "But, ma'am, I am the police!"

He'd pulled his wallet and spotted his badge with the flashlight, and she'd said, "All right, dammit, then do something."

Lockington had said, "Pull your hood release."

She'd said, "But—"

Lockington had said, "Please, ma'am, don't argue with me—pull your hood release, will you?"

She'd complied and Lockington had popped the latch and hoisted the hood, leaning under it, exploring the intestines of the Mercury with the aid of his flashlight. The hood had come down with a crash, slamming Lockington in the back of the neck, driving his face into the battery. Lockington had fought his way clear of the entrapment. He'd said, "Jesus H. Christ, guillotined at midnight! Why didn't you tell—"

"I tried to tell you—that damned hood just won't stay up!"

Lockington had appraised the situation and said, "Look, can you navigate this thing with no power steering?"

"But I have *power steering!*"

"You won't have power steering with the engine conked out. Can you handle it?"

"I can try. *Why?*"

"Then maybe I can nudge you into that parking space just ahead with my car."

"That won't get me home!" She'd been dark-eyed with a fairly prominent nose that was running in the cold, more than could have been said for her automobile. Lockington had said, "Ma'am, first things first—we have to start somewhere, don't we?"

They'd gotten it done after a fashion—the traction had been poor, the Pontiac's rear wheels had spun, its tires had screamed and smoked, and she'd had a terrible time maneuvering the Mercury without the aid of power steering. They'd left her car at the curb, more or less, its rear end protruding into the street at a dangerous angle and she'd gotten out, locking the door, saying, "Okay, now what?"

"Now we get to a telephone. There's a tavern just around the corner on Barry."

"I'll never get help in a storm at this time of night, and you know it!"

Lockington had spread his hands defenselessly. "Well, ma'am, if we don't give it a shot, we'll never be sure, will we?"

When she'd piled into the Pontiac he'd noticed that she had very good legs, and he'd driven her to Barry Avenue and a small neighborhood drinking place. He'd bought her a rum and coke, he'd ordered a Martell's cognac, they'd called a dozen towing services with no luck, and they'd sat in a booth looking at each other. She'd been *pleasant enough to look at, early thirties maybe, he'd liked her chestnut hair, rumpled by the hood of her parka, and he'd approved of the set of her dimpled chin. Above all, he'd appreciated her smile, a frank, open thing, when she'd finally gotten around to smiling, which had been during her second rum and coke. She'd shivered from the chill still in her, and she'd said, "Pardon me, but aren't you slightly drunk?"*

"Slightly."

"No problem with that—so am I. I was at a Christmas party."

"So was I. I could probably drive you home. Where do you live?"

"Des Plaines."

Lockington had whistled, and she'd said, "Long way in a blizzard, isn't it?"

"That's not all—you'd have to get back to your car in the morning."

She'd shrugged a dismal shrug. "So here I am at square one. Any suggestions?"

"Just one."

Her second smile had been every bit as good as her first, but it'd been of the knowing variety. She'd said, "Your place?"

Lockington had nodded.

She'd dropped her head, laughing. She'd said, "Oh, Jesus, am I ever easy!"

Lockington had said, "Well, look, I'll sleep on the couch."

She'd said, "The hell you will."

"Then you'll sleep on the couch."

"The hell I will."

7

Three hours later, he lurched to his feet, paid his tab, tipped his waitress, and headed back to his apartment. The rain had stopped but the respite would be brief because there was a stiff breeze out of the west. Muted thunder mumbled from that direction, and Chicago's night sky was a mass of writhing black clouds, reminding Lockington of a vast snake pit, a strange collation, since Lockington had never seen a snake pit, and he was glad for this because, the way his luck had been running, he'd probably have fallen into the damned thing headfirst.

He plodded homeward on the south side of Barry Avenue, picking his way through a maze of sidewalk puddles, staying close to buildings in an effort to avoid the spray from eastbound vehicles, passing a darkened shop doorway from which stepped a pair of Hispanics, sharply dressed young fellows, mid-twenties or thereabouts. Their white-toothed smiles were ingratiating. They could use a few bucks, they told Lockington.

Lockington took the revelation under consideration and said well, this was probably true, but then couldn't just about everybody?

The Hispanics said *sí, quizá*, but apparently Lockington was overlooking one highly-compelling factor—just about everybody didn't possess switchblade knives like theirs. They showed their switchblade knives to Lockington. They were expensive switchblade knives, chrome-trimmed, bone-handled with white plastic inlays; their blades glittering menacingly in the pinkish glow of the only streetlight on the block.

Lockington nodded. Magnificent, utterly magnificent, he said.

Ciertamente, the Hispanics said before inquiring as to how Lockington would like to have one of their utterly magnificent switchblade knives inserted in his *vientre boton*.

Lockington wasn't on speaking terms with the Spanish language, but he managed to interpret enough of the question to grasp its meaning, and he was duly impressed by the ramifications thereof. He was so duly impressed by the ramifications thereof that he hauled out his .38 police special and shot the Hispanics, one through the liver, the other through the left lung.

He stepped carefully over his twitching, groaning extormenters, retracing his steps to the little Italian restaurant where he telephoned the police, ordered another bottle of beer, and stepped into the men's lavatory. Following his first ten or twelve bottles, beer had a habit of going through Lockington like Grant tore through Richmond, although Lockington didn't know for a fact that Grant had ever been within fifty miles of Richmond. He had only his old

American history book's word for it—history is written by the winners—and Lockington had flunked American History three times running.

8

Monday's Chicago *Morning Sentinel* hit the streets with a bang—KILLER COP STRIKES AGAIN, SLAYS TWO! Gone were Stella Starbright's flowery phrases, Stella got right at it—the Hispanic kids could have been talked out of their aborted mugging attempt had Sergeant Lacey Lockington quieted his itchy trigger-finger long enough to appeal to their better natures. There was absolutely no excuse for an off-duty, thrice-decorated Chicago police officer gunning down two underprivileged lads in the flower of their manhood without making an honest effort to dissuade them. It was a hard-hitting column in which Stella branded Lacey Lockington as a man with two more notches in the handle of his gun, a creature driven by an irresponsible Dodge City mentality, prone to gross violence, a born exterminator, undoubtedly an incurable psychopath, and she concluded her terse piece by recommending that Lockington be suspended pending a painstaking investigation of his having transformed Chicago's northwest side into a shooting gallery. When, Stella

Starbright demanded to know, "Oh, Dear God in Heaven," *when* would some form of corrective action be taken?

Lockington, whose aging torso bore several switchblade scars accumulated in police service, was oblivious to Stella Starbright's third broadside—he didn't read the Chicago *Morning Sentinel,* he rarely read the Chicago *Chronicle* save for its excellent sports section, and he avoided as many television newscasts as were avoidable. He was a man fed up with reports of prissy-assed, self-serving congressional investigating committees telling military people how to conduct military affairs, he was weary of left-leaning, publicity-grabbing press piranhas boosting themselves to national star status by constantly harassing officials of state under the protective blanket of wanting to know the truth. The media angered Lockington greatly. Lockington was a conservative.

And so was Chicago Police Superintendent Nelson G. Netherby, to an extent—to a greater extent when the pendulum of public opinion swung pronouncedly in that direction, to a lesser extent when it didn't. Nelson G. Netherby was demogogically flexible, rolling with the tides, reading both *Sentinel* and *Chronicle,* never missing a television news program, keeping a finger on the pulse of politically sensitive issues local and national, particularly local. Netherby was a political creature with lofty political ambitions, gifted with the acutely responsive devices visited upon that vile and despicable breed, and the panels of his early warning systems were lighting up like Christmas trees. A storm was brewing here, a crusade was in the formative stages—that muckraking Chicago *Morning Sentinel* and its rabble-rousing Stella Starbright were out there in the concrete jungle, beating the drums, whipping up controversy where there was no controversy to be whipped up, gathering a posse, and posses must be cut off at the pass. Chicago Police Superintendent Nelson G. Netherby knew something about the interception of posses.

9

On the hazy Monday morning following his four-day break, Lockington sat straddling a splintered brown locker room bench, smoking a cigarette and sucking on a cup of atrocious coffee while awaiting muster and assignment. Chances were they'd send his ass back to Division Street, there to sit in the tail end of a stuffy Chevy van across the street from a run-down tavern he'd never set foot it, peering through a rusty chink, awaiting the arrival of a man he'd never laid eyes on who'd probably skipped to Emlenton, Pennsylvania, three months ago, and this would go on and on until somebody filled Grand Canyon with potato chips or Christ returned to set up His earthly kingdom, whichever came first. Well, what the hell, as long as he was doing that, he wouldn't be doing anything else. There was a heavy clomping out in the hall and the bulk of Officer Kevin O'Malley darkened the locker room doorway. O'Malley boomed, "Hey, Lacey, you in here?"

Lockington peered around the corner of a row of

battered olive-drab lockers. He said, "I'll let you know when I finish this coffee."

Kevin O'Malley said, "Super wants to see you in his office."

Lockington growled, "When?"

"Like pronto—he's probably gonna give you the fucking *croix de guerre.*"

Lockington frowned, checked his watch, tossed his coffee container into a trash can, and drove over there, reaching the dim, dingy foyer of the rapidly deteriorating three-story red brick building at 8:00 on the button. The Police Superintendent's suite was off a dusty blue-carpeted east wing hall and Lockington stopped at the receptionist's desk. He said, "Okay to go in? I got an appointment."

Henrietta Mosworth glanced up from a check list she'd been perusing, putting it down to study Lacey Lockington as she'd have studied a pile of steaming moose manure. She smiled the smile of a vampire in a blood bank. She nodded, rasping, "Oh, brother, do you *ever!* Certainly, hurry right in!"

There'd been a marked absence of cordiality in his dealings with Henrietta Mosworth since he'd nixed her explicit proposition of a few weeks earlier. He hadn't *nixed* it, exactly, he'd attempted to step around it. He'd told Henrietta that he had a ticket for the White Sox game that night. Henrietta's mouth had tightened at the corners. She'd said, "All right, tomorrow night then?"

Lockington, beginning to get that hemmed-in feeling, had said, "That'd be just great, but, oddly enough, I got a ticket for tomorrow night's White Sox game, too."

Henrietta Mosworth's eyes had glittered like little stainless steel ball bearings. She'd said, "You really dig baseball, don't you, Lacey?"

Lockington had said, "Yeah, great game, baseball—very scientific!"

Henrietta had said, "Well, you lying sonofabitch, you'd better take a look at a schedule—the fucking White Sox are in fucking *Seattle*!"

Lockington, a Chicago Cubs fan who'd known less about the Chicago White Sox than he'd known about nuclear fission, had said, "Oh," not knowing what else to say to a woman who stood six-one, weighed 233, and was said to trim her pubic hair with shrubbery shears.

Now he entered the lair of the mighty, removing his hat to approach Chicago Police Superintendent Nelson G. Netherby who sat behind a highly polished Philippine mahogany desk nearly the size of a carrier flight deck, tilting in his tall-backed genuine Corinthian leather swivel chair, watching Lockington with wary eyes. Netherby was a graying, florid-faced man, heavyset, pompous, an ex-bird Colonel in Army Military Police, a brassbound martinet by any standards. He had the visage of a bereaved water buffalo, the temperament of an arthritic bull crocodile, and the authoritative mien of a Roman emperor. He glanced briefly at the small note pad on his desk blotter and snapped, "Detective Sergeant Lacey Lockington?"

Lockington nodded, saying nothing, coming to the position of parade rest, his hat held behind him.

Netherby yawned, put a Zippo lighter to a cork-tipped cigarette, exhaled loudly, and suspended Lockington on the spot.

Lockington wanted to know what the hell for.

For transforming Chicago's northwest side into a

shooting gallery, Netherby told him.

Lockington wanted to know for how the hell long.

Until the painstaking investigation, Netherby told him.

Lockington wanted to know what the hell painstaking investigation.

The painstaking investigation of Lockington's transforming Chicago's northwest side into a shooting gallery, Netherby told him, dismissing the veteran detective with a perfunctory wave of a pudgy hand.

Lockington stood there, a Niagara roar in his ears, struggling to absorb the impact of the pronouncement, counting his years as a police officer, watching Nelson G. Netherby's overstuffed person half-dissolve into a strange reddish haze, not knowing whether to laugh, weep or blow Netherby's brains out. He ruled against these options, choosing the last available course of action, that of turning to depart the premises without a word or a backward glance.

Netherby drew a relieved deep breath. When dealing with these Dodge City mentalities a man hardly knew what to expect. He smoothed his silvering hair with the palm of one beautifully manicured hand, straightening his pale blue silk necktie with the other, a wisp of a smile fluttering across his sagging features. So much for Stella Starbright and her posse.

The great man pushed an intercom button, instructing Henrietta Mosworth to arrange a hurry-up luncheon press conference—at Cindy's on Wells Street, he said—12:30, he said—the Wicker Room, if possible, he said—he'd be making an announcement having to do with the Lockington matter, he said—oh, yes, the meal, well, let's see, he'd have beef barley soup, artichoke salad with vinegar and oil, a small filet medium well, buttered carrot discs, baked potato with sour cream, strawberry cheesecake, and black coffee with a double brandy, he said. *Good* brandy, he added.

Meanwhile, Lacey Lockington was driving northwest to the Shamrock Pub on Grand Avenue where he hoisted numerous hookers of tequila before going to bed with Edna Garson, which was unusual because Lockington hardly ever drank tequila.

10

His Tuesday had been pleasantly uneventful, and Wednesday morning found Lockington, unshowered, unshaven, still clad in pajama bottoms, frayed robe, and worn-out slippers, seated at his living room window, chain-smoking, drinking strong black coffee, watching pigeons peck at gravel along the Barry Avenue curbing. He'd received a telephone call shortly after eight o'clock—a local television station wanting to interview him for its evening news presentation. His sleep rudely shattered, Lacey Lockington had declined that honor with as much charity as he'd been capable of mustering under the conditions. There hadn't been a great deal of it.

The jackals were grouping now. Lockington's days as a Chicago police officer were numbered, that was an obviosity, if there was such a word. Since Nelson G. Netherby had assumed office some eighteen months earlier, investigations of the type confronting Lockington had been fixed—Netherby dictating verdicts long before they were officially arrived at. The procedures had been given an appearance of authenticity by the retention of traditional trappings—the highly-publicized selections of blue-ribbon panels, the haggling, the haranguing, the disputes, but the proof was in the pudding—not a single verdict had gone in favor of the accused. To the discerning eye there was no disguising it—the mavericks, or those perceived as such, were being systematically cut from the herd, branded as unfit, displayed as pariahs in this, the brave new era of sweetness, light, and gross permissiveness. Lockington saw his chances of acquittal as approximating those of a crippled rabbit at a timberwolf reunion.

Three months back, Matt Ryan had been canned for busting the jaw of a prominent alderman in a Wilson Avenue brothel. Two weeks earlier, Ace Webster had gotten the axe on charges of driving his police vehicle sideways into the rear end of Cardinal Tom Keough's brand-new Mercedes-Benz in the parking lot of Economy Liquors, this at a time when Ace Webster had been working on a bowl of chili at Mexican Joe's across the street. And on Monday last, Mule Merriam had been booted off the force for hopping into bed with the wife of a city councilman, the matter exacerbated when the cuckolded councilman had opened fire on the fleeing Merriam, blasting a hole in the radiator of an approaching sanitation department truck. The good old days were gone—the situation had degenerated to the point where a Chicago cop could be fired for scratching his balls in his own bathtub.

There was however one bright splinter protruding from the wreckage of Lockington's police career, bright only by contrast to the gloomy bulk of the ruins, but a notch better than nothing—his suspension hadn't been without pay, the usual sop thrown to those about to be pink-slipped, and he'd have a measure of adjustment time, possibly as long as six weeks, before his dismissal went into the books. Beyond that projection, Lockington's future was far too dim to contemplate—he'd been a cop for more than fifteen years, and police procedures were virtually all he knew. But there'd be severance pay, he'd receive six months of Illinois unemployment compensation, his pension fund would be available in a lump sum, and while he wouldn't be eating particularly high on the hog, it'd be a while before he starved to death.

The Wednesday morning was dismal, quite cool for a Chicago August, gray, damp, with billowing black clouds mushrooming ominously to the southwest of the city. If there wasn't rain, he'd probably accomplish something of breathtaking consequence later in the day, providing he could find something of breathtaking consequence to accomplish. Lockington considered his potential for breathtakingly consequential accomplishment and smiled wryly, hoping to Christ that there'd be rain.

He watched a silver Toyota Cressida ease to a halt in front of his apartment building to spook the pigeons of Barry Avenue, sending them flapping northward to Belmont Avenue. A great grayish glob of pigeon dung splashed audibly against his window pane, sticking there, partially obscuring his view of the thirtyish young lady who departed the expensive Japanese automobile to prance primly to the sidewalk. She was five-six or so, dark-haired, dark-eyed, and cuter than a termite's nightshirt. She was pert-nosed, full red-lipped, jutting-breasted, narrow-waisted, slim-hipped, long-legged, and she moved with the fluid grace of a young jungle cat. She wore a gauzy powder blue blouse with a navy blue tie at its collar, a pleated, short navy blue skirt with powder blue belt, three-inch-heeled powder blue pumps with navy blue bows at the toes, and she carried a large powder blue handbag, a beautifully harmonizing outfit that'd set her back a few shekels, if Lockington was any judge of female apparel and its accessories.

She paused on the vestibule step, a hand on a hip, gazing around the area, a once-neat, quiet, middle-class neighborhood that had begun to follow the rest of the city down the drain. Her brief scrutiny completed, she entered the building and in a moment Lockington's bell sounded. He squelched his cigarette before leaving his chair to open the door. He said, "Not today, ma'am—no magazines, please."

Her smile was quick, her upper lip curling over white teeth, one of which was attractively slightly out of line, Lockington noticed. She said, "Lockington—Mr. Lacey Lockington?" Her voice was husky, possibly a trifle too throaty for the slightness of her build, but Lockington liked it. It belonged, he thought, in a darkened bedroom between satin sheets—*black* satin sheets, and that got him to wondering if they'd ever manufactured black satin sheets. He decided that they hadn't—black would prove too vulnerable to leakage and spillage. The lady at the door was repeating herself—"Mr. Lacey Lockington?"

Lockington nodded, squinting quizzically at his visitor, and she went by him and into his apartment before he could stop her. She'd been quicker than a mongoose, and Lockington turned slowly from the door to face her. He said, "Lockington's just an alias, you understand. Another is Jack the Ripper."

She threw back her head and laughed, a fetching mannerism in Lockington's opinion—he'd always admired women who'd thrown back their heads when they'd laughed, especially when their laughs had been light and tinkly like the sound of a brook, as hers had been. She said, "Oh, really? My *gracious,* you must be terribly *old!*"

Lockington said, "Right about now, you don't know the half of it."

She said, "Perhaps not, but I learn rather quickly," and Lockington took her word for it, watching her sit on the arm of his overstuffed chair. She didn't *sit*—she *perched* there, long legs dangling, crossed at slender ankles—chorus girl legs, as Lockington saw them, delicate ankles—there was a fragile silver slave bracelet adorning one. "By the way, Mr. Lockington, may I come in?" she said, her lilting laugh floating through the shabby apartment.

Lockington said, "Suit yourself," kicking the door shut behind them and slumping on his sofa.

She said, "Are your neighbors aware of your identity?"

"Do they know that I'm Jack the Ripper?"

"No, do they know that you're Lacey Lockington?"

"I'd imagine that they do—I've lived here for thirteen years."

"And they aren't afraid?"

"Of what?"

"Of getting shot, of course."

Lockington sighed, fumbling for a cigarette in his robe pocket, finding one, firing it up. He raised his eyes to meet hers—they were large brown eyes, he observed, and they sparkled mischievously. He said, "Uhh–h–h, looky, ma'am, before this goes any further—"

She threw up her hands, cutting him off. "I know, I *know*—who am I, *what* am I, what the hell am I doing here right?"

"This could be your day to play the lottery."

She was frowning—not severely—a semi-frown, Lockington would have called it. She said, "All right, I'm a whore—after a fashion."

"Out of want or out of need?"

"What's the difference? If you're a whore, you're a whore."

"That's a rather unworldly opinion and you aren't a whore."

"Well, not *that* sort of whore, for God's sake!"

Lockington blew smoke in her direction. "Honey, we're *all* whores, every damned one of us. What sort of whore *are* you?"

She avoided the challenge of his stare, her eyes dropping to study the bows of her pumps. She cleared her throat self-consciously. "Well, you see, Mr. Lockington, I say things that aren't true—things that I *know* aren't true—things that I don't mean—and I get paid for doing it." She spread her hands, palms up. "Which makes me a whore wouldn't you think?"

"Probably not. A whore can hang onto to her integrity—a liar can't."

She rolled her eyes ceilingward. "Oh, Dear God, the semantics, the *semantics*!" It'd have been an excellent spot for her silvery laugh but she held it in check.

"All right, you're into politics. At what level—precinct —ward?"

"No, I'm not into politics—well, yes, possibly— indirectly, I suppose—but just occasionally, by coincidence."

"There was a politician's response, if I've ever heard one."

"You dislike politicians?"

"Not all of them."

"Why not all of them?"

"Because I don't know all of them." He was thinking that she might be a plant, one of Netherby's Internal Affairs gestapo, sent to clinch the case against him by tacking on a charge of attempted rape, or something equally ridiculous— heresy, perhaps, or counterfeiting, or attempting to dry up Lake Michigan.

She was saying, "Okay, I'm a journalist. How's that?"

Lockington's scowl was dark. "Well, it ain't good, but at your age there could still be hope."

She was pivoting on tight buttocks, slipping downward from the arm of the overstuffed chair to its cushion, like an otter into water, Lockington thought—not a ripple. He'd caught a flash of a navy blue half-slip. That'd make her panties powder blue, probably. He liked her spunky approach, her chipper personality, but he was beginning to experience grave misgivings about having permitted her to walk into his apartment—he was in enough trouble already, but she was *in* and the trick would be to get her *out,* short of *throwing* her out. These were perilous times—a man could get sued for next to nothing.

She was smoothing her skirt, leaning forward, brown eyes flashing. She said, "Mr. Lockington, I'm here to apologize—I'm late, I know—I should have come a couple of weeks ago."

Lockington sat on his living room couch, elbows on his knees, head cradled in his hands, face expressionless, weary eyes riveted to the faded pattern of his brown carpeting, a new line of thought weaving its way into his thought processes—he might have a tiger by the tail here, she might be a wacko. In his fifteen years of police service, Lockington had learned one thing well—all of the Chicago area loonies weren't confined to mental institutions, there were more of them out than in. He'd encountered his share of unapprehended crackpots and he knew the warning signs, one of the surest being a strange ability to construct imaginary platforms of reference capable of supporting kaleidoscopic networks of illusory injustices—rudimentary paranoia. But the human mind was a labyrinth with as many dead ends as thruways, and there were innumerable variations of the basic disease, at least one of these causing its victim to behold himself as offender rather than offended. Lockington hadn't dug into the self-accusatory bracket, nor did he intend to, but there existed a solid possibility that he'd just run into one of its prime exhibits. This female was wound to the limit, one more turn of the key and she'd fly to pieces like a two-dollar wristwatch. If she wasn't riding some sort of chemical high, she'd probably gone over the wall of the nearest funny farm. They'd never set eyes on each other, yet here she was, claiming that she was two weeks overdue with her apology. Obviously she wasn't playing with a full deck, and it was imperative that he proceed with extreme caution until he could distract her long enough to get to his bedroom telephone. Guardedly, Lockington said, "Apologize—apologize for *what*?"

She said, "We'll come to that shortly."

"That'll be fine." Lockington's tone was cajoling—he didn't know what the hell was in that big powder blue handbag.

She gulped in a deep breath, sitting erect, squaring her shoulders. She chirped, "Well, here goes—my *real* name is Erika Elwood."

Lockington nodded an approving nod. "Erika Elwood— Erika Elwood—yes, it has a nice ring, but I fail to associate it with anything that comes readily to mind. Uhh–h–h, how many names do you have, Miss Elwood?"

"Erika, please—you may call me Erika."

"All right, thank you, Erika. Now about your names— just how many, would you say?" She could be one of those quintuple-identity schizophrenics—Sunday school teacher, wild animal trainer, corporation executive, three-dollar prostitute, and hatchet murderess. Lockington eyed the big powder blue handbag. It'd hold a hatchet, sure as hell.

Erika Elwood said, "How many? Oh, just two. The other isn't mine, of course—I just *use* it, you see."

"Uh-huh—and for what purposes do you use this other name?"

Her eyes locked his. Very slowly, very clearly, she said, "I write for the Chicago *Morning Sentinel,* Mr. Lockington— under the name of 'Stella Starbright.'"

11

A silence pervaded Lacey Lockington's cluttered apartment on Barry Avenue—an awesome silence, vast, dense, profound, a silence to be encountered at the grave of Almighty God, and when Lockington ran a thumbnail along his grizzled jowl, the sound was not unlike that of a fifty-ton bulldozer plowing through seventy-five acres of rusty scrap iron. His visitor was saying, "Mr. Lockington, you must understand that coming here has been extremely difficult for me."

Lockington yawned. He'd been wrong—she wasn't an escaped mental patient, and he should have been relieved because now there'd be no sirens, no padded wagons, no men in white coats, no explanations to make, but he *wasn't* relieved. Crazy or not, he'd found himself rather liking the brown-eyed intruder in the silver Japanese automobile—she'd been amusing company and damned good to look at, and if they'd thrown a straitjacket on her and taken her away, he'd probably have visited her in Dunning or Elgin, or wherever, but this was a horse of another color. Her husky voice dispelled his thoughts—"Very well, *ignore* me—I suppose you feel that you *should,* and that's understandable, but, dammit, it took *courage* to bring me here—courage and a sincere desire to set this matter straight with you!" There was a quaver in her voice, but she wasn't about to weep, not Erika Elwood—Erika Elwood was pissed-off.

Lockington said, "Sorry, but my string ensemble is playing a gig in Baltimore."

She snapped from the overstuffed chair to her feet, brown eyes blazing, jaw set, fingernails digging into the soft blue leather of her handbag. "All right, I should have known better, but I've done what I came to do—I've made my apology, and I'll be boiled in oil if I'll kiss your ass! Good *morning,* Mr. Lockington!"

Lockington raised a detaining hand. "Aw, don't be that way! Why deprive an old man of an education? I've always wondered just what makes you newspaper bastards tick. Tell me about it."

She nodded curtly, throwing herself petulantly back into her chair, one slender leg tucked under her, her flare-up subsiding, the stridency leaving her voice. She said, "What makes us newspaper bastards tick? The same things that make you cop bastards tick—paychecks, no more, no less."

Lockington said, "Same holds true for assassins, doesn't it?"

"Oh, absolutely—we're all whores—*your* words, not *mine!*" She'd heard the bugle, and a trace of battle fever still sizzled in her eyes.

Lockington said, "That point's been established, but you get paid no matter *what* kind of trash you write, so why the banzai attack on a busted-down cop—and why the hearts and flowers for the scum of the earth?"

"That's my job."

"Some job—distortion of facts, blowing them clear the hell out of proportion!"

"It's a living."

"You do-gooders frost my ass—and *you*, you in *particular*—a *woman*, a *beautiful* woman who's fair game for these reptiles, *defending* the bastards! Why, in this town, you could lose your purse *and* your cherry before you get around the next corner!"

Her laugh was brittle. "My purse, yes."

"You know where I'm coming from! I'd think that you'd be *applauding* the police, not *denigrating* them! What's *with* the press?"

"I *do* applaud the police, Mr. Lockington, but not on paper."

"Yeah, you applaud! I'll bet you go around cutting hoses at five-alarm fires!"

"Don't *lecture* me, dammit! I know how it *looks*—now may I tell you how it *is?*"

"By all means." Lockington's fury was spent.

"Listen to me, please—the views I profess to espouse in the *Sentinel* are in no way related to the values I cherish!" She was underlining her words with quick gestures, driving them home like they were tacks. "The Stella Starbright column is written on instructions from management—it's ordered like you'd order a sardine sandwich!"

"I wouldn't order a sardine sandwich."

"But if you would, you'd get one, whether the cook likes sardines or not!"

"He probably doesn't."

"There's been nothing personal about my columns—you were my assignment and I wrote what I was told to write—it's been just that simple!"

"I think it's those slimy little tails that throw me."

She shrugged. "Spare me the non sequiturs, if you will. Do you have a drink?"

"Sure. What's your pleasure—hemlock, arsenic, strychnine?"

Her smile was tight. "I'd really prefer whisky."

Lockington said, "Then you haven't tried Old Anchor Chain." He put out his cigarette and left the couch to amble into the kitchen, his slippers sloshing against the cheap linoleum. He busied himself at the sinkboard, raising his voice to continue the discussion. "So a *Morning Sentinel* honcho grabs a telephone and says, 'Hey, I want a Stella Starbright column that links Mother Teresa to an international terrorist group.' He *gets* it?"

She jack-knifed forward in her chair to peer into the kitchen. "Of *course*, he gets it—he gets it or I start looking for a new job!"

Lockington returned to the living room bearing a dented, chipped black metal tray. On it were two cloudy glasses, a plastic bowl filled with ice cubes, a small pitcher of water, a nearly full quart bottle of Old Anchor Chain, and a butter knife. He didn't know what they dumped into Old Anchor Chain, but he suspected that the distillery had a working relationship with a nitroglycerine refinery. He'd bought a case of the stuff at a clearance sale three years earlier, and eleven bottles remained. He parked the tray on his coffee table, seated himself, poured, added ice and water, and pushed a glass in Erika Elwood's direction. He said,

"I'm fresh out of swizzle sticks, but you could stir with the butter knife."

She lifted her glass, murmuring, "Thank you—is a toast in order?"

Lockington said, "Why not? 'To mine own executioner' would seem appropriate."

"'*Surrogate* executioner' would be closer to the truth." She sipped at the drink, grimaced, shuddered, blinked, coughed, and gasped, "Oh, Jesus, Joseph, and Judas Iscariot!"

Lockington smiled a gratified smile, saying nothing.

After a struggle she regained her normal breathing pattern. "If I hadn't churned out that garbage, another eager beaver *would* have—the *Sentinel* has a battalion of them, all geared to create controversy. That's the *Sentinel's* gimmick— be outrageous, buck the tide of popular opinion. It sells newspapers, and that's Max's bottom line."

"Max?"

"Max Jarvis—*Sentinel* owner and policymaker. At one time or another that old shyster has taken a stand against everything from chocolate eclaires to motherhood. Last year I had to do a piece inferring that Joan of Arc was a switch hitter."

"Was she?"

"Probably not, but that particular issue sold over a million! Good old Maxie—one of these days he'll shit in his own hat—I hope."

Lockington offered his guest a cigarette and she accepted, digging into her handbag to produce a tiny blue-enameled Colibri, holding a light for them. He said, "So, it's 'Erika,' not 'Stella'—right?"

She nodded, tilting her head, directing a slender

gray plume of smoke at the ceiling. She had a striking profile—delicate, but there was strength along the jawline, Lockington thought. She said, "I leave Stella Starbright under my typewriter."

"Is she Erika's alter ego?"

"No connection, I assure you!" She took a nip of her drink. "My *God*, who *makes* this stuff—the *Apaches*?"

"I believe that the recipe dates back to Genghis Khan."

"A distant relative?"

"No, I'm in the bloodline of Aristotle."

"You don't look Greek."

"I'm not—Aristotle was an Irishman. You don't fit my image of Stella Starbright—not at *all*."

"I should be fat, fifty, splayfooted, and wear pop bottle spectacles?"

"Something like that."

"The others may be fat by now—but they're still a long way from fifty."

"The others?"

"The other 'Stella Starbrights'."

"Hold it! Run that one through here again!"

"There've been three 'Stellas'—I'm the third. The column's nearly ten years old—I've written it for a little over two."

"That's interesting. And the two previous Stellas took the same slobbering route—give us anarchy or we perish?"

"Of course. That's the *Sentinel's* creed."

"Uh-huh." Lockington leaned back on the sofa, crossing his legs, studying the coal of his cigarette, enjoying the conversation. This was a strange woman—unprincipled, yet principled to a degree—interesting. Lockington wondered how she was in bed. If he'd been ten years younger, he'd have taken a run at her. He said, "With the *Sentinel* being what it is, and the Stella Starbright column being what *it* is, it's a damned miracle that some crackpot conservative hasn't blown the Sentinel Building off the map."

"Oh, we've had threats at the *Sentinel*—several have been directed to me personally."

"From whom?"

"A radically conservative organization that calls itself 'LAON.'"

"LAON—which stands for what?"

"'Law and Order Now,' I've been given to understand—childish choice of names, isn't it? No class."

"Male or female caller?"

"No calls—typewritten postcards."

"Chicago postmarks?"

"Chicago area, yes—various stations."

"Addressed to your residence or to the *Sentinel*?"

"The *Sentinel*—I've moved from the lakefront to St. Charles recently. I receive quite a bit of mail at the *Sentinel*."

"What do you do with these postcards?"

"I give them to management. They were to be turned over to the postal authorities."

"What threats have been made?"

"Nothing specific, other than I'm to be eliminated."

"That's specific enough. When and why—does LAON get into that?"

"Soon—because I'm a menace to the human race, to the flag, 'and to the Republic for which it stands'—on and on—the typical fanatic spiel."

"Do these disturb you?"

"At first they did."

"But not now?"

"Not really—there've been so many—I've become calloused to them, I guess."

"What's the frequency of contact?"

She thought about it. "Oh, I'd say twice monthly, on the average. There's no predictable pattern."

"For how long now?"

"A few months—it goes back to early spring, maybe late winter."

"The most recent?"

"Let's see—last Thursday or Friday, I believe. Why? Do you take this stuff seriously?"

"There's one chance in ten that there's substance to it, but—well, there's still that one chance. How's security at the *Sentinel*?"

"Excellent—armed personnel at every entrance—everybody's carded."

"Do you live alone?"

"Uh-huh—a small house just off the Fox River, north of St. Charles."

"Rent or own?"

"Rent."

"Do you have a gun?"

"Yes—it's a Repentino-Morté something-or-other."

"Repentino-Morté Black Mamba Mark III—excellent piece, probably the best. Do you have it in your purse?"

"Heavens, *no*—I'm *afraid* of the damned thing!"

"You'd better get over that and carry it. Some of these screwballs are for real."

Erika Elwood stretched catlike in the overstuffed chair.

She said, "May I compliment you, Mr. Lockington?"

"That'd be a switch. For what?"

"For a precise line of questioning—I've never been, uhh-h-h—*grilled* before. Is that the word—*grilled?*"

"That's what the newspapers call it, the connotation indicating police brutality, of course."

"Oh, my, we *do* have a chip on our shoulder, *don't* we?"

"*Shouldn't* we?"

She considered the question, shifting slightly in her chair, her silver chain sparkling on her well-turned ankle. "Yes—yes, indeed we should. At any rate, Mr. Lockington, you've learned more about me than I know about you, which isn't fair. Might I ask you a question or two?"

"Concerning?"

"Concerning Julie—was that her name—Julie Masters?"

Lockington nodded. "Where do you get your information?"

"It was in our files—the *Sentinel* carried the story."

"The *Sentinel would.*"

"She died of multiple knife wounds—in February, wasn't it?"

"Look, Miss Elwood, I'd just as soon not discuss it."

"You two were happy?"

"Very. Let's drop it right there."

"Just one more question—just *one?*"

"I'd have to hear the question."

"Since Julie's death, you've killed four times—prior to it, just twice, and you were untouched by controversy in any—"

Lockington broke in. "I'd be untouched today if it weren't for the *Morning Sentinel.*"

"Granted. Mr. Lockington, you're a reasonable man,

fair-minded—you'd have thrown me out if you weren't—but isn't it just possible that you've seen in the people you've killed the man or men who murdered Julie Masters?"

Lockington throttled his temper, shrugging. It was a fair question—he'd thought about it before and he'd shrugged then. He said, "Look, how the hell can I answer that? Freud might—so, go see Freud."

"Freud is dead—so are four minor-league criminals."

"A minor-league criminal is a criminal working on becoming a major-league criminal."

"You sound like a crusader."

"No, I'm a cop—*you're* the crusader!"

"In effect then, you don't differentiate between an arsonist and an innocent shoplifter."

"Shoplifters aren't innocent—if they were innocent they wouldn't be shoplifting."

"You'd shoot one?"

"Circumstances dictate cases, Miss Elwood and, incidentally, that's *two* questions."

"No, that's two parts of one three-part question."

Lockington said, "I see." He really didn't.

Erika Elwood said, "It's obvious that you *had* to kill Joe Solano—if you hadn't killed *him*, he'd probably have killed *you*."

"Well, would you believe that I received that very same impression?"

"And it's just as obvious that Timothy Gozzen had to go—sooner or later, Gozzen would have killed a little girl."

"Or a dozen."

"But those Mexican kids on Barry Avenue last Sunday night—they had a couple of knives and you had a *gun*! That was a mismatch!"

Lockington grinned. "Oh, it was, *indeed* it was."

"They could have been bluffing."

"They *could* have been, but when you're looking at a pair of switchblade knives on a dark street, you just don't take that possibility under consideration. The Cook County morgue is stacked to the scuppers with switchblade victims!"

"*Now?*"

"*Any* damn time—check it out, and remind me to show you my old switchblade gashes."

"Then you have no regrets for those Mexican boys?"

"None that I can think of."

Erika Elwood got leisurely to her feet, tucking her big blue handbag under her arm, winking at him. "When you show me your old switchblade gashes maybe I'll show you my butterfly tattoo."

He got up to see her to the door. He ushered her ahead of him, liking her perfume—expensive stuff, whatever it was—vague. He said, "You see one butterfly tattoo, you've seen 'em all."

"Not so! Mine's *special!*"

"Okay, I'll bite. Why is that?"

"It's perched on my appendectomy scar."

"What's perched on your hysterectomy scar—a vulture?"

"I don't have a hysterectomy scar. Do you like butterflies?"

"Depends. What color?"

"Blue."

"I was attacked by a blue butterfly once. It was a frightening experience."

"You should have shot it."

"I did."

She threw back her head and laughed her musical laugh. He'd hoped that she'd do that. She turned to stand on tiptoes, stretching to kiss him on the cheek—just a lukewarm peck, but better than no peck at all. She whispered, "Oh, but you're *precious!*" At close range her perfume was heady stuff, nearly buckling his knees. She went out and he wished she hadn't.

He watched the silver Toyota Cressida pull away before he postponed the Pepper Valley baseball game.

12

There comes a time in the life of every mortal when he must take inventory of his life, reckoning his pluses and minuses, deducting his past from his future, providing that he *has* a future, and facing the results. That time had come around for Lacey Lockington on numerous occasions, and it'd just come around again. He sat at his Barry Avenue window, contemplating the ebony clouds that stalked the city, musing, nursing his tenacious case of snakebite, making his computations, and coming out no better than he'd come out at the conclusions of his earlier inventories—still a few digits short of zilch.

Then the rain struck, a hissing, snarling, gray wall of fury, a real tail-twister, even by Chicago standards. He listened to the storm for more than an hour, waiting for it to abate, then he turned on his radio. The bulletins were coming—Schiller Park's viaducts were impassable, this development failing to impress Lockington because Schiller Park's viaducts became impassable every time a dog pissed on an evergreen, but the situation was worsening, spreading like wildfire. Railroad underpasses were being closed on North Avenue, the already swollen Des Plaines River had topped its banks, submerging River Road under six inches of muddy water, the Chicago White Sox game had been postponed, Maywood Park had scratched its nightly harness-racing program, flash flood warnings were going up from Lawrence Avenue south to Roosevelt Road, from Harlem Avenue west to York, power failures were reported in numerous sections northwest of the Loop, that area having been converted into a fifty square mile quagmire, and Lockington's earlier plans for monumental achievement fizzled and drowned in the muck of that sodden August afternoon. No great loss, Lockington thought, he hadn't taken them seriously.

It was shortly before eight o'clock in the evening with the deluge continuing to hammer the city and Lockington approaching the dregs of a second bottle of Old Anchor Chain, when he threw in the towel, turning off the radio and killing the lights to stumble, crocked to the gunwales, into his bedroom where he flopped face-down on the rumpled bed, listening to rain claw at his windows. It was a horseshit world, he'd decided—it'd probably wash completely away before dawn, and Lockington just didn't give a damn.

He sprawled in the darkness, pulling a pillow over his head and plummeting into the dreamless, untwitching sleep of the chaste and the naive, a singular experience for Lacey Lockington because Lacey Lockington was not chaste, neither was he naive, and he'd known nights, a great many of them, when his dreams would have chased a fat woman out of a rummage sale.

His nightstand telephone awakened him at two twenty-five in the morning. Lockington didn't know how long it'd been ringing, but locating the sonofabitch required the better part of an eternity. He finally managed to dig it out of a jungle of crumpled empty cigarette packs, candy bar wrappers, matchflaps, and out-of-date sports magazines to mumble unintelligibly into it and hear Duke Denny snap, "Lacey, what the hell have you been doing?" Denny's voice was taut, urgent, half-an-octave higher-pitched than usual.

Lockington said, "Well, I *was* sleeping until some drunken barbarian blew me out of bed in the dead of the fucking night!"

Denny said, "Partner, this is important—are you awake?"

Lockington said, "No, this is a fucking recording."

"Listen, Lacey—the early edition of the *Morning Sentinel* just hit the stands!"

Lockington opened one eye to glare at the battered alarm clock on his dresser. He said, "You woke me up at two-fucking-thirty in the morning to tell me *that,* you prick?"

"Hear me out, damn it! When did you talk to Stella Starbright?"

"That ain't her real name—it's Erika or something."

"No matter—when did you talk to her?"

"You see, there ain't no real Stella Starbright—Stella Starbright's a *nom de plume* or whatever they call it—two other chicks wrote that column before she did."

"Lacey, are you drunk?"

"Well, if I ain't I just wasted a whole afternoon of my life."

"Tell me about Stella Starbright."

"She's stacked like—"

"Skip that—for the *third* time, *have you talked to her?*"

"Yeah, she drove out to see me." Lockington tried to whistle but his tongue was too thick. He said, "Some dish!"

"When was she there?"

"What day is this?"

"Wednesday—early Wednesday morning."

"It was probably yesterday—what the hell *was* yesterday?"

"Tuesday, for Christ's sake!"

"Okay, then it was Tuesday—she came around to apologize."

Duke Denny snorted, sounding like a bull hippopotamus in rut, Lockington thought. Lockington had never heard a bull hippopotamus in rut. His head was throbbing like a Comanche war drum. He'd never heard a Comanche war drum, either—he'd never been west of the Mississippi. He wasn't certain that the Comanches were *from* west of the Mississippi—for all he knew the Comanches were from fucking Alaska. Lockington was still intoxicated. Duke Denny was saying, "She came around to apologize, my rosy-pink *ass*! She came around to sucker you into sticking your neck out! You just gotta read her Wednesday column!"

The dark-brown taste in Lockington's mouth defied printable description. He growled, "Duke, I don't gotta do nothin' but kick the bucket."

Denny rasped, "Lacey, if you stood a fucking single ghost of a chance at that stacked investigation, it's long gone now! That floozie ripped your guts out! She had a tape recorder stashed in her purse, did you know that?"

Lockington made no response and Denny yammered on. "She says that you have no regrets for the taking of human lives, that you seem proud of killing the people you've killed, that the extent of a person's wrongdoing seems utterly irrelevant to you, that by your own inference you'd probably shoot a shoplifter as quickly as you'd shoot an arsonist! Lacey, did you *say* such damn-fool things to a *newspaper* woman?"

"She isn't completely accurate, but she's close."

"My God, where were your *brains*?"

"I dunno—she seemed sincere enough at the time."

"So did Fidel Castro—at the *time*!"

"Okay, so I blew it, but they're gonna can me anyway, so what's the difference?"

"This holier-than-thou scorpion calls for your immediate resignation from the force, she says that it'd spare the taxpayers the prohibitive costs of your hearing, that it'd be the first honorable deed you've ever performed for the citizens of Chicago, that—"

Lockington said, "How do you know that she had a tape recorder in her purse—did she state that in her column?"

"No, she says that she interviewed you in your apartment, but it *had* to be a tape recorder! She wouldn't have dared to go out on this kind of limb without something to back her up!"

"Well, to hell with it. Tell me, did she use that 'Oh, Dear God in Heaven' shot?"

"Yeah, probably half-a-dozen times."

"Touching—very touching. Well, Duke, I'm gonna catch some sleep."

"All right, partner, I just thought you oughta know about this. 'Forewarned, forearmed,' y'know."

"Yeah—Cervantes. Cervantes spent about half of his life in one lockup or another."

"Then he knew what he was talking about. Say, why

don't we have dinner tonight?"

"Good question. Why don't we?"

"How's the Ristoranté Italia at River Road and Irving Park—seven-thirty okay?"

"River Road's under water—so's that section of Irving Park."

"Now, yes, but not for long—the rain stopped three hours ago."

"Who's buying?"

"It's my turn."

"Real good memory you got there, Duke. Good night." Lockington hung up. He hadn't been stunned by the development, but there'd been a slight twinge of disappointment. He skirted it, returning to sleep, and this time he dreamed. He dreamed that he'd died and that the Devil had him. In his dream he was amazed by his ecstatic sense of relief at getting the hell out of Chicago, Illinois.

13

With dawn came the hangover, and with the hangover the customary melancholy. Lockington, awake briefly at six-fifteen, avoided a portion of the depression by rolling over and sleeping until nearly eleven o'clock, when he roused himself to smoke a cigarette, trying to assemble the scattered pieces of his fractured yesterday, remembering the whirlwind visit of Stella Starbright—or Erika Elwood or Mata Hari or whoever the hell she'd been—his losing tussle with those jugs of Old Anchor Chain, the violent rain storm, Duke Denny's late-night report on Stella Starbright's cutthroat column in the *Morning Sentinel,* and Duke's invitation to dinner at the Ristoranté Italia. That was all behind Lockington now and if there'd been perceptible changes in his situation, they certainly hadn't been for the better—except maybe the dinner invitation. A square meal and a couple hours of kicking the gong around with Duke would probably help.

He stared across the bedroom at the bleary-eyed, shaggy

apparition reflected in his dresser mirror—the Wolfman of Barry Avenue, he thought, shaking his sleep-tousled head. He eased to his feet, tottering into the bathroom, stepping recklessly into a steaming shower, scrambling hurriedly out of it, readjusting the water temperature to somewhere below the boiling point before stepping back in. He emerged to towel himself dry, shave, brush his teeth, and feel nearly human again. He slipped into his old brown flannel robe and headed for the kitchen where he scrambled two eggs and started the coffee while waiting for the toast to pop.

He ate his breakfast slowly, ruminatively, sipping coffee, paging through the yellowed volume of *Tom Sawyer* that had become a fixture on his kitchen table, his companion at virtually every meal. If he'd read it once, he'd read it fifty times, beginning back in his fourth grade days. He'd never tired of it. Tom Sawyer had been fortunate, his times had been simpler than Lockington's, and Lockington envied the youngster, feeling a nostalgia for Tom's sleepy little river town, his sun-splashed afternoons, his friends and acquaintances, even Injun Joe, that rotten sonofabitch.

He downed a second cup of coffee before washing the dishes. One of Lockington's many frustrated ambitions was to become neat and orderly, but he'd never quite gotten around to it—something was always in the wrong place. He returned to the bedroom to dress, choosing a short sleeved white shirt, gray cardigan, black slacks, gray socks, and black loafers from a wardrobe that fell considerably short of the extensive category. In the living room he squinted through his window at sunlight, blue sky, and fleecy white clouds, then turned on his radio to catch the noon roundup of the news. Lockington preferred taking his news from radio—he'd never been able to understand why news had become show business, why television required ninety minutes and a cast of a dozen posturing, smirking fruitballs to present a review of events that one reasonably literate radio announcer could have handled in fewer than ten minutes. After all, who the hell cared if Lane Technical High School had held a hayride on a farm near Gray's Lake? The horses, possibly, if there'd been horses.

The noon news radio reporter was low-key and to the point—on the international front, a bunch of Iranian maniacs had blown up a Paris rock concert, thereby terrifying a bunch of French maniacs. Locally, Chicagoland was bailing out following its most severe rainstorm in fifteen years—the Mayor and his city council had engaged in a free-for-all on the city council floor, the Mayor having been kicked in the groin—a light plane had crashed into a hotdog stand north of Wheeling, Illinois, breaking the pilot's arm and a gallon jar of mustard—the body of a Wilmette woman, one Eleanor Fisher, had been found in a dumpster behind a gas station in unincorporated Leyden Township—the weather would be clear and sunny with a high of eighty-two degrees—the White Sox would play a twinight doubleheader—the Cubs had lost in Los Angeles 11–4.

That was the news, such as it was, and Lockington stood at his front window, watching the pigeons—a man who had no place to go and nothing to do when he got there.

14

On their morning after, she'd rolled to him, smiling, her dark eyes alive with something that hadn't been there the night before. She'd whispered, "Oh, Jesus, how I hate to get up!"

Lockington had said, "Then don't."

"But you have to go to work."

"So?"

"Well, the least I can do is make coffee!"

"Okay, make coffee—I'll shower and shave."

She'd run her fingertips along his jowl. "Not bad there, but you'll probably need that shower. I was—uhh-h-h, dripping—we were making squishy sounds."

"Yes, we were."

"I want to thank you for last night—bailing me out of that situation—the warm bed, and, well, everything that went with it. Is breakfast included in the package?"

"Yep. We're out of bacon, but we have eggs."

"Scrambled—over easy—how?"

"Whatever you're pushing."

"*Over easy, then—look—thanks again.*"

"*The pleasure was mine.*"

"*Huh-uh—I've had the best of it.*"

"*Think you'll be here when I get home?*"

"*I'd like that, but there's my car—I should get it out of the middle of the street.*"

"*Give me your keys and I'll take care of it on my way to work. There's a good garage a couple of blocks from here.*"

"*You want me to be here?*"

"*Yes—very much.*" *And he did—very much.*

"*Honest injun?*"

"*Cross my heart and hope to die!*"

"*All right, I'll be here. What would you like for dinner?*"

"*What's your specialty?*"

"*If I have one, it's lasagna.*"

"*Say, why don't we have lasagna?*"

"*Excellent idea! Red wine?*"

Lockington nodded. "*There's money in the top dresser drawer.*"

"*No, sir—my treat! How far am I from a grocery store?*"

"*Block and a half west—Sanganiti's—all the fixings will be there.*"

"*Block and a half west means nothing to me. In Chicago I don't know my ass from a mint julep. Which the hell way is west?*"

"*From the front door, you'll turn right. Don't lock yourself out!*"

She'd laughed. "*Now wouldn't that be something? Out of the frying pan into the fire—no car, no roof over my head—I'd be a waif!*"

"*There's a key where the money is.*"

"*What time do you get home? Usually, that is.*"

"*Oh, five—five-thirty.*"

She'd sat up in bed, the sheet cascading into her lap. Her bosom was magnificent.

When he'd left the shower and come into the kitchen, she'd been seated at the table, still naked as a jaybird, munching meditatively on a slice of toast. His eggs had been ready and he'd sat across from her, eating rapidly. Between bites he'd said, "I have spare pajamas."

"Thank you—you're a trusting soul, do you know that?"

"Not all the time, but I get feelings about people—call it radar."

"You had feelings last night—I didn't quite expect—well, you were—you were very, very good."

"Put that down to the luck of the Irish."

She'd said, "Huh-uh—there's no luck in bed—either it works or it doesn't!"

He'd shrugged, glancing at his watch, gulping the last of his coffee, getting to his feet. "Gotta make tracks."

She'd said, "I don't want to seem presumptuous, but what's your name?"

"Lockington—Lacey Lockington."

"Mine's Julie. You're a cop?"

"Yeah—hi, Julie! What's your occupation?"

She'd smiled her wonderful smile. "Hi, Lacey! I'm trying to be a writer. The last name's Masters."

Nice, Lockington thought, knowing each other's names.

15

Late that afternoon, the Pepper Valley Crickets took two of three from the Scorpion City Stingers with Nick Noonan going 5 for 15 in the series, and Lacey Lockington was in a much-improved frame of mind when he returned the Cider Press Federation to its cardboard box and drove west to River Road, swinging north on River toward Irving Park. Northbound traffic moved at a snail's pace, River Road being heavily littered with flood debris and reduced to single-lane flow at several spots, but he reached the Ristoranté Italia without incident, parking his road-weary Pontiac Catalina in the large black-topped lot precisely at seven-thirty. He didn't see Duke Denny's black Cadillac convertible.

The Ristoranté Italia's lounge was dim, cozy, beautifully-appointed, and silent as a tomb. After vainly scanning the cavernous dining area for Denny, Lockington parked himself on a high-backed leatherette barstool, alone with the bartender, an oversize, beetle-browed glowering man wearing a New England Patriots sweatshirt, a tough-looking customer who looked like he could have gone bear hunting with a broomstick. He reminded Lockington of a B movie Foreign Legion top-kick, and he peered at the newcomer over the sheaf of invoices he'd been checking. He said, "Hey, would your name be Lockingworth?" He had a voice like a New Hampshire foghorn.

Lockington shook his head. "Nope, it'd be Lockington—been Lockington ever since I was born."

The bartender said, "Yeah, well, whatever it is, Duke Denny just called—said I should tell you that he'll be a few minutes late, but that he'll be here for sure, so you should stick around. Okay?"

Lockington nodded, ordering a bottle of Old Washensachs beer. He preferred hard liquor but, after the Old Anchor Chain, beer would be a welcome change of pace. He said, "Come to think of it, we got quite a few Lockingtons in my family."

The bartender dug a bottle of Old Washensachs out of the cooler, poured, pushed Lockington's money away, and said, "Your money's no good—Duke gave me instructions."

Lockington said, "My brother's name is Lockington, too—Casey Lockington."

The bartender said, "I've known Duke Denny since I started working here—gonna be four years come the middle of November, just before Thanksgiving—great guy, Duke is."

Lockington took a gulp of his beer. He said, "It probably got something to do with my father's name being Lockington."

Duke Denny was sliding onto the barstool to Lockington's right, chuckling, waving hello to the bartender. He said, "Don't let this guy throw you, Pete—sometimes he has a one-track mind."

Pete said, "Aw, Lockingworth ain't so bad—I've run into worse."

Denny nudged Lockington. "Finish your beer and we'll go into the mess hall."

Pete was yawning, rubbing his eyes with hairy bricklayer fists. "Off night tonight—must of been all that rain." He went back to the stack of invoices.

They ambled into the dining room. It was deserted save for a waitress who sat at a table, jotting notes on a large yellow pad. Lockington looked around the place, shaking his head. He said, "Just what is it with Italians and crystal chandeliers?"

Denny shrugged. "Don't forget red tablecloths, red carpeting, red candle-chimneys, and all the travel posters."

They took a table in a distant corner of the room. Denny said, "Why don't we kick this off with vodka martinis?"

"It's your credit card."

The waitress left her chair to bear down on their table. She was a half-pint peroxide-blonde bit of fluff wearing a shiny, short black dress, a frilly white apron, and enough makeup to camouflage the *USS New Jersey*. She was thirty-five, possibly. She was also fifty, possibly. Denny ordered a pair of vodka martinis on the rocks. He said, "No twists with those, sweetie—make it anchovy-stuffed olives."

The waitress said, "Okay, that's two vodka martinis for you." She swung her attention to Lockington. "How about you—how many?"

Denny rolled his eyes. "Just let him have one of mine until he makes up his mind." When she was gone, Denny said, "That was Laura—hardly a candidate for class valedictorian—a bum lay, incidentally."

Lockington winked at Denny. "Bum lays are bored

lays, usually."

Denny let that one go by. There was something bugging Duke or he'd have jumped right on it, Lockington thought. He looked his ex-partner over—he could have stepped right out of a haberdashery display window—white sports coat, brown silk shirt, white tie, brown slacks, white oxfords, and there was a brown chrysanthemum tucked into his left lapel buttonhole. Same old Duke—once a clotheshorse, always a clotheshorse. They differed there—clothes didn't interest Lockington. They served to create favorable first impressions, but when those faded, a man stood naked. Denny was saying, "By the way, I got one helluva coincidence for you!"

Lockington said, "Let's have it—I'm crazy about coincidences."

Denny leaned toward Lockington, starting to speak, then holding up as Laura arrived with their vodka martinis. He sampled his drink, smacking his lips. He said, "Pete makes the best goddam martini from here to Alexandria, Louisiana."

Lockington said, "I've never been to Alexandria, Louisiana," his eyes tracking Laura's return to her table at the dining area entrance. Laura had a magnificent ass. Lockington gave Laura a mental checkmark in the magnificent ass column. He said, "Uhh–h–h, the coincidence, if you will."

Denny said, "Okay, you're in the hot soup with this Stella Starbright column, right?"

Lockington said, "I'm beginning to get that impression."

"And last night you said that a couple of other broads have written under the Stella Starbright byline."

"That's what I was told. What's your point?"

"Well, partner, just this morning, the Cook County cops hauled a dead woman out of a garbage bin down at the corners of Wolf Road and Grand Avenue—quiff by the name of Eleanor Fisher—shot through the back of the head—very neat job. You hear anything about that?"

"It was on the noon news but there was no mention of how she died—only that she lived in Wilmette."

"Right—Wilmette, out where the long green grows."

"Okay, so she lived in Wilmette where the long green grows."

"So this afternoon I was talking to Information Brown. You know of a fella they call Information Brown?"

"*Everybody* knows Information Brown—little guy—looks like somebody's first husband—runs the newsstand at State and Randolph—spends most of his time in the Squirrel's Cage—knows everything and everybody."

"Check. Well, Information Brown was telling me that Eleanor Fisher was divorced and playing the field—however, until a year and a half ago, she'd been married to Gordon *Fisher.* Whaddaya think of *that?*"

Lockington said, "Not a helluva lot—if she'd been married and divorced, you'd get even money that it'd been to and from a guy named Fisher. Who's Gordon Fisher?"

"You've never heard of him?"

"The name fails to send little jingles up my spine."

"Why, Gordon Fisher's one of Chicago's top-flight corporation attorneys! He's filthy-rich, and his clients' list is topped by the Chicago *Morning Sentinel.*"

"All right, Eleanor married money—that ain't happenstance. She just might have done that on *purpose.*"

"Oh, sure, but *that* isn't the *coincidence,* that's just a sidelight. The *coincidence* is that Eleanor Fisher used to write the *Stella on State Street* column!"

16

Lockington worked on his vodka martini for a few moments. Denny was right, it was an excellent cocktail but, being a skeptic, Lockington charged that to accident. The next one would probably blow their socks off. He said, "Duke, I think you're seeing rats in your woodpile when you got no woodpile."

Denny said, "Well, *hell*, Lacey, stand back and *look* at it! Stella Starbright spooks Netherby into suspending you, then a woman who once wrote the column gets herself murdered, and it turns out that she'd been hitched to the chief attorney for the newspaper that *publishes* the damned thing! You don't see a coincidence in *that*?"

"If it's there, it's like getting two parking tickets in one day—a trifle unlikely, but no big deal. Where's the connection—what does it hook to *what*?"

Denny's face was beet-red. "Lacey, God damn it, I didn't *say* that there was a connection, I didn't say that anything was hooked to *any*thing—all I said was that it was a fucking *coincidence*—Jesus Christ, I—shit, forget it, will you? Just forget the whole fucking business!"

Lockington grinned. "Okay." He'd popped Duke's cork.

They finished their martinis in stony silence, Denny glaring at Lockington before waving to Laura and pointing to their glasses for refills. Lockington said, "On the other hand, and for whatever it's worth, the current Stella Starbright has been receiving death threats in the mail."

Denny hoisted an inquisitive eyebrow. "That right?"

"That's what she told me."

"Recent threats?"

"Tail end of last week, and several times before that—it dates back to cold weather."

Denny made no comment, and Lockington listened to the Ristoranté Italia's piped-in music—lush, swirling strings, muted brasses, throbbing basses—"Begin the Beguine"—"elevator music," according to the kids—if it didn't blast your eardrums halfway through your cerebellum, the kids called it "elevator music." "The kids"—a generation that could not read, neither could it write. Laura had pranced into view, bearing their fresh vodka martinis. She said, "Gotcha couple extra anchovy-stuffed olives this time!"

Denny reached to squeeze her leg, quite high on the thigh. "Good girl!"

Laura wiggled the tip of her tongue at Denny. "*Good girl—me?*" She giggled wildly, sounding like a jackhammer gone out of control, Lockington thought.

Denny said, "Busy later?"

Laura's smile for Duke Denny was the smile of a puma for a lamb chop with the lamb still attached. She said, "Not so's you could notice."

Denny said, "Still living on Damen Avenue?"

"Uh-huh—I always make that little joint on the corner before I go home—that's around midnight, usually." She giggled again, setting Lockington's teeth on edge.

Denny said, "The Brass Rail?"

"That's it—the Brass Rail." She whispered something into Denny's ear and went away, smiling mysteriously, scratching her magnificent ass. The tryst had been arranged Chicago-style, Lockington noted—lay it on the line—first come, first served. He gave Denny a look. "Bum lay, did you say?"

Denny shrugged defensively. "Yeah, but you know how it goes, partner—any old port in a storm."

Lockington said, "Some storm." He watched Laura seat herself at her table, her short black skirt rocketing to her thighs and beyond. He said, "Some port." After a while, he said, "She told me that these threats are made by an outfit identifying itself as LAON—a radical right wing group, apparently."

Denny was nodding. "LAON—familiar name—I believe LAON stands for Law and Order Now—it's been around for years—murky organization, all hot air so far as I know—no track record—threats, but no moves of consequence."

"What if there was a first time—what if the Fisher woman received threats and ignored them? That Stella Starbright column has been spouting ultra-liberal bullshit since its beginning, hasn't it?"

Denny frowned, "Yeah, but we're probably trying too hard. You hear of LAON on the streets and everybody laughs—a bunch of Don Quixotes, chances are."

Lockington didn't say anything. He'd never heard of

LAON on the streets.

Denny ordered spaghetti with clam sauce, Lockington tried the veal française. Laura dropped Denny's fork into Lockington's minestrone. Laura apologized. Lockington said, "That's okay." They had double Gallianos with black coffee. Lockington said, "Eleanor Fisher probably got picked up by the wrong jocker. These newspaper chippies swing—they get started during their working days and they never hit the brakes. Remember that society reporter from the *Chronicle*?"

"The one Luke Stark was banging?"

"Yeah, she'd been married for ten years, and screwing for twenty."

"Lucy Wallick—Luke didn't have a monopoly on Lucy—Lucy had a thing for cops—liked the macho image, probably."

Lockington yawned. The Eleanor Fisher thing was none of his affair. He was a cop in name only, and not for much longer.

Denny was saying, "Hey, how's about this—what's her name again?"

"Erika—Erika Elwood."

"Well, *she's* a newspaper woman. Does Erika get it on?"

"I'd think she does. When I told her that I'd show her my switchblade scars, she said that she'd show me her butterfly tattoo."

Denny smiled a wolfish smile. "Words uttered not completely in jest, perhaps. Where's her butterfly tattoo?"

"On her appendectomy scar, she told me."

Denny popped the table with the flat of his hand. "Hey, partner, get to that butterfly and her monkey will be just over the ridge!"

Lockington made a deprecatory gesture. "I'm old enough to be her father."

Denny snorted. "That *matters*? Give it a shot! Whaddaya stand to *lose*?"

"Uh-uh, not *this* one—if I never see that little conartist again, it'll be six months too soon!"

Denny signalled for another round of double Gallianos and turned back to Lockington. "*Use* the slut, Lacey—what the hell, she's certainly used *you*! That's the name of the game, isn't it?"

"*Is* it?"

"I asked you first." Lockington didn't answer and Denny lit a cigarette. "Well, brace yourself, partner—here comes the commercial."

Obviously ill-at-ease, Denny was studying the golden depths of his double Galliano, tracing an invisible design on the bright red tablecloth with the handle of his knife. He looked up at Lockington.

Lockington nodded. He'd sensed that there'd been considerably more on Denny's mind than the death of a woman unknown to either of them.

"Uhh–h–h, look, partner, I'm in one helluva bind— Moose Katzenbach checked out on me late yesterday afternoon—gave me all of fifteen minutes notice!"

Lockington said, "Moose moved to Brooklyn?"

"Guess so. That's his hometown, isn't it?"

"Naw, Moose was born and raised in Chicago—Helen's from Brooklyn."

"Well, anyway, on that kind of notice, where the hell do I find a man who knows his ass from a hole in the ground?"

Lockington shook his head. "Beats me." He knew

where Duke Denny was coming from, and he knew his intended destination.

Denny said, "I wanted to discuss this last night, but you were *embriagado*."

"Does that translate to 'drunk'?"

"Jesus, a linguist, yet!"

Lockington could see no point in delaying the inevitable. He said, "You want me to fill in for Moose."

Denny's green eyes were pleading. "Probably just for a week or so—seven-fifty a week, *double* what I was paying Katzenbach, cash on the barrelhead and piss on the IRS." He spread his hands. "Unless you'd want to stay longer, of course—the job's yours for keeps, if you can use it."

"Well-l-l-l—"

Denny broke in. "Lacey, they're gonna barbecue your balls at that kangaroo hearing, and you *know* it! Stella Starbright fixed your clock, and you'll just have to settle *some*where!"

Lockington fired up a cigarette, flipping the match into their tin ashtray, watching it shrivel to gray ash. He said, "All right, I'll pitch in for a few days, but anything beyond that will have to hinge on how things work out."

Denny shot a hand across the table, grabbing Lockington's shoulder, squeezing until it hurt. "Jesus, *thanks,* partner! It'll work out—we were the best team this town ever *saw*!"

"What's cooking at the agency—where would I fit in?"

Denny was mopping his brow with a brown silk handkerchief—obviously relieved. He said, "Yeah, the agency—well, let's see—okay, I'll put you on the Grimes thing."

"The Grimes thing. What's the 'Grimes thing'?"

"J.B. Grimes—he's news to you?"

"Yep. What about J.B. Grimes?"

"He has a big Oklahoma Mutual Insurance franchise on West Monroe—employs thirty-some people—first-class operation."

"Somebody's dipping into the till?"

"No, Grimes isn't my client—it's his wife."

"Uh-huh." Duke Denny had just switched to a familiar frequency.

"Well, she's always called him on working-day afternoons, right around two o'clock, and recently Grimes has never been available—he's always in conference, or he just stepped out, or he's with a client and he can't be disturbed—you know the route."

"And that's a departure?"

"*Drastic*—normally Grimes is in his office, hacking dutifully away, easy to reach."

"Does he know that she's been calling him?"

"At first he did, and he had alibis, but now Martha Grimes is changing her voice, or having friends phone in—same old story, Grimes is tied up."

"So he isn't avoiding his wife, he's avoiding *every*body."

"You got it! Martha isn't questioning him these days—she's lulling him into a feeling of security."

"Matinees, of course."

"Of course—you see, his receptionist-switchboard operator isn't taking afternoon calls—she has a slight Spanish accent, Martha knows her voice, and it's always another girl. Then Grimes becomes readily available between four-thirty and five and so does the regular switchboard chick—two and two make four."

"That's all you have going—this Grimes business?"

Denny chuckled. "That's *all?* Hell, partner, give me two or three a month just like it and I'm knee-deep in *clover!* The job'll gross seven grand!"

"Martha Grimes wants grounds for divorce?"

"What else? She should cash for upwards of a million! Grimes is in his mid-fifties, Martha's just a hair over forty—a bit on the pudgy side but she's straddling a steamy crotch and I got a hunch she kicks up her heels from time to time. With that kind of money she can rent some fancy jockers!"

Lockington said, "Well, I don't know the market, but isn't seven grand a shade steep for a run-of-the-mill surveillance thing?"

"I don't know that it'll be run-of-the-mill—it could take time, maybe *weeks*. So the deal was seven big ones, guaranteed results, no time limit—we dog him until we nail him. Martha says that J.B. won't come easy."

"You'll need witnesses to make it stick."

"Witnesses, shitnesses—we'll need *facts*—you get the facts, I'll *buy* witnesses. This is Chicago, partner—*everything's* for sale!"

Lockington nodded, remembering Duke Denny when he'd been an impressionable, almost-naïve kid out of someplace in Ohio.

17

At 10:15 A.M. on Friday, August 24, Lacey Lockington
stood on the West Monroe Street sidewalk, facing the New
Gebhardt Building, peering upward thirty-eight floors to its
pinnacle jutting into Chicago's morning smog like the dagger
into Julius Caesar's chest, or belly, or whatever. Lockington
wasn't up on his Shakespeare.

The New Gebhardt Building had replaced the old
Gebhardt Building, and for the life of him Lockington
couldn't understand why. The old Gebhardt Building had
possessed flair and individuality, the new one was just one
more of the antiseptic stainless steel and smoked glass
monstrosities that had begun to clutter the downtown area,
utterly devoid of personality, a carbon copy of the Alfred
Bartlett Building which was a carbon copy of the Wentworth
Building, which was a carbon copy of the Ajax Building, these
providing a disconcerting peek into Chicago's architectural
future. There was something Orwellian about the inexorable
transformation, Lockington thought, and he didn't like it.

He entered the New Gebhardt Building apprehensively, pausing to locate the J.B. Grimes listing on the satin-chromed, black-enameled foyer panel before stepping into a Flash Gordon-style elevator to meet a fat woman coming out. The fat woman sported red plastic earrings the size of barrel hoops, a purple-on-white tropical-flowered dress, green jogging shoes, and some twenty-three gallons of cheap perfume. The fat women of Chicago present a force to be reckoned with and Lockington should have known enough to get out of her way, but he was preoccupied with the chore ahead of him, and he didn't. The resounding impact and the stench of her stale three-dollar perfume left him with the distinct impression that he'd just collided head-on with an overdue cemetery truck chock-full of withered carnations. Overmatched, Lockington reeled from the elevator, his legs giving way, and she swept by him as a tidal wave sweeps by a minnow, hissing, "You better learn to watch where the hell you're going!"

From his knees, Lockington muttered, "Yes, ma'am," regaining his footing to stumble back into the elevator. The doors snapped silently open on the seventh floor of the New Gebhardt Building and he stepped from the cramped confines of the conveyance onto a blue-carpeted expanse the size of a tennis court, suddenly surrounded by a mausoleum-type silence, feeling out of touch with civilization as he remembered it. He peered bewilderedly about him before spotting the bold black block lettering on the frosted glass of the door to his left—J.B. GRIMES, OKLAHOMA MUTUAL INSURANCE, and below that, in smaller letters—Life, Accident, Fire, Casualty, Commercial Group Hospitalization. Lockington consulted his watch.

The time was 10:25. Here went nothing.

He took a small notebook and a ballpoint pen from a pocket, pushed his hat to the back of his head, squared his shoulders, adopted his very best jaded facial expression, and barged through the door, pulling up short in a walnut-paneled alcove no larger than his Barry Avenue bathroom, confronted by a narrow sheet of white plastic. He sat warily on a spindly-legged blue fiberglass chair, then got to his feet as the plastic panel slid to one side. He stared into the enormous liquid-brown eyes of a slender Latino female perched primly at an Olivetti ET225, the arch of a switchboard headset imbedded in her glossy-black hair. Her face was long, her nostrils slightly flared, her chin weak, her bosom nothing short of spectacular. She smiled the insincere smile of every receptionist on Planet Earth. She said, "May I be of assistance, sir?" speaking with a lightly staccato Spanish inflection.

Lockington nodded, dug for his wallet, dragged it out, flashed his tarnished police badge, and growled, "Lieutenant Nick Noonan, Chicago Fire Marshall's Office, ma'am—how many fire extinguishers do you have on these premises?"

She frowned. "Uhh–h–h, well, I'm not quite sure. What do they look like?"

Lockington said, "They're red, in most cases."

She brightened. "Oh *those*—yes, we have one here!" She nodded in the direction of the fire extinguisher.

Lockington said, "One won't be enough, ma'am."

"Oh, but there's one in the stockroom, one in the consultation room, one in the ladies' room, one in—"

"How about the men's room?"

She blushed through dusky high-boned cheeks. "I—

uhh–hh, I really don't know, sir—I've never been—that is—"

"I'm running late, ma'am. Is there anyone here who might provide me with an exact count?"

She was rattled now, she'd need help, precisely as Lockington had hoped. She said, "I'd better call Mr. Grimes—oh, there he *is*!" She spun on her tiny swivel chair, raising her voice to a portly, baldheaded man in a rumpled gray gabardine suit. "Johnny—er-r-r—Mr. Grimes?"

J.B. Grimes was seated at a large table with an angular, white-haired woman, and he turned slowly, peering over his shoulder at the receptionist. He had the anguished look of a bull moose in the throes of a hemorrhoidal flare-up, but his voice was gentle. "Yes, Maria?" Lockington had all he'd be needing. Now it boiled down to getting out of the situation gracefully.

Maria was saying, "Mr. Grimes, how many fire extinguishers do we have?"

J.B. Grimes pinched the bridge of his nose, head down. "Well, let's see—"

Maria said, "They're red, in most cases."

Grimes said, "Yes—seven, I believe—is it important, Maria?"

Lockington muttered, "Not unless the joint catches fire."

Maria nodded agreement with Lockington, speaking to J.B. Grimes. "There's a gentleman here, a Lieutenant Noonan from the Chicago Fire Marshall's office."

Grimes sighed. "Very well—I'll talk to him in a few moments."

Lockington said, "There'll be no need for that, ma'am—this is just a routine check." He riffled through several blank pages of his notebook, scrawled a couple of X's on one, dumped pen and notebook into a jacket pocket, tipped his hat to Maria, and said, "Sorry to have troubled you, ma'am—have a nice day." He went out, prepared for his assignment, the principals identifiable to him.

Martha Grimes's female intuition was firing on all cylinders—Lockington would have bet on it.

18

At high noon, Chicago's Loop was a sweating, swarming, snarling, snapping mass of confusion. Lockington had seen greater semblances of order in burning termite hills. He leaned against a lamppost across the way from the New Gebhardt Building, watching its entrance for J.B. Grimes and Maria. They emerged together, arm-in-arm, turning west, chatting, laughing. Lockington dodged traffic, crossing West Monroe Street at a dangerous angle to fall in behind them.

Maria was a leggy lass, she had a smoothly loose-jointed gait that appealed to Lockington's baser instincts. Her black slacks were so tight that Lockington could see the outlines of what was probably a small mole on her right buttock, and he couldn't help but wonder how she'd squeezed into them in the first place. Then he couldn't help but wonder how J.B. Grimes was going to pry her out of them in the second place. Following that, he attempted to anticipate the site of the afternoon's sexual festivities. Probably the Lochinvar Arms or the Hooper House, he figured, both establishments being seedy, no-questions-asked hostelries made to order for such arrangements. He decided that they'd hit the Lochinvar because it was on West Monroe, just three blocks from the New Gebhardt Building, while the Hooper House was across the river on Canal Street and several blocks north of West Monroe.

It was to be neither, at least not immediately. Maria turned right on North LaSalle Street, waving so-long to Grimes who waved back before swinging left. Lockington grinned—they weren't taking damned fool chances—by splitting they were hoping to convince a tracker that they had nothing on the fire. They'd rendezvous a bit later, of course, an ancient dodge, but worth a shot—it might befuddle a neophyte. Lockington, no neophyte, stuck with J.B. Grimes.

The big man in wrinkled gray gabardine slouched into a shabby little lunchroom a couple of blocks south of West Adams Street, and Lockington held back, entering a minute or so later. Grimes was seated at the counter, his broad back to Lockington, already working diligently on an order of thuringers and sauerkraut. Lockington slipped unobtrusively into a corner booth, ordering a swiss and tomato on rye and a glass of lemonade, not particularly proud of what he was up to. These weren't evil people, they weren't peddling drugs to minors, or setting fire to old people's homes, or attempting to overthrow the Government of the United States of America—they were merely kicking up their heels, enjoying a fling, a temporary diversion since all flings are temporary, and some are even shorter.

In six weeks, six months at best, it'd go the inevitable route of employer-employee romances—Maria quitting her job, or J.B. Grimes slipping her a thousand dollars, cutting her loose and they'd drift down other avenues into other beds, because Chicago is the world's biggest whorehouse and there is no critical shortage of beds.

Lockington chomped glumly on his sandwich. One helluva way to make a living—he'd dropped into the lawyer-used car salesman-politician class, but all men can't be Jesuit priests, and rent payments still fall due on the last day of every month on the calendar.

Grimes heaved himself to his feet, still chewing a portion of his last thuringer as he headed for the cashier—Lockington watching him wallow through the revolving door and turn north before departing the booth to pay his check. Grimes had a half-block lead and Lockington ambled leisurely, keeping as many people as possible between his quarry and himself. Grimes went into a liquor store and Lockington stopped to study the window posters of a health food shop, learning that this was the first day of a week-long special on Tibetan dried spinach sprouts. Then Grimes came out, carrying a bottle wrapped in a brown paper bag, and Lockington nodded a nearly imperceptible nod of approval—a few hookers served to enliven a matinee—oil for the blazing lamps of fornication.

Grimes seemed edgy now, flicking occasional glances over his shoulder—the moment was nearly at hand, it was going to be the Ellenwood Hotel. Another three-quarters of a block and he performed an abrupt right flank maneuver, disappearing through the grimy glass doors of the Ellenwood, a broken-down, four-story, twenty-five room roach ranch that was long overdue for a date with the wrecking ball. When compared to the Ellenwood, both the Lochinvar Arms and the Hooper House stacked up favorably with the Taj Mahal.

J.B. Grimes was standing at the desk when Lockington sauntered unconcernedly into the lobby, pulling up at the west end of the splintered mahogany counter to stare myopically at a rack of magazines, listening intently. The emaciated clerk was saying, "That's right, Mr. Kelly, they're talking rain tonight and probably all day tomorrow."

Grimes said, "Then that's what we'll get. Ever notice how them meteorologists are always right on wrong weather and always wrong on right?" He had a country drawl.

The clerk's smile was a humorless, worn and weary thing. He said, "It never fails, does it? I've assigned you to ROOM 315 for this afternoon, Mr. Kelly. That'll be okay?"

Grimes-Kelly nodded. "Good old 315—a room with a view."

"Yessir, right over the alley."

Grimes-Kelly said, "Oh, by the way, has my friend arrived?"

The clerk flashed an okay sign. "Your friend's in 315, waiting."

Grimes-Kelly departed the desk and Lockington eased out of the Ellenwood's lobby, crossing LaSalle Street to a tavern on the northwest corner. He chucked a five dollar bill onto the bar, ordering a shot of Martell's cognac before hiking to the pay phone in a dim corner of the place. He punched out the number of Classic Private Investigations and Duke Denny answered on the first ring. Lockington said, "Okay, her name's Maria—they're shacked in 315 at the Ellenwood on South LaSalle—Grimes is using the handle of Kelly."

Denny cackled gleefully. "Great, partner, just *great—*

where are you now?"

"Gin mill—half-a-block south—west side of LaSalle."

"Okay, we'll be there—should be no more than an hour!"

"'*We*'? Who's '*we*'?"

"Martha Grimes and me, plus whoever it takes—Martha wants to be in on the kill."

"Where's Martha Grimes?"

"Browsing around town—she calls in every fifteen minutes for developments. Stay right where you are and keep your eyes open!"

"No problem—I can see the Ellenwood's entrance from the bar."

"Good man, Lacey!"

Lockington straddled a barstool, downed his snort of Martell's and ordered another, eyeing his watch. The bartender said, "Watch yourself, good buddy—here comes Maybelle!"

Lockington said, "Maybelle?"

"She works Union Station for between-trains tricks—gets over our way about this time every day."

Maybelle popped onto a barstool next to Lockington's. She was a scrawny, washed-out blonde with flickering phony eyelashes. Lockington figured that she bought her mascara by the gallon. Maybelle said, "Well, hi, there! Lonely?"

Lockington said, "Usually."

Maybelle sized him up. She said, "What's your line?"

Lockington said, "I'm a brain surgeon."

Maybelle's eyelashes fluttered and she whistled, low and long. "Oh, wow, there must be big bucks in *that* racket!"

"I work for nothing."

"Welfare cases—things like that?"

"No—I'm not allowed to charge until I get a license."

Maybelle's eyes narrowed. "No license—how can you operate when you don't got no license—what hospital you with?"

Lockington said, "*Hospital?* I don't need no stinking hospital—I work right in the home."

Maybelle didn't say anything.

Lockington said, "Hell, I get by with a chain saw and a pocketknife."

Maybelle still didn't say anything.

Lockington said, "What's your address?"

Maybelle was headed through the door onto North LaSalle Street. The bartender returned to pour another Martell's for Lockington. He said, "Nice going, pal! How'd you manage it?"

Lockington said, "I told her I'm a cop."

The bartender said, "*Are* you?"

Lockington said, "No, I'm a brain surgeon."

19

The minute hand of Lacey Lockington's wristwatch, which had set him back $19.95, seemed riveted in place, but time passes, even on North LaSalle Street in Chicago, and eventually a Yellow Cab ripped to a tire-smoking halt along the curbing. Moments later the tavern door flew open with a bang and Duke Denny came bounding in, followed by an enormous woman in a brilliant orange dress. She wore spike-heeled white pumps slightly smaller than canal barges, she carried a bulging white plastic handbag slung over her shoulder, and she glared at Lockington with the searing, unblinking eyes of a pissed-off swamp adder—Martha Grimes, sure as hell. Denny had described Martha as being a bit on the pudgy side, an understatement akin to likening the Pacific Ocean to a Wisconsin trout pond, Lockington thought. Behind Martha Grimes came a long-haired, spidery, bespectacled creature with an eleven hundred dollar Japanese camera draped around his neck. Bringing up the rear of the strange procession were two shuffling, unshaven, bloodshot-eyed, red-nosed apparitions clad in tattered jackets and baggy-kneed pants. Lockington was staring incredulously at Duke Denny. He said, "Now, wait just a fucking minute! What're we gonna *do*—invade the fucking Soviet *Union*?"

Denny said, "What're we gonna *do*? We're gonna catch good old J.B. Grimes with his drawers off, *that's* what we're gonna do!"

Lockington said, "But who the hell *are* all these God damned *people*?"

Denny took the woman by an arm the circumference of a young banyan tree. He said, "Lacey, this lovely young thing is Martha Grimes." Lockington looked her over and that took a while. Her proportions approximated those of a Holiday Inn. Lockington nodded and she nodded back, smiling frostily.

"Yes, of course, but what about the rest of the regiment?"

"The guy with the camera is Fingers O'Shaughnessy—Fingers is a free-lance photographer—does his own developing, printing, enlarging, superimposing if necessary—whatever it takes."

Lockington gestured half-heartedly and Fingers gave Lockington a thumbs-up sign. He said, "Bongo, baby!"

Lockington lowered his voice to Denny. He said, "Uhh–h–h, *bongo, baby*?"

Denny shrugged. He said, "Fingers talks funny."

Lockington kept his voice down. "Tell me about the Lush Brothers."

"Murph and Dillingham."

"Which is which?"

"Murph's the one with his fly open—Dillingham's the one whose shoes don't match."

"Uh–huh, and what are *they* doing here?"

"They're witnesses—like you said, Lacey, we gotta have *witnesses!*"

Lockington shook his head. "Y'know, I'm beginning to get a dim feeling about this safari."

Denny waved a pooh-poohing hand. "Standard procedure, partner—it's gonna go off like clockwork!"

"Isn't that what Hitler told Goebbels?"

The bartender said, "Are you people going to hold up the joint or will you be drinking?"

Dillingham glanced hopefully at Denny. He said, "Drinking, ain't it?"

Lockington shoved his empty glass at the bartender. He said, "Martell's—a *double,* 'ere I perish.'"

Martha Grimes squirmed agitatedly. Martha Grimes squirming agitatedly reminded Lockington of something Lockington hadn't wanted to be reminded of. Martha said, "I doubt that we'll have time for a great deal of drinking."

Lockington said, "Apparently you've never seen Maria."

Dillingham said, "I'll have the same as this fine gentleman here!" He fetched Lockington a goodly wallop between the shoulder blades.

Denny said, "All right, set 'em up, but make it fast!"

Murph said, "*Cantate Domino! Transeat in exemplum!*"

Dillingham said, "Fix bayonets, men!"

Denny leaned toward Lockington, whispering, "Murph used to be an Archbishop or something."

Lockington said, "Which leaves Dillingham—what'd *he* used to be?"

"Hard to say—he's been on Skid Row ever since."

"Ever since *what?*"

Denny shrugged. "That's what's hard to say."

20

They came trooping into the Ellenwood Hotel's dismal deserted lobby, a sextet that could have stepped from a Gilbert and Sullivan operetta—the smiling Duke Denny togged out in a spiffy plum-colored leisure suit, the glowering Lockington looking like a middle-aging torpedo from a 1940's cops-and-robbers movie, Martha Grimes in her bright orange dress resembling a Goodyear blimp that had just burst into flames, Fingers O'Shaughnessy peering wild-eyed through his unkempt mane of hair, Murph and Dillingham ambling bewilderedly at the end of the parade.

The desk clerk was a hollow-checked, sunken-chested relic from the halcyon days of Boss Kelly. He gave the new arrivals an expressionless, rheumy-eyed stare. He'd been around the block a few times, Lockington could tell. Duke Denny stepped with knowing, businesslike mien to the desk, whipping out a twenty dollar bill to dangle it tantalizingly under the nose of the clerk. He said, "Sir, it is my desire to rent a passkey."

The desk clerk smothered a yawn. He said, "You're coming in a hair light, dear friend."

Denny's smile was ingratiating. "Why, certainly, but we had to start *some*where, didn't we? Now just how light am I coming in, would you say?"

The desk clerk took the question under consideration, scratching his testicles in the process. "Well, an educated guess would place that figure in the neighborhood of eighty clams."

Denny's smile faded abruptly. He said, "Sir, you would appear to be laboring under a false impression— you see, I am not interested in *purchasing* the Ellenwood Hotel—I am merely attempting to rent one of its passkeys for twenty dollars. Twenty dollars is the going rate at the Lochinvar Arms."

The desk clerk said, "Yes, twenty dollars is the going rate at the Lochinvar Arms, but at the Ellenwood Hotel the going rate is one *hundred* dollars."

Martha Grimes tapped Denny's shoulder with an impatient thuringer-size forefinger. She snarled, "Give the creep his hundred and let's get the hell upstairs!" Her face was taut, her voice like breaking glass.

Denny shrugged and complied, palming the passkey, motioning his mercenaries into a tight huddle at the foot of the Ellenwood's staircase, dropping his voice to super-secret level. He said, "All right, gang, here's the way it's gonna play—I'll go first and get the door open."

Dillingham was whispering to Murph. "I wonder, will they maybe have a bottle?"

Murph snorted. "Of *course*, they'll have a bottle! What's a roll in the hay without a *bottle*?"

Denny was saying, "Fingers, you'll be right behind me—when I pop that lock you'll charge in there and start shooting pictures before they have the slightest idea of what the hell's happening!"

Fingers said, "Blasto, baby!"

Denny turned to Martha Grimes. He said, "Are you certain that you want a piece of this action? It could get sticky up there!"

Martha's smile was the smile of a hangman for the condemned. She rasped, "Oh, but, Mr. Denny, I wouldn't miss it for the *world!*" She hefted her big white handbag, testing it for balance and weight, adjusting its shoulderstrap paratroop-fashion, five seconds before jumptime.

Denny said, "Murph and Dillingham, you'll go in after O'Shaughnessy—you'll just stay out of the way and observe the action—we'll be requiring your affidavits a little later in the ball game."

Murph nodded, his gaze a faraway thing. He murmured, "*Gloria Chivas Regal.*"

Dillingham said, "Press where ye see my white plume shine, amidst the ranks of war!"

Lockington wondered about Dillingham.

Denny clapped his hands together. He snapped, "All right, people, let's *hit* it!"

Lockington said, "One moment, please. Where the hell do *I* fit in?"

Denny grinned. He said, "Partner, you get twenty minutes with Maria!" He slapped Lockington on the shoulder and they climbed the two flights of dusty, creaking stairs, singlefile, Denny on the point, passkey at the ready, reminding Lockington of a white hunter in lion country, and

Lockington experienced a sudden inexplicable urge to return to Kenya Colony, which was odd because Lockington had never been within eight thousand miles of Kenya Colony. They tiptoed furtively down the third-story hallway through the clinging odors of rot and mildew. Behind a door to their left a man coughed a rapid-fire series of consumptive coughs. Behind a door to their right a television set blared a Budweiser commercial. Lockington detested Budweiser commercials.

Denny pulled up at the door of ROOM 315, raising an authoritative hand, very much in command, like Custer at the Little Big Horn, Lockington thought. Dillingham was nudging Murph, whispering, "I wonder what kind of bottle will it be?"

Murph shrugged. He whispered, "*Que sera sera.*"

Lockington wished that Murph and Dillingham were at the Little Big Horn, or *in* it, preferably.

Duke Denny was crouched at the door of ROOM 315, easing the passkey into the lock, turning it slowly, silently—Duke had been a first-rate cop, he'd learned all the wrinkles. He twisted the knob with the sensitive touch of a safecracker, opening the door just a crack. Then, stepping back and lowering his left shoulder, he went plowing into the room like a rogue rhinoceros into a Wednesday night prayer meeting, the nightchain snapping, twanging like a tenor banjo string. Fingers O'Shaughnessy skirted Denny to rocket into 315, hollering, "Bashwollo, baby!"

Martha Grimes, who'd been trailing the procession, came hard on the outside to rumble hot on O'Shaughnessy's heels, tearing open her handbag on the dead run. She negotiated the turn at a speed defying the laws of centrifugal force, Murph and Dillingham stumbling dazedly behind her, and Lockington was still several feet short of the doorway when he heard Martha screech, "Oh, Merciful, Crucified Jesus Christ of fucking blue Lake fucking Galilee, debauchery, *debauchery*, *DEBAUCHER-E-E-E-E!*" There was the shattering roar of a firearm, this followed by another and another and yet another. It sounded like the battle of Midway in there, and Lockington hit the deck flat on his belly as a slender, chalky-faced, stark-naked young man came barreling out of ROOM 315, carrying a pair of trousers and one shoe, vaulting Lockington's prostrate body like an Olympics low hurdles champion, babbling a steady torrent of terrified Polish.

Lockington didn't understand a word of Polish but he wished to Christ that he was in Warsaw.

He wormed his way, infantry-style, to the doorway of ROOM 315, peering cautiously around the corner. Martha was struggling with a Colt .45 automatic pistol, screaming, "This God damned thing is *jammed*—somebody *hold* that sonofabitch while I run out and buy a *machine* gun!"

Duke Denny crossed the room in two giant strides, ripping the pistol from Martha's grasp, ejecting the clip, and tucking the barrel of the weapon under his belt. The smoky room was filled with the acrid smell of spent gunpowder, and Lockington counted two holes in the ceiling, one in the north wall, a fourth in a window. He clambered warily to his feet, dusting himself, watching Murph and Dillingham crawl from under the bed. Dillingham had a strangle hold on the neck of a nearly full bottle of Smirnoff Vodka. Denny was addressing Fingers O'Shaughnessy. "Did you get the snaps?"

Fingers O'Shaughnessy leered. He said, "Bofferino, baby!"

J.B. Grimes sat huddled cross-legged in the middle of the rumpled bed, bald head buried in palsied hands. The big man was sobbing. He said, "Well, Marty, I guess you had to find out *some*time." Lockington's Chicago-calloused heart went out to J.B. Grimes.

Martha Grimes said, "Get dressed, you unthinkable pile of filth!"

Grimes raised his tear-streaked face. Quaveringly, he said, "I *can't* get dressed—he grabbed *my* pants by mistake!"

"Then wear *his*, you swine!"

"His won't fit—he has mine, and my wallet's in 'em!"

Lockington stood in the doorway, surveying the scene, shaking his head, wishing he was in Halifax, wondering where Halifax was. He left ROOM 315 to walk slowly down the hallway in the direction of the stairway, head down, hands thrust into his hip pockets. Behind a door on his right a woman shrieked, "Not *that* way, Harry! I don't *do* it that way, Harry!" Behind a door on his left a television set blasted out a McDonald's commercial. Lockington loathed McDonald's commercials.

21

It was Monday, and if it wasn't a clear blue Monday, it was as clear blue a Monday as is likely to be seen in Chicago. On Mondays Chicago is a very good place not to be. On Mondays Chicago registers more fistfights, more traffic accidents, more abortions, more just about any damned thing, than on all the remaining days of the week put together. Monday also happens to be an excellent day for quitting your job in Chicago, although few Chicagoans bother to formalize the act. The way most Chicagoans handle it is by simply failing to show up for work on Monday morning, and hiring out on a different railroad on Tuesday afternoon—it's a Chicago tradition of long standing, which was why Lacey Lockington was about to quit his job on a Monday. He'd made his decision shortly following the J.B. Grimes debacle, but being a firm believer in the preservation of traditions, he'd procrastinated over the span of the weekend.

At 8:30 on that particular Monday morning the Loop was busy enough, but it'd get busier—the clawing frenzy of its midday was poised in the offing like a headsman's axe. This two-hour stretch of utter insanity would commence with the riotous arrival of Chicago's fat women—the Lard Legion, as Duke Denny had dubbed them. They'd come boiling from trains, buses, cabs, elevateds, subways, fanning out to sack the city as the Huns sacked Danubia. There was a ferociously determined inevitability about the fat women of Chicago, and never were they more inevitable than on Mondays.

Lockington sat at the white-enameled counter of a Greek coffee shop on West Randolph Street, gnawing on a grease-soaked chocolate doughnut, sucking on a lukewarm cup of abominable black coffee, thinking of Martha Grimes, pondering the matter of obesity and its effects on the personality of the Chicago female. Turmoil was the Chicago fat woman's catnip, she *revelled* in it—if it was absent, she'd go looking for it—if it existed, she'd *double* it. Lockington knew nothing of Denver's fat women, or of Baltimore's, but he was convinced that one Chicago fat woman, smuggled into the Kremlin, could introduce a wave of pandemonium so awesome as to bring Russia to its knees within a fortnight. He wondered why the CIA hadn't considered the move. Such a plan might already be in the works, he thought, smiling craftily, marveling at its strategic potential. He finished his chocolate doughnut, gulped the rest of his coffee, paid his tab, and crossed West Randolph Street to an ancient red brick building and Duke Denny's one-horse private investigations agency in its basement.

Denny's place of business was a tiny, damp, cheaply-paneled single room, its concrete floor covered by dark brown outdoor carpeting which served to make it appear considerably smaller than it was. The Spartan severity of the enclosure had been slightly modified by a cheap beige throw rug that had steadfastly refused to lie flat, its cantankerous middle constantly bowed upwards in the manner of a cornered tomcat's. There were three straight-backed wooden chairs lodged against the east wall, and another parked next to the dented green metal desk that stood in the northeast corner of the place. There were a couple of black plastic-framed pictures suspended lopsidedly from the north wall—a reproduction of an excellent charcoal sketch featuring a lion and a lamb sprawled contentedly together under what appeared to be a dogwood tree, and a blown-up color print of Wrigley Field where the marquee sign said DEDICATED TO A NEW TRADITION. Lockington assumed that there was some sort of symbolic connection between these, but he'd failed to grasp it, Denny had never offered an explanation, and Lockington had never asked for one.

There was a tarnished brass pedestal-type ashtray, a wobbly wooden clothes tree, several outdated news magazines stuffed into a flowered cardboard basket, a small portable radio belting a song that Lockington hadn't heard before and certainly didn't want to hear again, and there was a sartorially perfect Duke Denny, wearing maroon sports jacket, white knit shirt, and tailored baby blue slacks, slouched at the desk in a squeaky swivel chair, watching Lockington's approach. Denny raised an arm in an exaggerated "*Heil Hitler*" salute, winking at Lockington. He said, "Well, partner, what can I say? You turned in one helluva job—you made it look easy!"

Lockington sat on the straight-backed wooden chair to Denny's right. "It *was* easy—the wrong thing usually *is.*"

Denny caught the burrs in Lockington's voice. "You sound sour, Lacey—how do you feel?"

"In a word—slimy."

Denny brushed that away with a brisk overhand gesture. "Hey, we brought it off, didn't we? Martha Grimes has her old man by the balls on a downhill pull—her lawyer's kicking off divorce proceedings this afternoon, and J.B. can't contest—she has prints of Fingers O'Shaughnessy's pictures, and she could destroy him!"

Lockington said, "She destroyed the poor bastard the day she married him." He lit a bedraggled cigarette, chucking the smoking match into the cracked ceramic turkey platter that doubled as Denny's ashtray. "Martha Grimes is a downright merciless, masculine, domineering, overbearing, grasping, hog-fat bitch-witch."

Denny threw up his hands defensively, warding off the storm of adjectives. "Granted, but she's a *rich* bitch-witch, and, baby, that's the bottom line!"

Lockington blew smoke into the speaker of Denny's portable radio. "My God, Duke, you sure got yourself into a sleazy racket!"

"Aw, look, Lacey, this is a *service* agency—if I don't handle this sort of crap, somebody else *will!*"

"There's a familiar self-justifying line."

Denny leaned forward, elbows on the cluttered desktop.

"A man's gotta eat, doesn't he? Martha Grimes is on the proper side of the road, isn't she? What the *hell*, J.B. Grimes goes to bed with *men!*"

"Uh–huh—well, after being in bed with Martha, maybe that ain't such a fucking radical departure."

"Partner, that's just none of my God damned business!

Martha Grimes came in here, she placed her order, and she laid her money on the line."

"It's just that simple, huh?"

"It's just that simple!"

"Tainted goods, tainted money—that's how simple it is!"

Denny shrugged the remark off. "C'mon, partner, let's go out for breakfast—I'll close the joint for a couple hours."

"I've already *had* breakfast. J.B. Grimes ain't such a bad apple. So he went queer—with Martha at home it's a miracle that he didn't get into something a helluva lot *worse*!"

"What's a helluva lot worse than going *gay*?"

"Try *religion*—he *could* be going around speaking in unknown tongues, y'know!"

Denny chuckled. "Lacey, I'll be damned if I can *figure* you! You poke fun at the churches, yet you're the quintessential rug-dusting, old-time evangelist, preaching up a storm!"

"Duke, listen—all I'm saying is that there are things a man can do for money—and there are things he *can't* do!"

"Depends on the man, if you ask *me*."

"I don't recall asking you—I'm just telling you how it looks from here!"

"Hey, partner, wake up—this is *Chicago*! I'm a Johnny-come-lately and I've adjusted to it—you've been here since you were born and you *haven't*. In this burg it's devil take the hindmost! When in Chicago do as the Chicagoans do!"

"To hell with how the Chicagoans do it, to hell with how *anybody* does it! Have you ever considered being your own man?"

"*You're* your own man and what's to show for it—what kind of car are you driving, how much money you got in the bank?"

"I drive a clunker and I'm damn near broke, but, God damn it, I can sleep at night!"

"Yeah, sleep at night, and starve all day—big fucking deal!"

Lockington was silent for a time, letting the heat of their exchange subside. Then he said, "Duke, someday I'm gonna find me a quiet little town where people mean what they say—where they do what they say they'll do."

There was no humor in Denny's laugh. He said, "Lacey, there ain't no such fucking place!"

"Maybe not, but they can't hang a man for looking!"

Denny squinted puzzledly at his ex-partner. "What the hell side of the bed did you fall out of this morning? Man, you're in some kind of *mood*! You better get your ashes hauled!"

Lockington said, "Looky, Duke, I'd appreciate it if you'd get yourself another boy—busting into people's bedrooms just doesn't turn my crank."

Denny shrugged resignedly, nodding. "Okay, I can see your point—you're too direct for this pea patch—but could you spare me just a *little* time?"

"I'd rather not."

"Well, hear me out before you say no—this is the spot I'm in—I gotta go to Ohio tomorrow morning—Cleveland—I have a manipulating stepsister down there who's trying to shoulder me out of my cut of an inheritance."

"If it's any of my business, what does that amount to?"

"I don't know, but I've been told it's in the ballpark of fifteen grand."

"Is she beating you out of it legally?"

"Probably—she's a very good Christian."

"Then why bother?"

"I want to check it out from the ground up—it may be worth a shot."

"You driving to Cleveland, or flying?"

"Driving—it's just seven hours or so."

"How long will you be gone—outside figure?"

"Offhand, I'd say a week—maybe slightly longer—I'll have to contact a Cleveland attorney."

"All right, what could I possibly accomplish here alone? I wouldn't be able to get out on the street—the best I could do would be scratch my ass and answer the telephone."

"Partner, that'd be good enough—you'd be my buffer, my good-will ambassador—you could stall appointments, sweet-talk people, freeze everything until the tail end of next week. I don't give a damn how you do it, just keep the ship afloat until I get back."

"And *then* what?"

"Then you can saddle up and hit the trail for Pepper Valley. I got a guy on the line—he'll be available by then. Whaddaya say, Lacey—just a few days—for old times' sake?"

Lockington sighed, banging the desktop with the flat of his hand. "I'm a sonofabitch—the damn-fool things a man will do for an ex-partner!"

Denny was grinning from ear-to-ear, digging enthusiastically into his top desk drawer, locating a key, sliding it across the desk to Lockington. "That'll get you in here tomorrow morning. Now get the hell outta here and get laid!"

They shook hands and Lockington said, "You'll be in touch?"

"I'll call from Cleveland at least once a day."

"How do I get hold of you in case the building burns down?"

"I'll leave a Cleveland number—I'll be staying with an old high school buddy—we chased a lot of pussy together. Don't look so downhearted, Lacey—maybe I can get this business ironed out sooner than I think."

Lockington went up the short flight of stairs, stepping onto the West Randolph Street sidewalk, thinking about Duke Denny—a rascal, but a lovable rascal—he'd never known one quite like him. Lockington didn't see the westbound fat woman and she piled into him, knocking him flat on the seat of his pants, plowing straight ahead, maintaining a steady course, never looking back. Lockington sat there, glancing dazedly at his wristwatch. It'd stopped at 9:32. 9:32 last night or 9:32 this morning, he wondered. He'd never know, and the realization saddened him.

22

Lacey Lockington was not a genius, nor was he a dimwit. He wasn't an optimist, neither was he a pessimist. He was, he figured, a skeptical realist, theorizing that all skeptics are realists, and all realists skeptics—that it's impossible to be one without being the other, but there were moments when he wasn't dead certain of that.

He was given to spending considerable time wondering about things that he had no business wondering about, because these invariably led to questions that no one had ever answered, and probably never would, at least not to Lockington's satisfaction. He had a habit of wrestling with such weighty matters while driving, and now he herded the rattling blue Pontiac Catalina west through a torrent of fender-to-fender Kennedy Expressway traffic, oblivious to the breakneck sound and fury of his immediate surroundings, his thoughts probing dark niches, considering once more the birth of Planet Earth and the origin of mankind. Had these been spinoffs of the legendary Big Bang, or had the entire kaboodle been deliberately set in place and motion by a Supreme Being? Lockington leaned heavily toward the Supreme Being line of reasoning, not necessarily because he preferred it—it just worked better for him. His realm of comprehension failed to encompass some twenty jillion planets roaring around out there at fifty skillion miles per split second in flawless synchronization for umptillion eons without timing and guidance from an intellect long preceding man's contrived and self-serving laws of physics.

And he was unable to accept the groundwork for his own existence having been laid with a couple of amoebas knocking off a quickie in some prehistoric Afghanistanian swamp, or wherever the theory of evolution claimed it had occurred. In lieu of that, Lockington liked Adam and Eve fornicating under a Wap-Wap tree in the Garden of Eden. He wondered about Eve—had she been an active lay, or had she ho-hummed the experience? Active, probably, Lockington thought, very active—a real stem-winder.

Crossing Kimball Avenue, Lockington turned to the human soul—was it an actuality, a tangible thing, or merely a wispy figment of man's wishful imaginings? How was it to be defined, what was its function, did it react before or after the fact, was it activated by senses or by thoughts, how did the damned thing work, *if* it worked—a cacophony of automobile horns was seeping into Lockington's consciousness and there was a thunderous pounding on the left front window of his Pontiac. His soliloquy shattered, Lockington took stock of his location and found himself parked under the traffic signal of the Kennedy Expressway's southbound exit onto North Mannheim Road, a spot not on his itinerary, because he'd intended to depart the Kennedy

Expressway at Harlem Avenue, some four miles east. He
was able to drum up vague recollections of having stopped
at a red traffic signal, but now the light was green, and a
fat woman stood at the door of his automobile, waving her
arms, stamping her feet, her beady eyes blazing, her face
livid, her chins quivering, every damned one of them. She
was screaming, "Are you gonna move this frigging pile of
junk or am I gonna call the frigging police?"

Lockington nodded, tipped his hat, and pulled onto
Mannheim Road, adding the incident to his already bulging
file of clashes with overweight females. There was a strange,
turbulent venom seething within these creatures, and the
fatter they got, the testier they became.

He turned left on Grand Avenue, tooling his old
blue car eastward through Franklin Park, River Grove,
Elmwood Park, pulling into the Shamrock Pub's parking lot.
Shamrock Pub action rarely picked up before five o'clock
in the afternoon, and the place was reasonably quiet, Mush
O'Brien standing behind the bar, one foot up on the sink
drainboard, watching the door with jaded eyes, the juke box
throbbing a tango—"La Cumparsita"—Joe Brothers and
Rosie Delancey dancing to its beat. They weren't dancing
to it, exactly—they were standing in a dim corner behind
a Hickory Barrel Ale display, glued pelvis to pelvis, *rubbing*
to it. Cheaper than a motel room, Lockington thought, but
there were certain drawbacks. At the bar Buster Weatherby
and Duffy Gray were discussing the destruction of Pompeii,
and Buster Weatherby was saying, "It wasn't Mt. Vesuvius—
Pompeii was bombed, baby, *bombed!*"

Duffy Gray said, "Yeah? Who bombed it?"

Buster Weatherby said, "Mussolini—who the fuck *else?*"

Duffy Gray said, "I didn't know that."

Buster Weatherby said, "Me, neither, till I figured it out!"

Duffy Gray said, "But Mussolini was *Italian*!"

Buster Weatherby said, "Uh–huh, and so was Joe DiMaggio!"

Duffy Gray said, "By God, I never looked at it in that light!"

Lockington took a seat at the bar and Mush O'Brien said, "Martell's, Lacey?"

Lockington nodded and Mush served him, rolling his eyes, lowering his voice. "You listening to them two lamebrains?"

Lockington nodded. "Highly enlightening conversation."

Mush said, "Now, Lacey, you know God damned well that Benito Mussolini *never* bombed Pompeii!"

Lockington said, "A doubtful premise, I agree."

Mush said, "It was that fucking Adolf Hitler, *that's* who!"

Lockington didn't say anything.

Mush said, "*Think* of it, a whole fucking *town*! Oh, my God, the *humanity*!"

Edna Garson came swinging in, ignoring Lockington. She went to the far end of the bar, waited for Mush O'Brien, ordered a screwdriver, took it to a rear booth, and sat with her back to the door. Her walk would have derailed a two hundred car freight train, and Lockington picked up his cognac, following her to the booth, sitting across the table from her. He said, "Hi, long time no see."

Edna scowled. "That's what the fat man said when he saw his dick in the mirror. Where in the hell have you *been*?"

"Around."

"*Around*? Around *what*—the fucking *world*?"

"I've been downtown, mostly. You aren't working today?"

"Apparently not."

"How come?"

"Possibly because it's my day off."

"I see."

"I'm so glad."

"Well, I got a new job, sort of."

"*Sort* of?"

"Yeah, it's a temporary thing."

"Doing what?"

"Not much of anything."

"So tell me about it."

"Okay, I'm—"

"Not *here!*"

"All right, let's go to your place."

"No, let's go to *your* place. I've never been to your place."

"What's to do at my place?"

"Same thing that's to do at my place."

"Oh, *that.*"

Edna gulped her screwdriver, getting to her feet, grabbing Lockington's hand to tug him from the booth. When they were in the Pontiac, she said, "For God's sake, *hurry*—this is an *emergency!*"

Lockington backed out of his parking spot, slanting the car toward Grand Avenue, stopping just in time to avoid a collision with a pink Cadillac coming down the wrong side of the road. He didn't get a good look at the driver, but over the years he'd noticed that Chicago fat women have strong preferences for pink Cadillacs.

23

On Monday, August 28, a scorching Chicago morning found Lacey Lockington seated at the desk in Duke Denny's unairconditioned office, mopping sweat, thoroughly mesmerized by the first game of a Pepper Valley–Delta River series. The contest was scoreless in the last half of the sixth inning, two Delta River hitters had been retired, one had walked, Buck Nesbitt was the Delta River batter, Carl Willis was the Pepper Valley pitcher, Buck Nesbitt tagged a Willis pitch deep into right field, and the God damned telephone rang. The caller told Lockington that her name was Millie Fitzgerald, and that she was calling in reference to her cat.

Lockington wanted to know what about Millie Fitzgerald's cat.

Missing, Millie Fitzgerald said. For two nights now, she said.

Lockington expressed grave concern.

Millie Fitzgerald wanted to know if Lockington had

seen him.

Lockington said well, no, not to the best of his knowledge.

Millie Fitzgerald advised Lockington to keep his eyes open.

Lockington assured her that he'd do that.

He was gray, Millie Fitzgerald said—gray with black stripes.

Lockington said uh–huh, just a moment while he made a note of that.

Millie Fitzgerald told Lockington that her cat's name was Geronimo.

Lockington said ah, yes—Geronimo.

Millie Fitzgerald asked if Lockington didn't regard that as being unusual.

Lockington wondered what was unusual about what.

Millie Fitzgerald said a Siamese cat with an Italian name was unusual, wasn't it?

Lockington said yes, by God, it was, it certainly was.

Millie Fitzgerald said oh, well, what the hell.

Lockington agreed, Millie Fitzgerald hung up, Jason Browne went to the wall to drag down Buck Nesbitt's long drive, but Delta River beat Pepper Valley anyway, and a big man in a dark blue suit came in, stopping to stare at Lockington before slamming the door, rattling Duke Denny's picture of Wrigley Field on the north wall. The big man advanced, scowling, approaching the desk with a lumbering, splayfooted gait, reminding Lockington of a tyrannosaur with fallen arches—a lousy collation but the best he could come up with on short notice. The visitor came to a grinding halt at the edge of the desk, placing skillet-size hands on it and leaning toward Lockington. He said, "*You,* sir, are a misbegotten, drunken, worthless, rotten, motherfucking, chowder-headed sonofa*bitch*!"

Lockington nodded. He said, "I know it."

The big man said, "For two cents I'd kick your balls up around your fucking ears!"

Lockington said, "For two cents you can't buy a stick of chewing gum."

The big man said, "All right, how's about I just do it for *nothing*?"

Lockington lit a cigarette. He said, "Up your keester with a blowtorch."

The big man grabbed the straight-backed wooden chair with his left hand, handling it like it was a bag of popcorn, hoisting it high over his head. He said, "Don't get cute with me, cocksucker—I'll scramble your fucking *brains*!"

Lockington didn't move. He yawned. He said, "You talk like a man with a paper ass."

The big man lowered the chair to its accustomed place near the desk, sitting on it, putting out his hand. Lockington took it. He said, "Moose, you bastard, how *are* you?"

Moose Katzenbach's smile was for days gone by. He said, "After that came the part where you hopped off your barstool and about fifteen customers jumped between us to keep somebody from getting killed."

Lockington chuckled. "Yeah, that routine really shook 'em up—we worked it at the Trocadero two or three times."

"The Troc, and Spud's Place, and the Poisoned Pup!" He squinted at Lockington. "Lacey, what the hell are *you* doing here—are you my replacement?"

"You didn't know I was here?"

"Not till I walked through the door, honest to Christ!"

"No, I'm not your replacement, Moose, not really—I won't be here longer than a week or ten days. I'm standing in for Duke—he has personal affairs to get straightened out in Cleveland. What about *you*? I thought you were in Brooklyn."

Moose Katzenbach's eyebrows arched like bushy black rainbows. "*Brooklyn?* I ain't been in Brooklyn since Helen's mother died, five, six years ago. What's in *Brooklyn?*"

"Duke said something about your brother-in-law buying a tavern."

"He did—three years back—it burned down. He was losing his ass, so he had it torched. What about it?"

Lockington shrugged, not carrying it further. He saw it now—Duke Denny had canned Moose Katzenbach to make room for his out-of-a-job ex-partner, cooking up the Katzenbach-to-Brooklyn yarn, not wanting Lockington to know that Moose had been the goat of the switch. "What's on your mind, Moose?"

"Duke owes me a week's pay—thought I'd come around and pick it up. Did he say anything about it before he left?"

Lockington shook his head. "Naw—Duke had a lotta things on his mind. I got a number where you can reach him in Cleveland. He'll be in there sometime this afternoon."

"I'll wait—y'know, Lacey, I can't figure why he let me go—hell, I was doing real good for Duke—never late, always on the job, did every damn thing he wanted, no questions asked. He tell you why he did it?"

Lockington lied, spreading his hands. "Economy measure, probably."

"Economy measure? Hell, I was making under twenty grand a year! How economical can you get?"

Lockington alibied his silence with the squelching of one cigarette and the lighting of another. Three-seventy-five per week as opposed to seven-fifty—ah, generosity, thy true name is Duke Denny! And, if he'd mention it to him, Duke would reply, "Skip it—that's what friends are for." Or something equally ridiculous. Duke was that way.

Moose Katzenbach was saying, "Hey, how'd that Grimes thing work out?"

"Just fine—providing that you aren't J.B. Grimes."

"That was the only thing Duke had cooking when he gave me the axe. What's next—who's gonna work with him now?"

"I don't know what's next, Moose, and I won't be here, whatever it is. When Duke gets back from Cleveland, I'm history."

"Maybe you oughta ask Duke if you can stay on—that investigation don't look too good for you."

"Naw, I'm through as a cop, but this ain't for me. I'll find something. How's Helen, Moose?"

"Not real good—about the same as when you used to come around on Friday nights—" His voice trailed away, and Lockington wished he hadn't asked. Helen Katzenbach had a heart condition. She was a fine lady, Helen Katzenbach—she'd baked Friday night apple pies, and she'd talked about Brooklyn, Brooklyn, Brooklyn. He should have called to inquire about her, but he hadn't. In Chicago nobody gives a damn for anybody, it's contagious—in Chicago you catch it early.

The silence was thickening when Lockington said, "You still got the same phone number?"

"Uh–huh—why?"

"Well, if you aren't working and I hear of something, I could let you know."

"That'd be good, Lacey—I'm gonna go on state unemployment and I'll tend bar a couple nights a week at the Roundhouse down near Pacific Junction—cash pay so it won't mess up my compensation. You know the Roundhouse?"

"Sure—before Julie, I used to bang around with the morning barmaid."

"Sadie Winters, probably—cross-eyed chick—big jugs?"

"That's her. What ever happened to Sadie?"

Moose thought about it. "I think Sadie married Elmer Klausen—Elmer was cross-eyed, too. You probably remember Elmer—he was a janitor at some west side high school."

It'd been a while for them, and they sat there, smoking, laughing, reminiscing, two veteran war-horses from palmier days, before Chicago had gone completely to hell.

It was noon before Lockington knew it.

24

Moose Katzenbach was gone—something about picking up a prescription for Helen, and Lockington sat in the sweltering basement office, feeling the rumble of West Randolph Street traffic, spinning the knob of Duke Denny's plastic radio to no avail. The Cubs were on the road, they'd be playing at Pittsburgh that evening, the White Sox would be at Comiskey Park for a night game, and there was nothing on the dial but rock stuff—soft rock, hard rock, acid rock, heavy metal—discordant five-note mishmosh with cookiecutter three-word lyrics, music geared to the mentality of retarded wart hogs. Someone had said, "Let me hear the music of a nation, and I will tell you the moral condition of that nation." With that remark in mind, Lockington found himself wondering if the United States of America would make it to the turn of the century.

His thoughts drifted back to Moose Katzenbach, and he was vaguely disturbed—Moose had a sick wife, he needed the job at Classic Investigations, but Duke Denny had cut him loose, and he was talking about hiring another man. Lockington didn't know the other man but he was certain of one thing—the new guy would never measure up to Moose Katzenbach. Moose was big, *too* big—grossly overweight, a condition that had cost him his job on the Chicago Police Force, but Moosè wasn't clumsy, he was remarkably agile. He looked stupid, but he was wilier than a fox, he had the guts of a Miura bull and he was just about that dangerous in a fight. With the possible exception of Duke Denny, they just didn't come any better than Moose, and he had one important plus—despite his size, he looked average. There was nothing about Moose Katzenbach that would draw attention—he could have tailed the Pope across the Gobi Desert and he'd have gone unnoticed. Moose was the neighborhood vacuum cleaner salesman, the proprietor of the corner used car lot, the bartender at the joint in the middle of the next block. Mr. Nobody.

Lockington glanced at his watch for the fiftieth time in that many minutes—it was 3:30. Duke Denny had been scheduled to leave Chicago for Cleveland, Ohio, at 7:00 that morning, and Cleveland was something like 375 miles east on Interstate 80. Lockington did a bit of grade school arithmetic—Denny drove hard, and if he wasn't already in Cleveland, he'd be blowing in there shortly. Lockington waited until 4:00 before picking up the phone and dialing the Cleveland number Denny had left in the top desk drawer. After a half dozen rings, a raspy male voice crackled on the line—"Shoot, you're faded!"

Lockington blinked at the 1930s crack before saying, "Is Duke there?"

"Duke?"

"Duke Denny."

"Who's this?"

"Lockington."

"Lockington?"

"Lockington in Chicago."

"I don't know no Lockington in Chicago. I don't even know no Lockington in Cleveland."

"I'm the guy who's running the agency while Duke's in Cleveland."

"Gotcha! Yeah, old Duke's here—well, he ain't here right this very moment, but he *was* here—pulled in, oh, maybe twenty-five minutes ago. What's up, Lockington?"

"Nothing—just checking to make sure Duke got there in one piece."

"Gotcha! Sure, he made it grand style—I'm nuts about that black Caddy, ain't you?"

"Yeah, nice car—Duke isn't there now?"

"Naw, old Duke went out for a case of beer— Rolling Rock—best damn beer in these parts—you like Rolling Rock?"

"I'm not a beer man. Cognac."

"Gotcha! Cognac! I can take cognac or leave it alone. Generally speaking, I leave it alone."

"Uh–huh, well, when do you expect Duke to get back? I want to discuss something with him."

"Gotcha! Say, man, I ain't real sure—he should be back in ten minutes, but you know old Duke—if old Duke runs into a snatch in heat, Christ only knows *when* he'll show up!" He chuckled a man-to-man chuckle, the kind with the built-in leer.

Lockington said, "Okay—looky, I'll be closing the

agency in about an hour—if I don't hear from him by then, he can call me at home sometime this evening—he has my number."

"Gotcha! I'll tell him—any friend of Duke's is a friend of mine!"

"Thanks—uhh–h–h, what's your name?"

"Jack."

"Thanks, Jack."

"Jack Slifka."

Lockington said, "Gotcha!" and hung up, suddenly not sure that he should bring up the Moose Katzenbach matter. After all, Duke Denny had told him that Moose had quit and was moving to Brooklyn, and there was nothing to be gained by proving Duke a liar—his heart had been in the right place, he'd fired Moose to help Lockington. Anyway, Lockington had just thought of another road to town, albeit a temporary route. He called Moose Katzenbach's number, and Helen answered. Lockington said, "To hell with St. Patrick!"

There was a long pause before Helen Katzenbach said, "Lacey Lockington, is that you, you shanty Irish bastard?" Helen sounded tired, but she was Irish, too, and she'd go down swinging.

"No, this is the Sheriff of Nottingham. Where's the big guy?"

"I recognized your voice—I got an ear for voices, Lacey—hell, I could pick out Cary Grant blindfolded!"

"So could I if he was blindfolded."

Helen swore. Helen could swear up a storm on occasion. Then she said, "Moose is in the shower, singing 'On the Road to Mandalay'! Have you ever heard Moose sing 'On the Road to Mandalay'?"

"Is that the one where the dawn comes up like thunder?"

"That's it, only thunder ain't quite the word for it. When are you coming over for apple pie, you ape?"

"One of these nights, Helen, *depend* on it!"

"All right, I'll depend on it. If you want Moose, I'll drag him out of the shower."

"Not necessary—you can handle this one. Just tell him to be at the agency in the morning—he gets his old job back for a week or so, and he'll be paid in cash—he can forget about Uncle Sam."

"Well, sure and God bless you, Lacey Lockington, but Duke Denny hasn't given Moose his last paycheck."

"I'll have the money for him—I'll get it from Duke later. Okay?"

"Lacey, you're one in a million!"

"A million *what?*"

"How's a million drunken Irishmen?"

Lockington said, "Right on the nose!" He broke the connection, grinning. Duke Denny was paying him seven-and-a-half per week, and that broke down to three-seventy-five for Moose Katzenbach, three-seventy-five for Lacey Lockington. It seemed no more than fair, and there was a bonus in it for Lockington—he'd have someone to talk to. The agency was dead, the hours were long, and the Pepper Valley Crickets wouldn't be able to take up all the slack. Lockington leaned back, lighting a cigarette, wondering about Millie Fitzgerald's cat.

And such is the diminuendo before the crescendo, the silence before the battle, the lull before the storm—it comes every so often, even on West Randolph Street.

25

The garage had located the '79 Mercury's problem. Gasoline hadn't been getting to the carburetor, this due to the gas tank being empty. The lasagna had been excellent, and that evening she'd driven to Des Plaines and brought half of her clothing. The next morning she'd announced that she'd made a serious mistake, and she'd driven back to Des Plaines and brought the other half.

On Christmas Day she'd roasted a small chicken because they'd never have gotten outside a turkey. She'd made a dressing from cashews and Lockington had wolfed the dressing and all but ignored the chicken, and this had pleased her. Her pumpkin pie had been laced with crushed pineapple, scoring big with Lockington, who'd wiped it out by bedtime.

They'd talked a lot, neither asking personal questions, the answers to the questions they might have asked coming voluntarily. Julie Masters had been an only child, her parents had been gentle, understanding people, and she'd had a well-to-do uncle whom she'd never met—he'd died when she'd been a baby—and he'd been terribly generous, providing her with a fully-funded college education and a monthly allowance that had lasted until her graduation. Uncle Oxford had been a fine man, no doubt about it, but Julie had never quite cottoned to his widow, Aunt Harriet, who'd brought the money every month, always on a Monday night. Aunt Harriet had been an extremely good-looking woman, but hard-faced, tough-spoken, and too-knowing.

Julie had grown up—after a fashion, as she'd put it—she'd attended Northeastern Illinois, a small school close to her Lincolnwood home. She'd studied journalism because her Uncle Oxford had wanted her to, and she'd stayed with it, liking it, one thought in mind— write a novel. She hadn't done that yet, but she was fiddling around with an idea, and she'd write one eventually, you just wait and see, Lacey Lockington.

Her parents were gone now, both with cancer, both at comparatively early ages, and she'd sold their Lincolnwood house to take a nice three-room apartment near Rand and River Roads on the northwestern edge of Des Plaines. She'd had male friends, naturally, but never one that she'd consider marrying—she wasn't certain that she believed in marriage—she didn't know that she believed in much of anything. She'd given up her virginity at the age of seventeen—to a tackle on the high school football team, a horrendous experience because she'd bled profusely and it'd hurt like hell, and it'd been all of two weeks before she'd cranked up enough courage to try it again, and this time she'd enjoyed the hell out of it, and she still did—she assumed that Lockington was aware of that, and Lockington had said well, yes, he'd gotten that impression.

There'd been one man about whom she grown serious—a fellow named Herzog, but there'd been facets of his personality that she hadn't liked, and they'd drifted apart—well, not completely, but they hadn't been getting together often recently, which was just as well, she thought, or said she thought, and Lockington hadn't made an issue of Herzog or the others, however many there'd been. She hadn't been explicit on numbers, but Lockington had figured that there'd been more than a *few—her knowledgeable, responsive behavior in bed having been far from sophomoric.*

For Christmas he'd bought her a hardbound copy of Roget's Thesaurus—to help her with her novel, he'd said, and she'd presented him with a black and chrome Zippo cigarette lighter engraved LL from JM. He'd kept it on his nightstand and they'd shared it during their long, dead-of-the-night, naked, sitting cross-legged in bed conversations, these leading them far afield but to nowhere, which was perfectly agreeable to both, because there'd been nowhere of importance to go. They'd been happy enough—not as happy as they might have been, but considerably happier than most, and they'd realized this, and they'd settled for it.

She'd stayed and she'd cooked and she'd kept the apartment neat, and she'd done some reading, and she'd jotted voluminous notes on a yellow legal pad—a rough outline for her novel, she'd told him, and before very long they'd fallen in love as lonely people are sometimes wont to do, their better judgement notwithstanding.

They'd spent their New Year's Eve in bed—fucking the old year out and the New Year in, she'd giggled—and then they'd tied into a few fifths of cheap champagne, and he'd gotten his first chance to see Julie Masters drunk. She'd been an utter delight until dawn— she was a topnotch mimic, he'd found out—and she'd sung, providing the harmony to Lockington's lead of "When You Wore a Tulip," then doing a commendable solo on "My Rosary." She'd hypnotized him with a naughty little dance, performing naked with the stem of a plastic rose tucked between her legs and another protruding from between her buttocks. On this note they'd returned to the bedroom where they'd started on the bed and finished on the floor. They'd slept through the Sugar Bowl game, and the Rose Bowl game, and halfway through the Orange Bowl game, awakening with the flame sputtering but hot enough to kick off another round which Lockington had felt fortunate to survive. They'd regrouped in the kitchen over a can of cream of mushroom soup, toast and black coffee, and when they'd gone back to bed, there'd been no shenanigans, none at all, and Lockington had been glad for this.

Quite a pair—Julie Masters, who would never write her novel, and Lacey Lockington, who'd never know what her novel would have been about.

26

The muggy Chicago afternoon struggled by on tortoise feet, and Lockington closed the Classic Investigations office at 5:00 sharp. He hadn't heard from Millie Fitzgerald concerning anything. It figured. Geronimo and Duke would be rendezvousing with females of their respective species—Geronimo pouring it to a feline *femme galante* under a backporch somewhere in Chicago, Duke Denny holed up with a third-rate Cleveland floozie in a fourth-rate Cleveland motel. Geronimo would return to Millie Fitzgerald when he was damned good and ready, Duke Denny would get back with the Rolling Rock beer, possibly before Jack Slifka succumbed to dehydration.

Of all the pussy-chasers Lacey Lockington had ever known, Duke Denny was far and away the pussy-chasingest. The man seemed equipped with some sort of incredible sensory device, a built-in apparatus akin to sonar that winnowed the chaff from the grain, separating the ladies who wouldn't from those who just might, then those who just might from those who sure as hell would, and it was downright amazing how many sure as hell would. Duke Denny was gifted beyond belief, an absolute cinch for the Pussy-Chasers' Hall of Fame, which Lockington assumed would be built in Chicago.

One evening at the Roundhouse Café, Lockington and Denny had been sucking up a few draft beers, watching a svelte little blonde article dancing juke box polkas with a Soo Line switchtender. Denny had studied the blonde through a polka and a half, and he'd nudged Lockington and said, "She's wearing green panties with a poker hand embroidered on them."

Lockington had said, "What sort of poker hand?"

Denny had said, "Wait'll she turns this way again." Then he'd said, "It's a straight, Jack-high."

Lockington had said, "Horseshit."

Denny had shrugged, leaving his barstool to cut in on the switchtender. A few moments later he'd whirled the blonde toward the bar, pulling her up short at Lockington's knee. He'd said, "Honey, I just bet this guy 300 billion dollars that you're wearing green panties with a Jack-high straight embroidered on 'em."

The blonde had winked. "You lose—it's a King-high straight *flush*—hearts."

Lockington had said, "That's a crock."

The blonde had sighed, "Well, what's a girl to do?" She'd hoisted her skirt and half-slip to the belt line, holding it there while Lockington stared. Green panties—King-high straight flush in hearts. She'd dropped her skirt and smiled fetchingly at Denny. She'd said, "Close, big boy, but no cigar."

Denny had said, "Is there a consolation prize?"

The blonde had said, "Damn betcha, but you don't get it *here!*"

They'd gone out arm-in-arm and Lockington had gotten drunk with the Soo Line switchtender who'd been every bit as puzzled as Lockington. He'd said, "Katy's panties usually got *birds* on 'em!"

The Katy's panties affair had been a departure from Denny's form, because Duke believed that simplicity is the essence of success, and he'd based his phenomenal string of conquests on a singularly inauspicious approach. At the initial tallyho, Denny could swap colors as effortlessly as a chameleon, suddenly projecting an aura of innocent bewilderment, his customary suave and outgoing demeanor giving way to fumbling, bumbling reticence—he became the kid from the barnyard, overwhelmed by the big city. Development of this facade had required a great deal of practice but it'd been worth the effort expended—it was convincing, and when presented with Denny's innate thespian skills, it served to endear him to the hearts of women, striking resounding chords within them, arousing nigh uncontrollable desires to protect and mother this wide-eyed defenseless bumpkin. That lure, working in tandem with striking good looks and the physique of a Roman gladiator, made Duke Denny a withering force in the field of pussy-chasing, and small indeed was the wonder that his intended quarry of the hour, no matter how worldly-wise, was very apt to find herself stripped, bedded, and impaled before she was fully cognizant of which the hell end was up.

Lockington drove directly home from the Loop, or as directly as it was possible to drive to West Barry Avenue from downtown Chicago at 5:00 in the afternoon, which was not directly at all, the twelve-mile trip consuming upwards of an hour. He shucked his clothing, showered, slipped into pajamas and robe, opened a can of beer, made a salami sandwich, and had his evening repast while reading a chapter of *Tom Sawyer*, the one in which Tom and Becky emerge safely from the cave. Lockington liked that part best—it gave him goose bumps.

He was smoking his after-dinner cigarette when the doorbell rang. He checked his watch. It was 7:05. Edna Garson stood in the vestibule. She stepped into the apartment, shoving a fifth of Martell's at Lockington.

She said, "Dammit, I was lonely!"

Not knowing what else to say, Lockington said, "Oh?"

Edna closed the door, locking it. Her fingers went to the top button of her blouse. She said, "Now or later?"

Lockington said, "I have that choice?"

Edna's blouse was open, slipping downward to expose one creamy shoulder. Her gaze was rapt. She said, "Quite frankly, no."

27

The bedroom was silent and the vague scent of Edna Garson's hyacinth perfume washed over Lockington like a light purple fog. Or maybe it wasn't hyacinth—Lockington didn't know one scent from another—well, onions, garlic, boiling cabbage, and roses—he could identify those readily enough. But Edna was wearing good perfume, whatever it was. She lay on her left side, her back to him, breathing slowly, deeply, barely audibly, her honey-blonde hair splashed fan-like on the crumpled pillow, Lockington cupping her right breast, a man closer to heaven than he had any right to be. Once in a while she'd twitch in her sleep, mumbling softly, unintelligibly. Then, at exactly 2:30 A.M. Lockington's telephone went off like a seventeen-dollar firecracker, nearly knocking him out of bed. Muttering a curse on Alexander Graham Bell, he lunged across Edna's shoulder to seize the offending instrument and hear Duke Denny's voice rolling over the wire. "Lacey?"

Lockington grunted, "Uh–huh."

Denny said, "Did I wake you up?"

"Uh–huh."

"Well, partner, I'm sorry about that, but I just came in and Jack Slifka left a note saying you'd called this afternoon."

"Uh–huh."

"Making sure that I got to Cleveland okay, Jack's note says."

"Uh–huh."

"There was something that you wanted to discuss?"

"Uh–huh."

"Oh—well, what happened here was I went out for beer, and I ran into this big blonde tomato—wow, these Cleveland chickies!"

"Uh–huh."

"I guess that hitting the hay is about all there is to do in Cleveland—hell, the Indians are in the cellar, and the Browns don't start regular season play for three weeks yet."

"Uh–huh."

"I dunno, maybe I shouldn't say that—I suppose a few of 'em play bingo—they sure got a lot of bingo in Cleveland."

"Uh–huh."

"Say, Lacey, I'll be digging into this inheritance business first thing tomorrow morning—I'm probably outta luck, but there might be a loophole."

"Uh–huh."

There was a long silence before Denny said, "Uhh–h–h, correct me if I'm wrong, but I got a hunch you ain't alone."

"Uh–huh."

"Oops, sorry! Well, have fun—I'll be in touch sometime tomorrow."

"Uh–huh." When Lockington returned the telephone

to the nightstand, Edna Garson reached to loop her arms around his neck, pulling him down to her, speaking into his mouth. "Locky—Locky, now that we're both awake and everything—well—"

"Uh–huh?"

She grasped him firmly by the ears, lifting his head, peering at him through the darkness. "Look, don't you *ever* say *anything* but '*uh–huh*'?"

Lockington sat up. "Why, sure! You think you're in bed with a dummy? Hell, I even recite poetry!" He slipped a hand under her buttocks, lifting her slightly, swinging her to the middle of the bed. "Want some?"

"Some *what?*"

"Poetry."

"Well, no, not particularly—you see, what I really had in mind was—"

Lockington had sucked in a deep breath. He said, "Under the wide and starry sky—"

Edna groaned. "Locky, for Christ's sake, knock that off!"

Lockington's voice was sonorous. "Dig the grave and let me lie—"

"Hold it, Locky—hold it! What in the name of God are you *doing?*"

"Glad did I live and gladly die—"

"All right, I *see*—yes—*yes*—well, I'll be damned, this is certainly news to *me*—but *good* news, you understand—how long—when—what—hail, Columbia—you've never—"

"And I laid me down with a will—"

"Come on, you big bastard—come on—come *on*— *come* ON!"

"This be the verse you grave for me—"

"Faster, dammit, *FASTER!*"

"Here he lies where he longed to be—"

"Will you hurry, please? You're down to the last two God damned *lines*—oh, what the hell, Locky, *Locky,* LOCKEEEEEE—"

"Home is the sailor, home from the sea—"

Edna clamped a violent scissors hold on Lockington's rib cage, pummeling the small of his back with frantic heels, her fingernails digging into his shoulders, shrieking *"QUOTH THE RAVEN, 'NEVERMORE'!"*

When the prolonged shudder had departed her body, she lowered her legs, sprawling spread-eagled under him, ruffling his hair, gasping for air. She said, "*Damn,* I blew it—wrong line."

Lockington said, "No problem—you'll get it right next time."

Dreamy-voiced, Edna said, "Where in the hell did you *ever* learn *that?*"

"In junior high—eighth grade—it was an absolute must in Miss Lavagetto's class."

"Yes, but that's not what I meant—"

"Hey, I'm here to tell you, Miss Lavagetto was one very tough cookie! One day she—"

"I don't want to hear about Miss Lavagetto—I want to know where you picked up that sex with poetry routine!"

Lockington smiled into Edna's shoulder. "That ain't the whole shot—I can do a couple or three verses of that thing about the raven—with *gestures,* yet!"

There was newly kindled interest in Edna's voice. "Is that right? What *kind* of gestures?"

Lockington said, "Like this." He made great flapping

motions with his arms, sort of like a raven, he thought.

Edna Garson's sigh was a dismal thing. She said, "Uhh–h–h, tell me, what ever became of Miss Lavagetto?"

28

When Lockington reached the agency building at 9:25 on Wednesday morning, Moose Katzenbach was seated on the stair, a pair of large white styrofoam coffee containers and a brown paper bag on the top step beside him. He said, "At your service, Master."

Lockington said, "Sorry I'm late, Moose—had to stop at the bank."

Moose hoisted his bulk to a standing position, looking Lockington over. He said, "Where in blazes were *you* last night?"

"Why, did I miss something?"

"Apparently not—you look like you got dragged through a very small knothole."

Lockington nodded, "Yeah, well, it wasn't last night, it was this morning—a fat woman just rammed into me with the handle of her umbrella!"

"Where?"

"Right in the balls!"

"Okay, but *where?*"

"Half-a-block from here—she was walking east, looking west!"

"Her *umbrella* handle?"

"Yeah, and it ain't even gonna *rain*! Moose, something's gonna have to be done about these God damned *fat* broads—they're a *menace*!" He handed Moose his back pay as he unlocked the agency door. "What's in the bag?"

"Couple chunks of apple pie. After you called last night, Helen went right to work. You didn't eat breakfast, did you?"

"Naw, didn't have time." It was a lie—he'd fixed scrambled eggs and sausage before he'd left his apartment, but there was always room for Helen Katzenbach's apple pie. They went in, seating themselves at the desk to wash down apple pie with coffee. Lockington said, "No doubt about it—Helen makes the world's greatest apple pie!"

Moose was silent for the better part of a minute. Then he said, "Helen ain't doing too well, Lacey. I don't know how much longer I'll have her."

Lockington munched the last of his apple pie, the taste going out of it now. He lit a cigarette to go with the dregs of his coffee before speaking into the thickening quiet of the office. "Moose, I can reach for you but I can't touch you—I know where you're coming from, but I've never been there."

"The hell you haven't—you lost a woman. I heard about it."

"Yeah, but that had to be different—with her it was sudden and the shock damned near killed me, but it was probably a helluva lot easier than the long haul—you've been looking this thing in the eye for how many years now?"

"I dunno—seven, eight, maybe nine."

"Moose, if I can be of help—"

Moose shook his head. "Nobody can help, Lacey—drugs, surgery, nothing—it's a dead-end one-way street—just a matter of time."

"We're all on that street, Moose—Helen's gonna outlive a lotta people who don't even know they're *on* it!"

They lounged around the office. Moose killed a fly, swatting it with the flat of his hand. He was quick, and for a *big* man, he was greased lightning. The telephone rang at 10:12—wrong number—a woman looking for DeHoff's Delicatessen.

They talked, they discussed the Cubs, the Bears, the Bulls, the Blackhawks, the Mayor, the City Council, the weather, the condition of Chicago's streets, women they hadn't taken to bed and wished they had, women they'd taken to bed and wished they hadn't, virtually everything within mutually discussable range. Moose was slouching back and forth in front of the desk like a short-leashed grizzly. He said, "Duke Denny ain't exactly tearing up the league in this private investigations business—you know that, don't you?"

Lockington shrugged. "Duke's getting by—he grossed seven-thousand on that Grimes thing—he doesn't need a helluva lotta those."

Moose spun like he'd been stung by a hornet. "Seven *thousand*—who told you *that?*"

"Duke. Who else?"

Moose jerked a hand from a pocket to level a forefinger at Lockington. "Lacey, Duke got seven *hundred* and expenses for the Grimes job—I *know*, because I was right here when he swung the deal with that female rhinoceros! You know *why* I was right here? I was right here because there was nothing for me to do anyplace *else!* Duke hadn't turned a wheel for two weeks before she got here and he ain't turned one since she *left!* Which is probably why he fired my ass— the sonofabitch just couldn't afford to *pay* me!"

Lockington kicked it around in his mind. He said, "Well, hell, Moose, he *has* to be turning a buck—he's driving a brand-new Cadillac convertible, isn't he?"

"Sure, but—well, look, Lacey, I know that Duke's a friend of yours, but if you want my opinion, I think he's hustling women for money—I think he's a gooddam *gigolo!*"

Lockington shrugged it off, grinning. "Duke's qualified."

The phone rang at 10:38—wrong number again—a guy with a southern accent, looking for Stacey's Model Railroad Shop.

Moose said, "Lacey, let's go out and do something magnificent."

Lockington said, "*How* magnificent?"

"*Very* magnificent."

"Okay, I haven't done anything very magnificent in a long time."

"This is just about the most magnificent idea I have ever had!"

"Then it must be extra magnificent because you have had any number of very magnificent ideas, one of which was to goose that waitress at the Ham and Egger on Elston Avenue."

"Well, how was I to know that she was gonna call the fucking police?"

"And it turned out to be O'Malley and Kerrigan, and when they spotted us, they sat at our table."

"And when she came over to register her beef, O'Malley pinched her tit."

"Back to your magnificent idea."

"Ah, yes! Lacey, this time I have outdone myself!"

"Speak, oh, thinker of profound thoughts!"

"Thou art with me?"

"Fear not!"

"Okay, let's go blow Nelson G. Netherby's ass off."

Lockington said, "Moose, you shouldn't tempt me like that."

"Well, *some*body's gotta get that fat fruit! You can't fuck as many people as Netherby's fucked without paying the piper! I'm a few pounds overweight and you shoot a few assholes, and we're *both* out of a job!"

Lockington stretched and yawned, ditching the subject. He said, "It's almost eleven o'clock. Why don't you go to lunch and leave me to contend with this avalanche of clients? Take an hour."

"Hell, *both* of us could go to lunch and take a *week*! Nobody'd know the difference!"

"Yeah, but Duke may be calling from Cleveland. Incidentally, if that phone rings when I'm not here, let the damned thing ring—I'm supposed to be running this joint all by my lonesome."

Moose nodded. "See you in an hour." Lockington watched Moose Katzenbach go out—a big guy carrying an emotional load that would have broken the average man. It'd been good to see him swing his mind from his troubles, however brief the respite.

Lockington sat at the desk, elbow on the chair arm, chin in the palm of his hand, his boredom returning. He found himself hoping that Millie Fitzgerald would call with tidings of Geronimo, but she didn't, and he mused, half-dozing.

29

It'd been a Thursday, a trying, tiring, February Thursday. Lockington had begun the day just two jumps behind a west side rubber check artist. When he'd closed it out, he'd been three jumps behind. His quarry had been a hit-and-run will-o'-the-wisp—he'd had a dozen names and two dozen addresses, over a period of three months he'd bounced more than thirty thousand dollars worth of paper, and his trail had been so muddled that all the bloodhounds in Transylvania couldn't have tracked him around the next corner.

Early that morning over coffee, Julie had told Lockington that she'd probably be home late—she was going to Park Ridge in the afternoon to meet a couple of Northeastern Illinois classmates, and he'd know how those things went. Lockington had said no, how did those things go? Julie had said well, there'd be lunch, and some drinking, and looking back, of course, and a touch of jealousy and a few snide remarks. Lockington had remarked that the afternoon had all the earmarks of a jolly fine affair, particularly the drinking part, and he'd toddled off to pursue the phantom check writer.

At 4:30, cold, weary, and lonely, he'd called Classic Investigations, *hoping to lure Duke Denny to some friendly near northside tavern where they'd have beer and conversation, but Moose Katzenbach had answered the telephone. Moose had said, "Now, Lacey, Duke's been out most of the day on a Missing Persons thing—he's been working it since Monday."*

Lockington had said, "I thought you were the leg man."

"I am, but Duke wanted to get out of the office—I don't know anything about the case—all I can tell you is that he said something about trying the morgue—good a place as any, I guess."

They'd exchanged a few pleasantries and Lockington had thanked him before hanging up and feeling guilty as sin for not having contacted Moose in a coon's age. He'd driven homeward, feeling sorry for himself—it'd be a lackluster evening until Julie got home. Lockington wasn't a lone wolf but he'd never been known as a glad-hander—he was acquainted with hundreds of people, most cops are, but he kept his own counsel, and his immediate associates could usually be counted on the horns of a goat. Earlier, he'd hung around with Moose and Helen Katzenbach. Then Moose had been kicked off the force, and that relationship had ebbed to a considerable extent. More recently, it'd been Duke Denny and Julie Masters, with heavy emphasis on the latter—so, to have described Lacey Lockington as outgoing would have been a misrepresentation of the coarsest variety, because cultivating new friends had never been particularly important to Lockington—he'd concentrated on keeping his old ones.

He'd stopped to pick up a bottle of Martell's cognac, his course clear—he'd read a few chapters of Tom Sawyer, it'd be one of those cozy hearthside evenings, and that'd been the way it'd begun. He'd assembled a liver sausage, sweet pickle, and mayonnaise sandwich, devouring it while listening to the six o'clock radio news, then he'd killed the radio, read half a dozen chapters of Tom Sawyer, drunk at least that many double hookers of Martell's cognac, and fallen sound asleep in his overstuffed chair, a warm sensation of well-being immersing him.

He'd awakened, startled by the urgently repetitious ringing of his doorbell. He'd peered groggily at his watch—11:30. He'd started to get to his feet, learning that his left leg had gone to sleep, and he'd hobbled to the door, opening it to admit a nattily attired Duke Denny—white western Stetson, fur-trimmed range-rider's cowhide jacket, sharply creased brown corduroy slacks tucked neatly into expensive short-topped boots. Denny's cheeks had been rosy and he'd been rubbing his hands briskly together. He'd said, "Colder than a witch's tit out there!"

Lockington had stared at Denny. He'd said, "Well, Jesus Christ, if it ain't the fucking Lone Ranger!"

Denny hadn't smiled.

Lockington had said, "Called you this afternoon, here you come tonight." He'd limped back to the overstuffed chair, collapsing into it, flexing his tingling left leg, gritting his teeth at the avalanche of needles he'd stirred up. He'd growled, "Care for a drink?"

Denny had shaken his head, sitting on the arm of the sofa, crossing his legs, balancing his white Stetson precariously on his knee. His face had been drawn, his lips taut, his voice sombre. He'd said, "Lacey, I—uhh–h–h—well, I was at the Cook County morgue a little over an hour ago."

Lockington had said, "Yeah, Moose Katzenbach told me that you'd be going by there. Is that where you found your missing person?"

Denny had said, "No—Cooney Richards was on duty and we checked every drawer in the joint. Remember Cooney Richards?"

Lockington had thought about it. He'd said, "Yeah, vaguely."

"Well, Lacey—you see—there's something—something you're gonna have to know."

Lockington had peered at his ex-partner. Duke Denny had been wound tighter than a voodoo drum. "You sure you can't use a drink?"

Denny had thrown up both hands defensively. "Not this time, partner! Look—well, God Almighty, Lacey—I just don't know how to tell you this!"

The electricity had gone out of Lockington's leg. He'd said, "Okay, Duke, so you need money—it happens to all of us. I got something like seventy-five bucks if it'll help."

"No money, Lacey—that ain't it, but thanks a bunch anyway—you see, when I was at the morgue, talking to Cooney Richards, they brought a girl in—dead of knife wounds."

Lockington had shrugged. It'd been a stiff shrug. He'd said, "Hispanic—switchblade—Humboldt Park area—right?" He'd said it to span the gap between where they'd been and wherever the hell Duke Denny had been struggling to get to, realizing that all was not well with his old sidekick.

Denny had been staring at the floor with an intensity that had threatened to drill smoking holes in it. Leadenly, he'd said, "No—she was Caucasian, and—well, I watched Cooney Richards type out her form—her driver's license showed Des Plaines as her address—her name—her name—Good God, Lacey, her name was Julie Masters!"

30

The sound of the office door banging shut straightened him in the swivel chair. The visitor was a burly man who wore a snap-brimmed pearl-gray straw hat, brown suede sports jacket, white shirt with its top three buttons open, black slacks, and tan loafers. The hat was bent out of shape, the coat was sweat-stained, the shirt was wilted, the slacks needed pressing, the loafers were badly scuffed—he wasn't in Duke Denny's sartorial league. Quick, intelligent, beady eyes were imbedded in a red-veined face, his clefted, protruding jaw could have been hacked from a block of granite, and his name was Curtin—Lieutenant Buck Curtin. They knew each other, but only from a distance—they'd never worked together, but over the years they'd waved or nodded on a few occasions.

Curtin was out of homicide on South State Street—he didn't handle narcotics or vice or rape or theft as Lockington had—Curtin was a trouble-shooter, homicides and homicides only, working one case or two or three, whatever the demand for his considerable talents. He was a no-nonsense cop, canny, abrasive, tough, and when he smiled he was dangerous. He'd busted the headline Sister Rosetta murders ten months earlier and several less-publicized cases before and since. He was short-fused and violent—Lockington had it on reliable authority that he'd whaled a surly young hood in the mouth with a tire iron and that the kid's front teeth had gone through the upper lip before they'd bounced on the sidewalk. Buck Curtin was a two-fisted cop in a two-fisted town, and when the going got sticky down at Homicide, Curtin was the man they whistled for.

He dropped his battered straw hat in the middle of the desk, extending a thick-fingered hand to Lockington. Lockington shook it briefly. Curtin parked one beefy buttock on a corner of the desk, helping himself to one of Lockington's cigarettes, lighting it, inhaling deeply—Lockington knew the routine—violate hell out of the territorial imperitative, establish yourself as top dog. Sometimes it worked, sometimes it didn't. With Lockington it didn't. Curtin said, "Whaddaya say, Lacey?"

Lockington said, "Save your money."

Curtin said, "Sorry to hear about your woman. February, wasn't it?"

Lockington said, "Yeah—February."

Curtin said, "I didn't draw that one."

"No, Homan and Theodore got it."

"You look into it at all?"

"Not much—I'm waiting."

"For what?"

"I don't know, but I'll recognize it when it goes by."

Curtin nodded, dragging deeply on his cigarette. "I'd

heard that you'd gone into private investigations, but I didn't believe it."

"You'd heard? From whom?"

"I forget—word gets around."

"Why didn't you believe it?"

"Because you don't got no P.I. license."

"Don't need one—I'm just answering the phone for Duke Denny until he gets back from Cleveland. You remember Duke Denny—he was my partner a few years back."

"Yeah, I rember Duke Denny—cunt-crazy, shifty bastard."

"And one helluva cop."

Curtin shrugged, changing subjects. "Don't look too good for you at that hearing, Lacey. When they gonna hold it?"

"No idea—maybe three, four weeks—you know the route."

Curtin was silent for a moment, sizing Lockington up. Then he said, "Uhh–h–h, Lacey, you ain't carrying a gun, are you?"

Lockington flipped open his jacket. "You see a gun?"

"Not from here."

"Well, that's as close as you're gonna get. Why the question?"

"Just curious—didn't wanta rile you if you were. Holy Christ, four guys in about a week, wasn't it? Not bad, baby, not *bad*!" He snickered.

Lockington leaned back in the swivel chair, stretching, locking his hands behind his head. He said, "Looky, you aren't here to discuss old news."

"No, now that you mention it, I dropped in on account of I figured you could probably help me clear up a little matter."

"Such as?"

"Such as your whereabouts on the night of Wednesday, August 22."

Lockington frowned. "I'd have to think on that one. What time of night are we talking about?"

"Well, let's see now—I'd say between two ayem and maybe four."

"I'm usually home in bed at that hour."

"Usually?"

"That's right. Usually."

"'Usually' would imply that there've been exceptions."

"Yes, wouldn't it, though?"

"To your being home in bed between two and four in the morning?"

"To my being anywhere at any time."

"Which indicates you got a playmate."

"We won't get into that."

"Maybe we should."

"Maybe we *shouldn't.*"

"I think we *should.*"

"All right, we *should,* but we ain't *gonna*—turn the fucking page."

Curtin eased up, grinning to bare crooked tobacco-stained teeth. "Okay, okay, Lacey, cool it. So tell me about the night of August 22—it was the night we had that God-awful rain storm."

"On that night I was home—all day and all night—I wiped out a bottle and a half of Old Anchor Chain."

"All by *yourself?*"

"All by myself."

"What was the occasion?"

"I haven't the foggiest."

Curtin whistled. "They mix Old Anchor in rusty locomotive boilers!"

Lockington didn't say anything. He didn't like Curtin and he didn't swap humorous asides with people he didn't like.

Curtin hung on like a pit bull terrier. "Anybody who'd verify your being home all night on the twenty-second?"

"Duke Denny phoned me at 2:30 in the morning."

"What for?"

"To invite me to dinner."

"Who'd believe Duke Denny? How about *last* night?"

"I'll bite. How *about* last night?"

"Where were you—same hours—2:00 to 4:00 approximately."

"Again, home in bed."

"Old Anchor Chain?"

"Martell's cognac."

"Alone?"

"Not necessarily."

"Somebody'll back that up?"

"If need be."

"Your playmate?"

Lockington got to his feet, kicking the swivel chair against the wall. "All right, Curtin, let's have it! What's on your mind?"

"Aw, don't get pissed, Lacey—it's been a bum morning—I keep drawing blanks. Ever have one of those mornings?"

"Seven every week. Now, why don't you just run along home?"

Curtin slid from the corner of the desk, lifting another cigarette from Lockington's pack, tucking it behind his ear.

He said, "See you around."

Lockington said, "Not if I see you first."

Curtin winked. "You won't—they never do." He went out, pleasing Lockington no end.

Moose Katzenbach checked in at noon on the dot, flipping his hat at the rickety clothes tree, missing, leaving the hat on the floor. He said, "I never *have* hit that sonofabitch—not even *once!*"

Lockington said, "Try not to lose any sleep over it."

Moose said, "Hey, they got beef stew for the special at Dugan's Cafeteria—good stuff."

"No beef stew—you never know what they put in that stuff. I know a guy who ordered beef stew and found an old wedding ring."

"Lucky. He could have hocked it."

"He did—right after he got it off the finger."

Moose said, "Say, Lacey, a bunch of the *Morning Sentinel* people have lunch at Dugan's, and I heard them talking—one of the women who used to write that *Stella on State Street* column was found dead."

"Yeah, I heard—shot through the head."

"I didn't catch how it happened. Was it on the news?"

"Yeah, a week ago. Where you been?"

"How could it have been on the news a week ago? They just found her this morning. She was in a ditch along the Soo Line grain track on Green Street out in Bensenville."

Lockington nodded, the chilling significance of Lieutenant Buck Curtin's visit washing over him, heading for the door, one thoroughly bewildered six-foot-one, 205 pound, forty-eight year old ex-police detective with the damndest case of snakebite he'd ever heard of.

31

He tottered eastward, numbed to the bone, covering the two-and-a-half busy blocks to the corners of State and Randolph in the fashion of a man who's just endured a ten hour heavy artillery barrage. Just three weeks earlier, everything had been peaches down in Georgia for Lacey Lockington—his horizon might not have been as rosy as he'd have liked it, but there hadn't been a cloud in sight. Now he was a suspended, about-to-be-fired cop with a jury-acceptable motive for murder in the first degree, Chicago's hottest homicide detective snapping at the seat of his pants. You never miss the sunshine till the raindrops start to fall—a line from a song in a minstrel show he'd attended as a youngster. He couldn't remember the tune but all of a sudden the words made sense.

The newsstand had stood at State and Randolph since Lockington could remember. You could buy London newspapers there, Paris newspapers, newspapers from every major city in the United States. There was a gangly, pimply-faced kid tending the stand when Lockington got there. He was the cocky, belligerent type. He wore a five-dollar pair of threadbare blue jeans and an eighty-dollar pair of Nike jogging shoes. A cork-tipped cigarette dangled Bogart-style from his lower lip. Lockington said, "Pardon me—could you tell me where I can find Information Brown?"

The punk blew smoke through his nose in the approved manner of 1938 B movie detectives. He gave Lockington that look reserved by the Now Generation for the ancient and infirm. He spoke from a corner of his mouth, the same corner used by Edward G. Robinson. He said, "Whaddaya want with Information Brown?"

Lockington said, "I'm putting together a hit squad to assassinate the Prince of fucking Wales."

The punk didn't blink. He said, "Hey, grandpa, if you know Information Brown, you know where he *is*."

Lockington said, "Mum's the word, kid." The boy's answer had been insolent but adequate. He crossed Randolph Street, doubling back to the west as far as the Squirrel's Cage Tavern, entering to spot Information Brown seated at the far end of the bar, alone and looking forlorn. Lockington sat next to him. He said, "Howdy, Info, what're you gargling?"

Information Brown's hangdog expression brightened perceptibly. He said, "Well, Lacey Lockington, you dog— Walker's DeLuxe!"

Lockington said, "Walker's DeLuxe? That looks like beer."

Information Brown said, "I was drinking beer till you got here—now I'm drinking Walker's DeLuxe—you see, Lacey, in this town there just ain't no fucking invariables."

Information Brown was a smallish, wiry man, graying,

wearing a Knights of Columbus windbreaker with a Masonic emblem high on its left chest. There was a Chicago Cubs patch on one sleeve, a Chicago White Sox patch on the other—Information Brown never took sides. He was a walking encyclopedia of Chicago affairs—he could tell you who was who and who wasn't ever gonna *be* who, he knew the city as Robin Hood had known Sherwood Forest, every nook, every seam, every cranny, and he knew its denizens—every hack, every hustler, every hood, every whore. Information Brown possessed the retentive powers of a five-million-dollar computer, he could have blackmailed half the populace of Chicago, and he was concentrating on drinking himself to death, his only excuse being that he didn't want to die sober. He studied Lockington with glassy bloodshot eyes. He said, "Been a while, Lacey. Why now?"

Lockington said, "Well, for the moment, let's file it under self-preservation." He slid a twenty-dollar bill onto the bar, spurring the barkeep to action—in Chicago's Loop, nothing smaller than a twenty will do it. He said, "Info, this ex-*Sentinel* writer who got scragged last night—who was she—how was she killed—what do you have on that?"

Information Brown said, "You working that case? I heard you got suspended."

"I did. If I was working it, I'd know this stuff. Curtin got it."

"Then God help *some* poor sonofabitch! Curtin don't strike out often."

Lockington made no response.

Information Brown said, "Well, for whatever it's worth to a guy who got no business being interested, her name was Connie Carruthers, and she was strangled—small hours of this morning." He downed his Walker's DeLuxe, pointed to his empty glass, and cleared his throat, warming to his task. "Connie did a six year stretch with the *Sentinel,* about half of it grinding out that *Stella on State Street* thing—she tossed in the towel a couple years back when she married Jason Carruthers—Carruthers owns a string of photoengraving houses, Chicago to Florida—big bucks there, but she blew the marriage—she couldn't keep her pants on."

"What was her maiden name?"

"Mmm-m-m-m—Mandell, maybe—no, Kendall—yeah, make it Kendall. She was a swinger before and after she got hitched—skated high, wide, and upside-down—hung around The Boiled Ostrich up on the Gold Coast, Rush Street—fine-looking chickie, scored at will, took most of the local sports celebs to bed—went every goddam route known to mankind—French, Greek, Bedouin—you name it, Connie Carruthers was good at it."

"Just one moment—*Bedouin,* did you say?"

"Never completely understood that one, Lacey—it calls for a camel, I've heard."

"Look, Info, let me take a shot in the dark—the character who runs the *Sentinel*—any way he could be involved? They say he'll go to the moon on a manure wagon if there's a headline in it. A couple of murdered Stella Starbrights ain't gonna damage the *Sentinel's* circulation numbers."

Information Brown shook his head vehemently. "No way! The *Sentinel* ain't cashing on the Stella Starbright stuff—no mention of it. No, he's clean, and he's concerned as hell, I understand."

"What sort of character is he—what's his name—Jarvis?"

"Yeah, Max Jarvis—Max is sixty, plus or minus—born

into North Shore money—graduate of Loyola University—ultraconservative—brilliant mind—he led the—"

"*Hold* it, for Christ's sake! Ultra-*what*?"

Information Brown grinned a bleary grin. "Conservative, like I said—he's a flaming *radical*—he helped found the Grayfriar Society!"

"Grayfriar Society?"

"You wouldn't want to live under the Grayfriar Society's rules—that bunch is so far right it's outta *sight*! That ain't all—Jarvis is a charter member of God knows how many similar organizations—he's a drum-pounding, flag-waving sonofabitch from the old Yankee Doodle school!" Lockington sat in silence, shaking his head, and Information Brown continued. "He's never been married, but he was an expert cocksman in his day—he had a few hundred affairs, but none of 'em got out of the chute except the scorcher he had with a Michigan City honky-tonk stripper—Bonita Berea—that one trailed smoke for a *decade*!"

"When was this?"

"Long time ago—early fifties, ran into the sixties, as I recall. Bonnie could really grind that thing—saw her get it on a few times back when Michigan City was a fast track. Bonnie's dead now, incidentally."

"Dead how long?"

"Not very."

"*How* not very?"

"Well, let's see—only a couple, three months—got her head bashed in right in her own bedroom, assailant unknown—they put it down as robbery—they thought some jewelry was missing."

"Never heard of it."

"It didn't make much of a splash—run-of-the-mill suburban murders don't rate big copy in Chicago. She was an easy mark—had a nice a secluded property out on Deerfield Road—she lived alone—no watchdog, and her nearest neighbor was a quarter-mile away. Nothing to it."

"Let's get back to Jarvis—he interests me."

Information Brown hoisted his Walker's DeLuxe, putting it away with an expert flip of the wrist, shoving his glass to the rim of the mahogany, winking an okay at the man behind the bar. "Jarvis had a bundle going in, big inheritance—bought the *Sentinel* at ebb tide, got it dirt-cheap. He overhauled editorial policy, moved to the sensational, made a ton of money—Jarvis got to be worth fifty million."

Lockington said, "A fifty-million-dollar asshole—he's a conservative, yet his stinking newspaper pisses on everything that's American in concept. Info, that just don't *rhyme!*"

"He's a conservative *politically*, which don't mean that he ain't an opportunist in the *business* field! The Chicago *Morning Sentinel* is a hot rag, and controversy made it that way—there just ain't nothing like *controversy!*"

"All right, you said that Jarvis belongs to various right-wing factions—how many *are* there—right here in Chicago, I mean."

Information Brown shrugged. "Hell, no more than half-a-dozen that anybody's ever heard of, I suppose." He polished off his Walker's DeLuxe and made a motion to the bartender. "There's Concerned Conservative Citizens of Chicago—that's probably the most influential of the locals—Jarvis contributes heavily to it—then there's—"

Lockington cut in on him. "LAON—tell me about LAON."

"*You* tell *me*. What's LAON?"

Lockington watched Information Brown's fourth Walker's DeLuxe vanish down the hatch. He watched Information Brown gesture for a fifth. He watched his twenty-dollar bill shrink to a ten. He said, "LAON is a conservative outfit, maybe *dangerously* conservative—L—A—O—N—Law and Order Now, I've been told."

"By whom?"

"Duke Denny."

Information Brown snorted. "Duke *Denny*? Jesus Christ, Lacey, Duke Denny don't have enough sense to pound sand into a fucking knothole!"

Lockington shrugged. "Duke didn't claim to know anything about it—all he said was that nobody takes LAON seriously."

"Well, I've never heard of it."

"Then who *might* have?"

Information Brown pondered the question while quaffing his fresh Walker's DeLuxe and smiling a yes to the bartender's questioning eyebrows. Eventually he raised a prescient forefinger. "There's a refugee from the loony-bin out in Franklin Park—"

"Franklin Park's *swarming* with refugees from loony-bins!"

"Yeah, but this one's a *preacher*—he made up his own religion. Can you imagine that—a home-made religion?"

"When you find one that *ain't* home-made, give me a call—any old time of the night will be just dandy. What is the name of *this* one?"

"First Church of Jesus Christ Our Glorious and Crucified Redeemer, I'm pretty sure."

"Well, if you're wrong, don't sweat it. What about the

preacher—who is he?"

"The Reverend Abraham Wright. He's got a whole bunch of people following him."

"So did John Dillinger. Wright could know something about LAON?"

"He's your best bet in the Chicago area—he's hooked up with rightist movements from coast to coast. LAON—how come you're interested?"

"I got a bet with Duke Denny."

"You're a loser already—Denny never paid a bet in his life—he owes every bookie from here to Muncie, Indiana!"

Lockington sighed, slipping from his barstool as Information Brown wiped out another Walker's DeLuxe.

"I probably just better have one for the road, don't you think?"

Helplessly, Lockington said, "Sure, what the hell, why stop *now?*" He salvaged a five-dollar bill, leaving the loose buck for the barkeep, waving so-long to Information Brown and going out to walk west on Randolph Street, his thinking more disorganized than it'd been when he'd left the agency, not certain that he'd gained fifteen dollars worth of knowledge—more like ten, he figured, but it'd been a seller's market, and Information Brown had been aware of that.

There was something squirming in the undercurrent, something hairy—Lockington could *feel* it. He was stumped. He was an aging, trail-wise hound with a strange scent in his nostrils—he was on a track and he didn't have the remotest idea what he could possibly be tracking, but whatever it was, it was deadly.

On a sudden hunch he turned into Leo's Hamburger Palace, a fly-plagued, roach-infested, greasy spoon eatery. He hustled into the kitchen, flashing his badge. He said, "Police matter—gotta use your backdoor!"

The emaciated old man washing dishes didn't look up. He said, "Leave the damned thing open—I could use the air."

Lockington turned left in the alley, found a rear door ajar thirty yards to the east, and used it to place himself in a dim room where a woman was slipping dresses onto hangers. She had frizzy red hair, glaring dark eyes, a mouth constructed along the lines of a bear trap, and she weighed two-seventy-five if she weighed a gram. She stepped in Lockington's direction, not stopping until they'd made bodily contact. She said, "What do you want from me, you monster?" Her breathing was hotly ragged.

Lockington said, "Nothing, ma'am, nothing at all—this is police business."

The woman said, "I give you fair warning—if you rip my panties off and rape me, I may scream!"

Lockington said, "I'm not going to rape you, ma'am—I'm not even going to rip your panties off. Where the hell am I?"

"You're in the stock room of Flora's Fashions on West Randolph Street. Who *are* you, you beast?"

"Chicago Police Lieutenant Buck Curtin, ma'am."

"I'm Flora—Flora Hapsburg—I get off just a little after five."

Lockington said, "I have to move along, ma'am—there's a Martian loose in the area."

Lockington departed Flora's Fashions by way of the front door, emerging into the tide of traffic on Randolph Street. One fat woman after another. He made his way west a couple of doors. Every now and then a hunch pays off. Buck Curtin stood in a shop doorway, watching the entrance to Leo's Hamburger Palace the way an eagle watches a gopher hole. Lockington ambled up behind him, tapping him on the shoulder. He said, "Hey, Buck, did you hear the one about the dinosaur and the dragon?"

Curtin turned to peer at Lockington as you'd peer at a centipede in your omelette. He said, "You're a cute guy, Lockington—real cute."

Lockington said, "Modesty would dictate that I make no comment."

Curtin said, "There never was a fucking private dick who wasn't a complete asshole."

Lockington nodded, yawned, and walked away. It was nearly 1:00. He'd give Moose Katzenbach a simple assignment for the afternoon, thereby allowing himself some thinking room. Moose glanced up from a tattered girlie magazine. He said, "We had one telephone call—I didn't answer it." When Lockington had nodded approvingly, Moose said, "There was a guy here—seemed wound mighty tight—didn't say a helluva lot except he wants to be contacted immediately. He left a business card."

Lockington took the card, studying it—Gordon G. Fisher, Attorney at Law, 440 West Randolph Street, Chicago, Illinois. 440 West Randolph Street was just a couple of blocks west. In Chicago a couple of blocks is like just next door.

32

Lacey J. Lockington sat in Duke Denny's spavined swivel chair, leaning back, feet up on the cluttered desk, lord of the manor, master of all he surveyed, and the odds-on choice as murderer of a pair of free-wheeling ex-newspaper floozies—probably the *only* choice, as matters stood. *Stella on State Street* had been highly instrumental in costing Lockington his police career, so he'd brooded over it and gone on a killing rampage, a vendetta against the column's proprietors—or such would appear to be Lieutenant Buck Curtin's theory—logical enough in essence, but without a leg to support it. At the approximate hour of Eleanor Fisher's death, Lockington had been at home, talking to Duke Denny on the telephone—on the night Connie Carruthers had been murdered, he'd been in bed with Edna Garson around the clock, seven-to-seven, so unless Lockington's witnesses got struck dead by lightning, Buck Curtin could take his theory and shove it where the sun didn't shine.

Lockington's smile was wry. Right about now, Erika

Elwood should be spooked half out of her skivvies. Erika was the last of the Mohicans, the current Stella Starbright, and the Stellas were a vanishing breed, going down in order. Well, the backstabbing little minx had earned herself a few sleepless nights, but if these killings hadn't been the most far-fetched coincidences imaginable, her life was in considerable danger, no doubt about it.

The telephone rang at 2:00 and Lockington grabbed it. Duke Denny was on the line, bright, chipper as always. "Howdy, partner—called earlier—guess you were out to lunch."

"Yeah—how's it going in Cleveland?"

"Not sure yet, but I just may come out with a few bucks. I should know more by the time by lawyer closes shop for the day, so I have three hours to sweat. Anyway, I should be in Chicago no later than Monday afternoon. How're things at that end?"

"How much time you got?"

"Hey, are you telling me that we've come up with a new client?"

"Not yet, but that's a possibility. By the way, another of the *Stella on State Street* writers got knocked off last night."

"I've heard nothing on it here in Cleveland—I don't believe that *Stella on State Street* is syndicated, so the case would be of little interest in Ohio. You see a pattern?"

"Why, hell, *yes*, I see a pattern, don't *you*?"

"Right about now I don't see much of anything—I'd have to think on it."

"Look, this LAON organization we've discussed—I can't find a thing. Seems like only you and Erika Elwood have ever heard of it."

"Well, to tell you the truth, Lacey, I haven't heard much myself—just casual mention on a couple of occasions."

"Who made the casual mention?"

"Christ, I don't remember—it was probably *months* ago! Lacey, for God's sake, don't get yourself involved in this mess!"

"Don't get *involved* in it? I'm *already* involved in it! I got the number one homicide bull in Chicago tailing me all over town!"

"Who's tailing you?"

"None other than Buck Curtin!"

"Buck Curtin—Curtin's bad news—what's he got for you?"

"Well, think about it, Duke—the Stella column helped get me suspended, it branded me as a trigger-happy lunatic—then a couple of Stella Starbrights bite the dust— so, who's *likely* to fall under suspicion?"

There was a lengthy silence before Denny said, "God *damn*, yeah, I get the picture—Curtin sees motive and means. How about opportunity?"

"That's where I have the bastard by the balls—no opportunity!"

"Good—another tempest in a teapot! Say, not to change the subject, but you said something about a new client."

"A man close to these murders has requested me to contact him."

"Why?"

"I don't know."

"You haven't talked to him?"

"Not yet."

"Who is he?"

"Guy named Fisher—the name ring a bell with you?"

"Fisher—*Gordon* Fisher—the cat who was married to the first Stella Starbright?"

"Got to be."

"And you think this may have something to do with the murders?"

"I'd imagine so, be it directly or indirectly."

"Fisher's a good man to know—a legal whiz!"

Lockington sighed a desolate sigh. He said, "Duke, this is one bewildering bucket of bagels."

Denny said, "Well, partner, I gotta hand it to you—you have a special knack!"

"Yeah, everything I touch turns to shit."

"So check Fisher out and I'll call you this evening."

"Calling me may not be that easy. I got a sinister urge to get crocked immediately after I close this firetrap."

"Nothing wrong with that—wish I could join you. Where do you do your drinking—still that joint on Grand Avenue?"

"Right—Shamrock Pub."

"You got a shoo-shoo there?"

"A *what?*"

"A lady-in-waiting?"

"Only if she waits."

Denny chuckled. "Have a blast, partner!" He hung up and Lockington lit a cigarette, blowing smoke rings, thinking. For a sliver of a second there, he'd had hold of something, but now he'd lost the damned thing. He shrugged clear of it—Alzheimer's Disease, chances were—like hay fever, very bad in August. He checked Gordon G. Fisher's business card and punched out the number. A sultry female voice answered. "Gordon G. Fisher offices—Andrea Kling speaking."

Lockington asked to speak to Gordon G. Fisher.

Andrea Kling said that Mr. Fisher was on another line—would the caller care to hold?

Lockington said no, he'd ring back in fifteen minutes.

He rang back in fifteen minutes. Andrea Kling said that Mr. Fisher had just left the offices on an emergency matter—was there a message for Mr. Fisher?

Lockington said no, when would Mr. Fisher be back?

Andrea Kling said that she was unable to say—possibly before closing time, but she couldn't guarantee that.

Lockington asked what time Mr. Fisher's offices closed.

Andrea Kling said 5:00, of course—the same time *all* legal offices closed.

Lockington said that *all* legal offices *didn't* close at 5:00, because he'd known a lawyer who'd closed at *noon*.

Andrea Kling noted that he'd probably been a charlatan.

Lockington said no, as a matter of fact, he'd been a Presbyterian. He'd asked if it'd be possible to call Mr. Fisher at his residence.

Andrea Kling said absolutely not, Mr. Fisher accepted nothing but personal calls when at home.

Lockington gave Andrea Kling his name and the Classic Investigations telephone number, thanked her, and hung up.

He located a dog-eared Chicago telephone directory in a bottom desk drawer. Gordon G. Fisher's law offices number was shown but no residence number was listed. He called Information. The operator advised him that there was no Gordon G. Fisher in any of Chicago's suburban directories. She said that this was because Gordon G. Fisher's number was unlisted.

Lockington said aha.

The operator said true, but life was like that. Lockington dropped the phone into its cradle, frowning. He'd just located his lost wisp of thought. He toyed with the truant, weighing it, balancing it, studying it from a variety of angles, unable to make head or tail of it, and this disappointed him because at first sight it'd seemed important. Early impressions are so often deceptive.

Lockington wasn't a storybook detective. He didn't smoke pipes and wear deerstalker caps, nor did he sit by his fireside, staring into the embers, assembling the pieces of a puzzle before rounding up a cast of seven or eight people and picking an unlikely killer from the bunch. Lockington had been a rather unimaginative, reasonably honest, heavy-footed, often heavy-handed detective, plodding doggedly through the muck of the most corrupt city on the face of God's once-green earth. He'd made arrests by the hundreds and he'd shot a few people, the bigger chunks of his action coming after long and patient stakeouts, or simply because he'd been told to go to such-and-such a number on such-and-such a street and bring in a man named something-or-other, and Lockington had complied, oftentimes not knowing the particulars involved. He'd rarely considered hunches, possibly because he hadn't gotten many, he'd played the cards he'd been dealt, always anticipating the worst and usually getting it. By and large, hunches were for neophyte horseplayers, but there's a difference between playing a hunch and catching a slip-up, if it'd been a slip-up rather than a simple mistake. It was the little slip-ups that tripped people, and *if* was still the biggest word in the English vocabulary, antidisestablishmentarianism notwithstanding. If those people had been able to find that horseshoe nail, they wouldn't have lost the shoe, the horse, the rider, the battle, the war, and eventually the whole flaming kingdom. The first inning error can cost you the nine inning ball game, and on that note Lacey Lockington filed his pesky thought under 'H' for horseshoe nails, dug deeply into the recesses of the desk's knee well, and dragged out the cardboard box housing the Cider Press Federation.

To hell with the deep thinking—Pepper Valley was at Delta River.

33

Trailing by two at the end of seven, the Pepper Valley Crickets had pulled it out, beating the league-leading Delta River Weevils on Nick Noonan's eighth-inning, two-out, bases-loaded double into the right field corner. That happy turn of events had put the Crickets on a one game roll, and Lockington was seriously tempted to play one more until a look at his watch changed his mind. Cider Press Federation games averaged an hour in length, and he didn't have an hour. It was 4:30. He set the league records straight, and he was returning his imaginary athletes to their temporary quarters under Duke Denny's desk when he heard the agency door click open, then closed. There were light, quick footsteps and Lockington straightened in the swivel chair to see a slender young woman approaching the desk. At sight of Lockington the visitor's eyes grew wide and she stopped dead in her tracks, throwing up her hands in a defensive gesture. She gasped, "Oh, my God, not *you!*"

Lockington said, "Excuse me, but that should have

been *my* line."

Erika Elwood spun on her heel to leave, then hesitated, turning back to face Lockington. She said, "Perhaps I'm mistaken. You see, I was looking for Classic Investigations."

Lockington said, "You've found it, according to the sign on the door."

"You—you're working here now?"

"Just filling in—temporary thing, but it'd make one helluva column—Mad dog killer cop terrorizes West Randolph Street."

Erika Elwood didn't smile—her brown eyes were frosty. She said, "All right, since I'm here, I'd like to speak to the gentleman in charge."

Lockington said, "You're looking at him. What's next—another show-and-tell session—followed by a Judas kiss?"

She said, "Mr. Lockington, *please*—this is *business!* I'm desperately in need of assistance!"

Lockington nodded. "Yes, I'm sure you are."

"I—I believe my life is in jeopardy!"

"So do I, Miss Elwood, so do I."

She shuffled nervously on the cheap brown carpeting, clutching her handbag tightly to her impressive bosom with both hands. "Well, then—what can I say—or *do*?"

"I'd recommend that you consult good old Stella Starbright, because good old Stella Starbright has all the answers. Should you doubt that, just ask good old Stella."

She winced, standing slightly pigeon-toed in her tailored gray gabardine business suit, tiny, frail, defenseless, looking a great deal like a drenched mouse, Lockington thought. She said, "I suppose I had that coming—but isn't there someone I can talk to, someone who'll help me? Mr. Lockington, I'm afraid to go home alone!"

Lockington put a match to a cigarette, relishing the moment, however perversely. He said, "Turn off the tape recorder in your purse, and sit down before you fall on your face."

She nodded uncertainly, cranking up a wan smile, wobbling to the straight-backed chair next to the desk, sagging onto it, not at all the brash, confident young thing who'd breezed unannounced and uninvited into his apartment just a week earlier. She said, "I don't *have* a tape recorder in my purse!" She turned to plunk her handbag onto the desk top with unsteady hands. Tremulously, she piped, "See for yourself."

Lockington waved her offer away. "I'll take your word for that, seeing as how you're such a straight-shooter."

Erika Elwood searched his face with great, round, brown eyes. "Mr. Lockington, do you know—do you know what's been *happening?*"

"Yes, Miss Elwood, I know what's been happening, but be explicit, if you will. You're in serious trouble, that's obvious, but why are you *here*—what do you *want?*"

"I—I want a man to spend the night with me!" She'd blurted it out like a first grader reciting a nursery rhyme.

Lockington said, "That's what I call laying it on the line! Well, shucks, there must be a million guys who'll take you up on that one."

"Don't pretend to misunderstand! You know what I mean—I'm talking about a *bodyguard!* He'd sleep on my living room couch, of *course!*"

Lockington frowned. "Well, Miss Elwood, no matter *where* he'd sleep, Classic Investigations gets five hundred dollars a day, and that's pretty steep for a working girl."

The matter of financial capability didn't seem to faze her. She said, "I don't worry during my working hours. The *Sentinel* has beefed up its security—I feel completely safe at the *Sentinel*—it's the nights alone—particularly since—since Connie Carruthers was—"

Lockington jammed his elbows onto the desk top, leaning forward to cut her off. "Now, Miss Elwood, here's the way it stands—I don't like you and you don't like me, but in spite of that I'm going to give you some Dutch uncle advice. For Christ's sake, *don't* go around shopping at nickel-and-dime detective agencies, looking for a helping hand! A woman in your position should hightail it to the nearest police station, explain the situation, and request protective custody!"

"Protective custody—what would that entail? It would mean around-the-clock coverage, as I understand it."

Lockington shrugged. "Probably—or you might be stashed in a safehouse until the smoke has cleared."

"Well, Mr. Lockington, there'll be nobody stashing *me* anywhere. I have a job to attend to, and there'll be no tangle-footed lame-brain dogging my footsteps twenty-four hours a day! I can't *use* that kind of attention!"

"A bit odd, isn't it—this sudden shrinking from attention? The *Stella Starbright* column is geared to attract all the attention it can drum up—favorable or *un*favorable—by legitimate means, or whatever is required."

There was a current crackling through the room, electricity generated by the abrasiveness of two strong personalities in proximity. Erika Elwood glared at Lockington. "You are *not* talking to Stella Starbright, can't you *understand* that? You are talking to *Erika Elwood*, a woman who goes to church every

Sunday and votes a straight Republican ticket! Believe what you will, but they are in *no* way related!"

Lockington pursed his lips, directing a stream of cigarette smoke at the big picture of Wrigley Field. He said, "Miss Elwood, you wouldn't bullshit an old bullshitter, would you?"

"Oh, don't give me that tongue-in-cheek treatment, God damn it! Can Classic Investigations possibly spare a man? Answer my *question, will* you?"

Lockington's grin was tight. She was scared spitless, but her dander was up, she still had fire. He tilted back in the swivel chair, stroking a jowl that could have used a shave. He said, "Well, let's take a look at Classic's manpower potential. The boss is in Cleveland until Monday, my assistant is on an assignment and won't be in until tomorrow morning." Lockington winked at her. "At the moment, your choices would appear to be limited."

"I have *one*?"

"That's it."

"*You*?"

"Yep, *me*—a kill-crazy vigilante with a Dodge City mentality." By nature, Lacey Lockington wasn't a cruel man—he'd never kicked stray dogs or torn the wings from flies, but he'd cut this vixen and he couldn't resist salting the wound. He said, "Take it or leave it."

Erika Elwood considered her options and groaned, "Oh, shit, I'll *take* it!" She lunged for her purse, opening it to jerk out a lace-trimmed gray linen handkerchief, burying her face in it, and coming apart at the seams like a three-dollar football. Lockington sat watching her, saying nothing, listening to her hoarse, racking sobs, waiting for her to come up for air. Eventually she got around to that, catching her breath, drying her eyes. She said, "Excuse my outburst, please."

Lockington said, "Why, sure. Hell, you're entitled."

She flared again, the flame not quite extinguished. "You sonofabitch, I've already *explained* how it goes at the *Sentinel*—I do what I'm told to do—I write what I'm told to write—" Her voice cracked and she lapsed into stony silence, gnawing on her lower lip.

After a while, Lockington said, "Uhh–h–h, Miss Elwood, just how long would such an assignment be likely to last, would you say?"

"Quite frankly, I just don't know—it could go on until the Millennium, I suppose."

"That'd consume some time, because there ain't gonna *be* no Millennium."

"All right—until the Cubs win a pennant—how's *that*?" A meager smile twitched a corner of her mouth—she was perking up, sensing a change in the wind. "Will you accept this—this assignment?"

"At five hundred clams a throw, you could be talking serious money."

"That's not my concern—Classic Investigations will bill the *Sentinel* for its services. I have a letter of authorization from Max Jarvis, if you'd care to see it."

"I wouldn't."

"But, Good Lord, this can't go on *forever*, can it—they'll catch up with these people sooner or later, won't they?"

"Who'll catch up with *what* people sooner or later?"

"The Chicago police—they'll corner this LAON organization shortly!"

"Without your complete cooperation, I wouldn't bet a dollar on them finding LAON or whoever the hell is behind this."

"It isn't a matter of my cooperating with the police—it's a matter of the police cooperating with Max Jarvis. They'll hustle or Max will ride them out of town on a *rail.*"

Lockington murmured, "They're hustling, take my word."

"I didn't catch that. What was it you said?"

"I said, 'The pen is mightier than the sword.'"

"Precisely."

"You get something from LAON?"

"Yes—this morning—a card in the mail."

"And what did it have to say?"

"It said that *my* time is coming *soon*! What's your decision—are you going to help me?"

Lockington stretched and yawned. He said, "Where's your automobile?"

"In the *Sentinel's* underground garage, and that's where it'll stay until this is behind me. LAON probably knows my car."

"I'd think so. How did you get here?"

"By cab—I'd hoped for a lift home."

"Where's that?"

"St. Charles."

"That's right—you've mentioned it."

"I have? Honestly, I don't recall that—I've been so shaken by these—these *horrors*!"

Lockington gave it a final shuffle, but his mind had been set before he'd riffled the deck. What the hell, it was beyond personalities now. Whatever Erika Elwood was, she was in danger and she had no champion. He slapped the top of the desk with the flat of his hand, the spanging sound echoing like a gunshot in the tiny office. He snapped, "All right, you'd better lock that door—we're stuck here for another few minutes."

He scowled, remembering that his .38 police special was in the drawer of his bedroom nightstand. Well, armed or *un*armed, here came the Twentieth Century's answer to Don Quixote, astride a swaybacked Pontiac Catalina, clattering to the rescue of the besieged Erika Elwood, which came as no great shock to Lacey Lockington. Knowing himself as he did, he realized that he'd have done the same for Lucrezia Borgia, who'd been no bargain, either.

Giddy-up!

34

The Wednesday late afternoon was hot, Chicago's Loop was an airtight gray cauldron. They walked the three blocks to the Randolph Street parking lot, Erika Elwood's right sleeve brushing the store fronts, Lockington close on her left, a half step off her pace, his slouching, unconcerned walk belying the alertness of his eyes. The parking lot attendant dug the floppy-fendered blue Pontiac from between a Mercedes and a BMW, and Lockington tooled the tired vehicle south to the Eisenhower Expressway, swinging west into the sluggish triple stream of traffic that trickled into infinity. He said, "I'll take Roosevelt Road into Geneva. Then what—to St. Charles on 25 or 31?"

Erika Elwood said, "Take 31—I'm just a couple of miles north of 64. Are you familiar with that area?"

Lockington's half smile was wry and distant. "Vaguely—it's been a while."

He could feel Erika's interested gaze penetrating him. After a brief hesitation, she said, "A woman?"

Lockington said, "Of a sort."

"What *sort* of sort?"

"Confused."

"It didn't work out, obviously."

"Obviously."

"What happened?"

"I'm not sure."

"Where is she now?"

"At the bottom of the Fox River—I strangled her and threw her in."

A smile sidled into her voice. "Why?"

"I forget, but you could stick it in your Stella Starbright column and make up your own reason."

She laughed—a lilting sound, pleasant. "You, sir, are a paradox."

Lockington said, "I'm not up on my Latin."

"*Seriously*, now—you can kill and think nothing more of it, but you're a *kind* man—at heart you're a kind man."

Lockington growled, "That's opinion only."

"Well, my gosh, what else *is* there? 'Opinion guides the feet of man to now from where he once began.'"

"Go ahead, finish it."

"There's more?"

"Sure. 'He walks his brief and troubled span, opinion tending ev'ry plan, and, at the end, Hell's smoking hole cooks his opinionated soul.'"

"Why, my God, that's—that's *cynical*! Who wrote it?"

"A cynic, probably. Does it matter?"

"I don't think so."

They were on Roosevelt Road, boring west through Wheaton into a blazing sunset. Erika lit two cigarettes, handing one to Lockington. She said, "Y'know, there are times when I could almost *like* you—you certainly aren't a hypocrite!"

"We've *all* been hypocrites at one time or another."

"Oh, boy—a week ago you said that we're all *whores*—now we've all been *hypocrites!* You don't like the human race, do you?"

"I like it—I just don't *trust* it."

"Define hypocrisy! What *is* it?"

"A guy in a restaurant men's room—if there's another man in there with him, he pisses and he washes his hands—if he's alone, he pisses and he *doesn't* wash his hands. *That's* hypocrisy."

"And you don't wash your hands?"

"What's to be gained? The cooks never wash *theirs.*"

"You're certain of that?"

"Absolutely—I know a whole bunch of cooks."

Erika Elwood shook her head. Her sigh was audible above the roar of the old Pontiac's engine. She said, "Oh, Jesus, there's just nothing like stimulating conversation, is there?"

35

Erika Elwood's place had turned out to be a small, white single-story dwelling on ten or more heavily-wooded acres, situated well back from a lumpy macadam side road that branched northwest from Route 31. From its site, no other buildings could be seen. The property was surrounded by a split rail fence, corn fields, and silence. Lockington was familiar with none of these. Lockington was a city boy.

She'd let him in, following him closely, slamming the door, locking it hurriedly behind them. She'd pitched her handbag onto the padded seat of a John F. Kennedy rocking chair. She'd peeled off her gray suitcoat and draped it over the handbag before settling into a large overstuffed chair that had a flouncy, flowered slipcover. She'd exhaled relievedly. Lockington had parked himself in the lefthand corner of a four cushion black leather sofa, a luxuriously comfortable piece of furniture, but far too masculinely severe to be in keeping with the feminine appointments of the living room, its starkness tending to make it a focal point. He'd looked around. "Nice little place—cozy—how long have you lived out this way?"

She'd said, "Not long. I tired of a lakefront condo—the constant hubbub, the sense of being closed in—it's better here."

"All but for the long drive—that must be a bastard."

She'd shrugged. "Well, there is no free lunch. Do you want television?"

Lockington had said, "Oh, Christ, *no!*"—a trifle bluntly for a guest, he'd thought after he'd done it, but he'd justified it by reasoning that he wasn't a guest, he was an employee.

Then she'd come up with a more agreeable idea. She'd said, "Martini?"

Lockington had said, "Yes, if you will."

"Gin or vodka?"

"Vodka, please—gin is for fairies."

"Dry?"

"Very."

Within a couple of minutes she'd been back in her flowered chair, raising her frosty slim-stemmed glass to him in an unspoken toast. She'd said, "Well, Mr. Lockington, here we are."

Lockington had thought about it. He'd said, "Yes, we sure as hell are."

"You have your—your gun, I trust."

Lockington had shaken his head. "It's at home—I haven't carried it since I was suspended. I'll use yours, if necessary. Incidentally, I'd like to take a look at it."

She'd nodded, getting up to go into her bedroom, returning with the Repentino-Morté she'd mentioned during her visit to his apartment, carrying the weapon gingerly.

Lockington had taken it, balancing it in the palm of his left hand, studying it. It was an exquisite piece of workmanship. He'd said, "This is the most expensive handgun in the business—deadly accurate. How did you come by it?"

"It was a gift." She didn't elaborate.

"Has it been fired?"

"Not to my knowledge—certainly not by *me*!"

Lockington had ejected the round from the chamber, popped the clip, squinted down the barrel, squeezed the trigger several times, feeling the hammer click home with deadly precision on a reasonably light pull. He'd jammed the clip back into the pebbled handle, snapped a round into firing position, engaged the safety, and slipped the Repentino-Morté into a jacket pocket.

Erika Elwood had watched the process, mesmerized by his deft handling of the pistol. She'd lowered her gaze and said, "Thank God you're on *my* side!"

Lockington had winked at her. "*Am* I?"

She'd glanced up quickly, evaluating his smile. "Don't even *joke* about that!"

"Okay. Sorry."

Her vodka martinis had been first-rate, and during their second he'd felt the tightness begin to come undone. So, apparently, had Erika Elwood. She'd cleared her throat and said, "Uhh–h–h, look, would it be all right if I call you 'Lacey'?" 'Mr. Lockington' sounds so—so doggoned *stiff*."

"Yeah, and that ain't all—you're wasting three syllables every time around."

"Right—and call me 'Erika.' Back at Classic Investigations, you remarked that we don't like each other, and that isn't entirely true, at least not from where *I* sit. I know you have cause to detest me but I have nothing against *you*—nothing at *all*. You're brusque, you're to the point—'unpolished' could be the word, I suppose—but I appreciate that. In my field I seem to meet so many of the other kind—the suaves, the effusives—you know the types."

"Too well."

"And, honestly, I admire the *hell* out of you, please believe that!" She'd shrugged apologetically. "All right, I thought I should get that off my chest."

Lockington had said, "Well, I've found it difficult to reconcile what Erika Elwood probably *is* with what Erika Elwood *does*. She may be quite a decent young lady, but she makes her living as a character assassin. I might get over that."

"I hope so—Lacey." Her smile had been a warm, frank, outgoing thing, and Lockington had liked it. She'd said, "You and I can be friends."

"We can try."

"Then we'll be friends, because I just can't imagine you trying and failing."

"It's happened more often than not."

They'd had a third martini, then, while Lockington had worked on his fourth, Erika Elwood had headed for the kitchen.

It'd been a simple meal, served at a small, round maple table with a brown-checked tablecloth. There'd been green salad, broiled porterhouse steaks, baked potatoes with sour cream, sliced tomatoes, butterscotch pudding, and coffee laced with an excellent dark rum. Lockington had gone through it like a Sherman tank goes through a tool shed. She'd shooed him back into the living room while she'd washed the dishes. He'd paged through a couple of old news magazines, noting that her address on the mailing labels had been 814 N. Michigan Avenue. Swank area, and she'd dumped it in favor of a little white house in gongaland. That was a plus for her in Lockington's ledger.

She'd brought in a chromed bucket, placing it on the coffee table. In the bucket, packed in ice, had been a bottle of Bailey's Irish Cream. They'd drunk it from tiny glasses, smoking, talking, running a gamut of subjects, feeling each other out, the lights low, the blinds drawn, Lockington in his corner of the black leather couch, Erika in her big chair, the Repentino-Morté Black Mamba Mark III on an end table to Lockington's left, looking every bit as dangerous as Lockington knew it to be. In the early light chatter Lockington had learned that Erika detested basketball, and Erika had learned that Lockington was wild about blackberries.

Yes, she'd loved *Tom Sawyer,* also *Ivanhoe,* and *Tale of Two Cities*—so much for novels, what was Lockington's favorite short story? Well, "The Lady or the Tiger," probably, what was hers? Oh, "The Gift of the Magi," *easily.* She'd added that William Sidney Porter must have been a wonderful human being despite the fact that he'd done a portion of his best writing in the Ohio State Penitentiary.

The haphazard talk had gone on, the cuckoo in her kitchen clock screeching 8:00, then 9, 10. Lockington abhorred cuckoo clocks—they were thought-disrupting.

The Bailey's Irish Cream had gone the route of all Bailey's Irish Cream, replaced by a bottle of blackberry brandy, because he was wild about blackberries, she'd told him, and he'd thanked her. They'd gotten into the subject of dogs—German Shepherds, Belgian Schipperkes, curbstone setters. She'd owned a toy poodle once but he'd bitten the mailman and she'd been forced to give him to a couple that lived on a farm. They'd drifted to movies—*The Third Man, Bridge on the River Kwai, Elvira Madigan,* motion pictures with substance—then music—Herbert, Friml, Romberg. She liked most music, excluding the new country stuff and rock, which wasn't music in the first place, and Lockington had been forced to give her another plus for that. He'd asked if she cared for ragtime, and she'd said certainly, Scott Joplin's "Solace" had been a work of pure genius. Lockington had agreed, wondering if she'd ever heard a ragtime number called "African Violet" by an Australian contemporary ragtime composer named Dave Dallwitz. She'd said no, was it good? He'd told her that it was a haunting song, that he had it on a cassette at home and he'd play it for her sometime. Inevitably, their conversation had drifted to the threats she'd received. She'd said, "What do these people want, anyway— what's their *purpose*?"

Lockington had said, "Whoever they are, they want the same thing Mussolini wanted, the same thing Hitler wanted—nationwide attention, then political power, then control of government, then a shot at world domination. The shortcut is fear—fear, hell—stark *terror*."

"And they'll kill?"

"Of course, they'll kill. If you want to see what a man's made of, threaten his *life*!"

"That won't necessarily alter his political viewpoint."

"No, but it'll sure as hell influence his *behavior*!"

"LAON can't be big, it's certainly not national in scope—how many people have ever heard of LAON?"

"The two previous Stella Starbrights, possibly. Were you

in contact with them—had they received warnings?"

"I have no idea—I haven't seen Eleanor or Connie in *months*. Their ex-husbands might know."

"Doubtful. They'd have said something, wouldn't you think?"

"Yes, if they didn't put it all down as crank stuff. The media hasn't picked up on this—I wonder about that."

"The media protects its own. If a couple of singers had been killed, or a few football players, the press would have aired it out in grand fashion, looking for parallels, but newspaper people are involved so it's being soft-pedaled."

"But why?"

"To aid in the investigation."

"You don't like the press, do you?"

"Not at all, but in this case it's doing the right thing— this group wants attention, recognition as a force to be dealt with, and it isn't getting it. It has to be damned frustrating."

"How many of them are there, would you say?"

"'They' is an *assumption*. LAON, or whoever, whatever it is we are dealing with, could be one man, one woman. Numbers be damned, it has to start *some*where, and a few dedicated lunatics can get you around that first corner in a hurry—providing you get the desired publicity."

"You think that we're dealing with insane people?"

"Look, Erika, the mentally sound don't kill except in self-defense or to enforce the law."

The telephone had jingled and she'd gone into her bedroom to take the call, unsteady on her feet, feeling her drinks. There'd been evenings like this with Julie, conversation, laughter, agreement, differences of opinion. Julie's opinions had been unshakable, chiseled in granite, and they'd clashed on a variety of subjects, but their first few minutes in bed had ironed out the wrinkles. He'd sat there in Erika Elwood's dim living room, nursing his blackberry brandy, trying not to think about Julie because Julie was gone and there was no way to bring her back, and Lockington had been half-crocked on martinis, rum, Bailey's Irish Cream, blackberry brandy—Christ, what a horrendous mixture!

His hostess-employer had returned to the living room in short order and a single glance had told Lockington that the party was over. Erika Elwood had been stone-sober, ashen-faced, walking straight. In awed tones, she'd said, "They've just found Gordie—dead in an Evanston motel room—shot in the chest!"

Lockington had reached to take her by the elbow, tugging her gently onto the couch beside him. He'd said, "Gordie—who's Gordie?"

She'd said, "That's right, you wouldn't know—Gordon Fisher, the *Sentinel*'s chief attorney."

36

Lockington frowned, telling the truth. "I wasn't acquainted with the man. Who was on the phone?"

"One of the *Sentinel* pool secretaries—she heard it on the 10 o'clock news."

"You knew this Gordon Fisher well?"

"No, not *really* well, but well enough to have talked to him dozens of times. He came to the Sentinel Building twice, maybe three times a week—legal matters to be discussed with Max Jarvis. He always bought coffee for the house— pleasant man, excellent sense of humor—everybody liked Gordie."

"I wouldn't say that—somebody *didn't*."

"Gordon was Eleanor Fisher's husband."

"The first Stella Starbright?"

"Yes—they met at the *Sentinel*—they clicked instantly. They were married within a matter of a few weeks. That was when Eleanor quit and Connie took over the column."

"Were they happily married?"

198

"What's 'happily'? Apparently they got along. Eleanor was a cutter—probably alcoholic, certainly nympho—couldn't say no to a drink or a man. It was what they call an open marriage—Gordie got around a bit, too—I've heard that he swung both ways, but that was only hearsay." She was steadying now, the tremor slipping from her voice. "Whatever—the marriage didn't last."

Lockington said, "Fisher's political leanings—pronounced?"

"Oh, God, *yes—left—*just as far left as you can *get!*"

"Uh–huh—how far left is that?"

"Gordie was a card-carrying member of the Communist Party—he'd handled God knows how many cases for the ACLU."

Lockington lit a cigarette. "On the basis of that, you're thinking LAON."

"Oh, *certainly,* it *has* to be! Gordie was outspoken in his criticism of this administration *and* of the Government."

Lockington was shaking his head slowly. "Why LAON? LAON can't take on the job of killing all the Commies in Chicago—that'd take a brigade of infantry six months!" He sat staring at the ash of his cigarette. "Fisher's ex-wife is killed, then Fisher's gone in a week. He had to know something—something he had no business knowing."

"Information connected to Eleanor's death?"

"Five'll get you ten."

"Then he had news having to do with this goddamned guerilla group. This is too coincidental to be a coincidence!"

Lockington's scowl was dark, brooding. "How does the killer manage to get this close—obviously his victims know him and they trust him—or her—right?"

Erika Elwood was sitting hunched over. She said, "Oh,

Jesus H. Christ, where's that God damned Italian revolver?"

"It isn't a revolver, it's a pistol—it isn't Italian, it's Japanese, and it's right here on the table beside me. I think you'd better get some sleep. What time do you roll out in the mornings?"

"Sixish, and if you think I'll be able to sleep tonight, think *again*!"

Lockington said, "Well, take a whack at it—I'll be right here on your couch."

"I'm *scared*!"

"Don't be—I'm a light sleeper and one helluva pistol shot."

She bounced to her feet, moving in front of him, placing her hands on his shoulders. She said, "Lacey, come to bed with me—I'll be damned if I'm going in there *alone*!"

"Not because you're afraid—I'd need a better reason than that."

"I have one—I'll show you my butterfly tattoo—will *that* do?"

"Uh–uh."

She took his head between her hands, mauling it, tilting it back to peer down into his eyes. "All right, I need a screwing, and I need it very *badly*—is that a little better?"

"It's better, but it's probably a goddam lie."

She smiled, shaking her head. "If it's true—*would* you?"

"If it's true, of course I would, but I have only your word that it's true."

"Put your hand under my skirt, Lacey."

"Is that an order?"

"No, it's a challenge. *Do* it, damn you!"

Lockington complied, his right hand moving to a

position north of her knee, halting there. He looked up, saying nothing.

She said, "Don't stop *there*! You know where the transmission is!"

His hand inched upward, leaving nylon to hit hot flesh, pausing again. He said, "You're sure?"

"Lacey, for your information, I am *not* a virgin—*feel* me!"

Lockington slipped a finger upward under the elastic of her panties leg before altering course ninety degrees to reach the crease of one of the most enticing women he'd ever set eyes on.

Her feet shifted to left and right, granting him unhindered access. Her fingers dug into his shoulders. She twitched and gasped, "Am I wet?"

"Yes, you're wet."

"*How* wet?"

"Very."

"Would my condition indicate that I'm ready to be entered?"

"My limited experience leads me to believe that you are rapidly approaching that point."

She threw back her head and laughed. She said, "In the bedroom we'll speak English."

Lockington said, "Suits me."

He stood and she slipped an arm around his waist, guiding him toward the bedroom. She said, "Tell me, do you strip your women or is that *their* responsibility?"

"My *women*? I lost my harem in a poker game."

"You've avoided the question. Do you peel me, or do I?"

"Your choice."

"You're a gentleman. I'll take care of it. You'll watch?"

"Like a hawk."

"Lights on or off?"

"On, please."

"Yes, I'd prefer that—after all, why show it if you can't see the damned thing?" She turned to push him to a sitting position on her bed, stepping to the middle of the room. "Will this do something for you?"

"Undoubtedly."

"That's nice, because it'll certainly do something for *me*. Say when."

"Go."

She undressed slowly but without hesitation, Lockington watching for the blue butterfly on her appendectomy scar. Erika Elwood didn't have a blue butterfly on her appendectomy scar. Erika Elwood didn't have an appendectomy scar—her glorious rigid-nippled body was without a mark. She curtsied, blew him a kiss, and turned out the lights.

Later, her legs clamping him deep into the hot cream of her, her tight, tawny buttocks rolling to the cadence he'd established, she whispered, "You're—you're *gentle!*"

Lockington muttered, "You were expecting to be ripped limb from gut?"

"Oh, no, but—no, but you—never mind about that— just never *mind—oh, fuckest thou ME!*"

Lockington smiled into the darkness of Erika Elwood's bedroom. It would have taken a newspaper woman to come up with a line like that.

37

They drove from St. Charles toward Chicago through a sunny Thursday morning, saying little, Erika's mind elsewhere, apparently, Lockington looking back on the most memorable Wednesday night within his memory range. Erika Elwood's shameless baring of a body that would have chased Venus de Milo into seclusion had been an elixir for the middle-aging Lockington, and he'd made love better than he'd ever known how. She'd responded in feverish fashion, coming at him like a tigress, tossing, turning, moaning, groaning, crying out, pawing him, clawing him, biting his shoulders, heaving upward to meet his thrusts with a wiry strength that had made her difficult to control. Lockington said, "Sleep well?"

She said, "Yes, thank you," the first words she'd spoken in twenty miles. Then she drifted back into her thoughts, whatever and wherever they'd been. Lockington would have given a pretty penny to have been privy to what went on in that lovely head, but the thoughts of a woman are difficult to come by, and the thoughts of a *beautiful* woman are next to impossible. For a splinter of a second he wondered about the thoughts of Chicago fat women, abandoning the subject in haste.

He dropped his passenger at the entrance to the Chicago Morning Sentinel Building, ignoring the impatient blasts of automobile horns, watching, waiting until she was safely within the doors before pulling away. Pick her up at 5:15 sharp, she'd told him, kissing him before she'd left the car, and Lockington had promptly driven through a red traffic signal.

He parked the Pontiac in the Randolph Street lot, walking east to stop at the shabby Greek restaurant across from Classic Investigations. He ordered a cup of coffee, and he was valiantly attempting to drink the dreadful potion when Lieutenant Buck Curtin slid onto the counterstool next to his. Curtin's smile for Lockington was something considerably less than a smile. He said, "Well, heavens to Betsy, Lacey *Lockington*, fancy meeting *you* here!"

Lockington frowned into his coffee. "Yeah, downright amazing, ain't it?"

Curtin filched one of Lockington's cigarettes from the pack on the counter, lighting it with one of Lockington's matches. He said, "Say, by the way, Lacey, a fella got killed out in Evanston late yesterday afternoon."

Lockington nodded. "It happens all the time in Evanston—also Skokie, Park Ridge, Mt. Prospect, North—"

"This guy's name was Fisher, Gordon Fisher—he was an attorney for the Chicago *Morning Sentinel*—the *Sentinel*—that's the newspaper that got your ass suspended, if I ain't mistaken."

"You ain't mistaken."

"Well, as one detective to another, you got any opinions on this Fisher thing?"

"Yeah, I got an opinion. If he was a lawyer, he probably had it coming—particularly if he was a *Communist* lawyer."

"What an unsympathetic outlook."

"I'm an unsympathetic guy. Make a note of it."

"I'll do that. Fisher was the ex-husband of the chickie who got her brains blown out back a week or so—that former *Sentinel* columnist."

"That right? Coincidence, probably."

"No coincidence, baby, take my word for it! Somebody got an axe to grind with the Chicago *Morning Sentinel!*"

Lockington shrugged, sipping at his coffee.

Curtin said, "Now, here's the interesting part—according to Gordon Fisher's secretary, he had a telephone call from a man named Lacey Lockington of Classic Investigations—late afternoon call—she got the impression that it concerned something important. What was *that* all about?"

"I'll be brief."

"Don't hurry, you might make a mistake."

"Fisher stopped at the agency while you and I were playing peek-a-boo yesterday afternoon. He talked to Moose Katzenbach—said he wanted to be contacted. I called Fisher twice—the first time he was on another line, the second time he was out of the office. That's it, *all* of it."

"Katzenbach—Katzenbach—yeah, another busted-down ex-cop. What's Denny running, a fucking refuge for washouts?"

"It's temporary, only temporary."

"Any idea what Fisher wanted?"

"I figure it may have had something to do with his

wife's death."

"Why would he come to you instead of the law?"

"Why did the mule shit in the church yard?"

"Where were you late yesterday afternoon?"

"On my way to St. Charles, Illinois."

"How about last night?"

"In St. Charles—or just north of it."

"Doing what?"

"Talking to a client of Classic Investigations."

"All *night?*"

"That's the way it worked out."

"The client will corroborate that yarn?"

"I expect so."

"Sex?"

"Not often these days—getting old, y'know."

"The *client's* sex, asshole!" Curtin's eyes were bloodshot chips of ice.

"Female, I believe."

"Well, God *damn*, Lockington, you *do* get around, don't you? Okay, let's have her name."

"I don't have to divulge such information, you know that."

"You don't have to divulge such information if you're a private detective, but you ain't no fucking private detective."

"No, but I'm a paid employee of a private investigations concern. Same applies."

"Uh–huh." Curtin got up, slapping Lockington on the shoulder, digging in, feeling for a holster strap. "Watch yourself, grifter—this time tomorrow, your keester could be sucking buttermilk."

"This time tomorrow there'll be fucking bluebirds over

the fucking white cliffs of Dover, just you wait and see."

The Greek behind the counter glanced up sharply. He snapped, "Watching yoom language—sometimes ladies come this place!"

Curtin said, "Any lady comes *this* place ain't no lady."

The Greek bristled. "Hey, yoom wanting me throwing yoom ass *out?*"

Curtin jerked his wallet, flipping it open to flash his buzzer. He said, "Hey, yoom wanting fast visit from fucking Health Department?"

The Greek's smile was a ghastly thing. He said, "No troubles, mens—too early in morning."

They went out, Lockington and Curtin, Lockington crossing Randolph Street to Classic Investigations, Curtin walking east toward State Street. Curtin waved. Lockington waved back. For a few moments there, they'd been on the same side.

38

It was 9:50 A.M. and Lockington was seated at the agency desk, tangled in a web of cigarette smoke and somber thoughts, staring at nothing in particular, mulling matters over and over and over, trying to get a grip on a thing that had no handle, grabbing big, slippery chunks of thin air. At 9:55 Moose Katzenbach came lurching in, sinking onto the client's straight-backed wooden chair with a whooshing sigh. He backhanded sweat from his forehead. He growled, "Thursday mornings suck."

Lockington nodded. "You are a sage for the ages. You manage to turn anything on the Stella Starbrights?"

Moose made a wry face. "Well, yes and no—mostly no."

"Give me the yes part."

"Yesterday afternoon, I did just like you said—I went over to the main library and threw the *Chronicle's* obit wrap-ups on the microfilm screen." He tugged a small paper notebook from a shirt pocket, opening it, leafing rapidly through it. "So, this is what I come out with—the Fisher woman was born April 12, '53—Connie Carruthers was born June 6, '56. You registering this earthshaking information?"

"For what it's worth, consider it registered."

Moose pawed for a cigarette, found that his pack was empty, accepted a Marlboro and a light from Lockington before peering owlishly at his notebook. "Eleanor Fisher graduated from Northwestern University in '75, Carruthers from DePaul in '78—both were journalism majors. Fisher's maiden name was Leavitt, her parents live on North Olcott Avenue—Carruthers's maiden name was Kendall—her father's dead, her mother lives on North Ozanam. No brothers, no sisters involved."

Lockington said, "North Olcott, North Ozanam—same neck of the woods—any connection there?"

"Like what?"

"Like maybe Fisher and Carruthers attended the same school or the same church, or some God damned thing—*parallels*, Moose—we're looking for *parallels*!"

"There was nothing sticking out—you know the obits, Lacey—bare bones."

"Both were journalism majors—that looks like a parallel."

"Yeah, but what can we do with it? What the hell, if two doctors get murdered, both studied medicine—two pianists, both studied music—naw, there ain't much there."

Lockington was silent through a few heartbeats. Julie Masters had studied journalism. Fisher and Carruthers had scored—Julie hadn't. Julie never would. The cemeteries were full of dead journalism majors. Lockington shrugged it off. "Okay, anything else?"

"Not yet."

"Whaddaya mean, 'not *yet*'?"

"Well, I went from the library over to City Hall, but Bugs Grayson had taken the afternoon off—baseball flu. By then it was time to go home, so that's what I did."

"Logical, by God. Who's Bugs Grayson?"

"Bugs runs the City Hall data processing center."

"All right, what can he do for us?"

Moose said, "He just might scare up something you could hang your hat on. Duke used him from time to time. I came by City Hall this morning—took me fifteen minutes to find Bugs—he was feeling up a skinny blonde typist."

"Where?"

"All over, but he seemed to be concentrating on the groin area."

"Yeah, but—"

"In the water fountain alcove."

"That's better. Duke used this Bugs Grayson?"

"Oh, sure—you see, City Hall's data banks are loaded with offbeat information. When what little we have hits those computers, we could pick up a lot of minor league fallout—unpaid parking tickets, traffic violations, teen-age shoplifting raps—or maybe something bigger, like DWI's or drug charges or—well, you name it, and it's somewhere on a silicone chip."

"It ain't on a silicone chip if it never happened."

"Yeah, and Bugs wants fifty bucks—it probably ain't worth the shot."

Lockington said, "Give him fifty and we'll find out. What was Duke using Bugs for—what sort of information?"

"I dunno—I never handled that end of it. Looking for character background, no doubt. Take that J.B. Grimes, for instance—Duke told me that Grimes got pinched in '65 for messing around with a choir boy."

"Duke knew that Grimes was queer?"

"Yeah—I tailed Grimes—he was shacking with some immigrant kid at the Ellenwood on North LaSalle."

"Then why didn't Duke throw the switch on him?"

"Probably trying to raise the ante."

Lockington tried not to smile. Denny had handed him a piece of cake and all the credit. "Duke was paying Grayson fifty a throw for data bank information?"

"Naw, Duke was fixing him up with sure things—Bugs is a gash-hound."

Lockington dug into his thinning wallet and shoved a pair of twenties and a ten across the desk. "Is Buck Curtin still hanging around out there, making like fucking Philo Vance?"

"Uh–huh, he's stashed in an unmarked black Ford in the no parking zone out front—about as inconspicuous as a hog in a synagogue."

Lockington thought it over for a few moments. "Okay, Moose, get back over to City Hall and see if Grayson has anything of interest. Here's the office key—you'll probably be back before I am."

"You're cutting out?"

"For a couple hours, I figure."

"With Buck Curtin snapping at your ass."

"Not this trip. I'm using the rear door."

"Mind if I stick around and watch? We ain't *got* no fucking rear door."

"I know it." Lockington winked. "So does Curtin. I'll take the vestibule stairs up to the Polack's gun shop—the gun shop has a rear door."

"Will the Polack let you use it?"

"He'll let me use it if I tell him that I'm in the market for a new gun. When Curtin sees you come out, he'll think that I'm still in here, minding my own business."

"Where you headed?"

"I've got to swing by my apartment for a few minutes, and make a stop on North Michigan Avenue—I should be back about 12:30."

"Lacey, what the hell's going on? You can tell me—we're working the same beat, ain't we?"

"Moose, I don't *know* what's going on."

"Well, I don't wanta piss on your parade, but I think we're beating the shit out of a dead donkey. After all, what do we *have*?"

"Well, we got two ex-Stella Starbrights and one ex-Stella Starbright's ex-husband, all deader than Kelsey's balls."

"Ex-husband—*whose*?"

"Eleanor Fisher's—that Gordon Fisher who dropped in yesterday afternoon was hitched to the first Stella Starbright."

"And he's *dead*?"

"Shot—in an Evanston motel room."

Moose scratched his head. "I didn't hear about it. Sonofabitch! Small world, ain't it?"

"Yep, and shrinking by the minute."

"There's a hookup?"

"You'd better *believe* there's a hookup!"

"Well, baby, we'd better find it pronto! Buck Curtin thinks you killed the Stella Starbrights because that horseshit column got you suspended!"

Lockington shook his head. "I doubt that Curtin sees it that way. Curtin's a fox—he pretends to look north when he's looking east. He's pouring the heat to me because he thinks I'll tell him something or lead him to something. Curtin thinks I know more than I do, and he could be right, but if he *is*, it's dormant information—I can't wake it up."

"This guy Fisher—he was killed because he'd been married to one of the Stella Starbrights?"

"I don't think so."

"Then *why*?"

"Well, for one thing, he was the *Morning Sentinel's* chief attorney. For another, he came to Classic Investigations looking for help, apparently. There's a loose thread hanging somewhere, Moose—there always is. Say, just for the hell of it, have Bugs Grayson run Fisher through the computer— that's Gordon G. Fisher. Got it?"

Moose Katzenbach heaved his bulk from the straight-backed chair. "How about the telephone—I still don't answer it?"

Lockington said, "Look, it's unlikely, but if I need you, I'll ring twice, hang up, ring twice, hang up, and ring again— pay no attention to anything else. Duke Denny would skin me alive if he called here and got Moose Katzenbach, the guy he'd just fired."

Moose said, "I'm gonna give Curtin the finger." He headed for the door, then held up, turning to Lockington. "Hey, if we bust this one, you think maybe Duke would take me back?"

"Moose, this has all the earmarks of a national interest item. If we bust it, you could wind up being interviewed by Carson."

Moose grinned, slapping his knee. "God *damn*, Lacey, Helen would sure like that! Helen never misses Carson because once in a while he gets animals on the show."

Lockington nodded. "More like five nights a week, wouldn't you say?"

39

Chicago's west suburban telephone directory had the listing—Wright, Rev. Abraham J., 2397 Scott Street, 455-7600.

The old Pontiac clanged into Franklin Park, rolling west on Grand Avenue, turning south on Scott Street, the roughest thoroughfare in the northern hemisphere, Lockington was certain. The building stood on the southeastern corner of the Scott and Fullerton Avenue intersection, a dilapidated, one-story, red-brick affair that'd once been a coffee and tea warehouse if Lockington's dim memories of Franklin Park were serving him correctly. He pulled into the gravel parking lot, stopping there to kill the engine.

Lockington checked out the scene. There was a crude wooden cross, fashioned from 2x4's, nailed lopsidedly over the entrance, and on the northern wall of the structure was an amateurishly-lettered black-on-white sign: FIRST CHURCH OF CHRIST OUR GLORIUS AND CRUCIFRIED REDEEMER–REVEREND ABRAHAM J. WRIGHT, PASTOR AND TRESUROR. Lockington noted that

TRESUROR had been underlined. He left his car to crunch across the gravel and try the door. It was locked. Then he spotted the buzzer and punched it a couple of times, waiting until the door swung groaningly inward, sounding very much like a medieval drawbridge being lowered, Lockington thought. Or raised. Lockington possessed no authoritative knowledge of medieval drawbridges. A tall, bony, scraggly-haired woman stood in the doorway, listing perceptibly to starboard, eyeing him up and down. She was either a young-looking older lady or an old-looking younger lady. She had a black eye, a swollen jaw, a lacerated upper lip, a few gaps in her mouth where teeth once were, and she was at least six months pregnant—and drunker than forty barrels of owl manure. "Yesh?" she lisped, experiencing difficulty with her balance.

Lockington shrugged a non-committal shrug, not prepared to go on record at such an early stage in the ballgame.

The woman grabbed the doorframe for support. "Look, oshifer," she said, "thish whole thing all horbull mishtake— he never laid hand on me like I tole you on phone—whah happen wash am fall down goddam stairsh, sho you go way, okay?"

Lockington said, "Ma'am, I'm seeking an audience with Reverend Abraham J. Wright, and I don't know what you're talking about." The hell he didn't—Lockington had pulled more than his share of Chicago southside assignments.

"You not cop?" She fell forward, inflexible as a redwood, and Lockington crouched, catching her on a jutting shoulder, planting her in a more or less upright position. He said, "No, ma'am, I not cop."

She nodded, stepping unsteadily aside to grant him

entrance, closing and securing the door with fumbling hands before leading him through a deserted meeting area that would have handled approximately seventy-five people, the room furnished with unfinished backless wooden benches, a splintered piano, and a lectern that had once been a packing crate. Lettered on the front of the makeshift lectern were the words JESUS WANTS YOU FOR A SUNBEEM.

They proceeded down a long dim hallway that reeked of fried onions, his guide ricocheting from wall to wall like a ping-pong ball, and Lockington wondered if she'd gotten whacked in the mouth because she'd been drunk or if she'd gotten drunk because she'd been whacked in the mouth, deciding that it'd probably been one of those chicken-or-the-egg things, and that whichever had come first hadn't been first by much.

The woman raised her hand, halting Lockington's advance, this immediately prior to her opening a door and reeling into a room where she fell flat on her face. From the hallway Lockington could see a stout gray-haired man of some fifty years who sat behind a desk, peering through thick-lensed spectacles. He wore a red sweatshirt on which was emblazoned ABRAHAM J. WRIGHT MINISTRIES, INC., and he smiled at Lockington, saying, "A good mornin' to y'all, brother!"

Lockington entered the office, stepping carefully over the untwitching woman on the floor. He said, "Likewise." He scanned the room in search of a place to sit, settling for a stack of telephone books. He said, "You're Reverend Abraham J. Wright?"

"The same, brother, the very same!" He reached to shake Lockington's hand and Lockington observed that his knuckles were skinned and bruised. Reverend Abraham J. Wright smiled expansively. "Now, brother, y'all juss gonna hafta 'scuse the good Sister Lucy Penrod—Sister Lucy Penrod done receivin' the Holy Ghost and there juss ain't no predictin' the behavior of them as is privileged to host His Divine Presence!"

Lockington nodded. "Yeah, I notice that for openers, the Holy Ghost kicked the good Sister Lucy Penrod's front teeth out."

The Reverend Abraham J. Wright cleared his throat, checking a desk calendar. "Wall, brother, since y'all the gentleman interested in the comin' of the anti-Christ—"

Lockington said, "Uhh-h-h, well, Reverend Wright, there seems to be some misunderstanding here, because—"

"Ain't no misunderstandin', brother, no *how*—the anti-Christ ain't made his appearance yet, but he gonna git here, yes-siree, he gonna come in with a *bang*! He gonna be accepted worldwide as the rat man at the rat time, and, brother, thass when the manure gonna hit the windmill, thass when—"

Lockington said, "Yes, this is extremely interesting, but the reason I'm here is to inquire about—"

The woman on the floor moaned, heaving herself to sitting position. She looked bewilderedly around the room, rolled her eyes, said "Shit!" and collapsed, spread-eagled on her back.

The Reverend Abraham J. Wright said, "Oh, glory, the Holy Ghost rilly doin' a number on the good Sister Lucy Penrod this mornin'—she sho' nuff in ecstasy!"

Lockington didn't say anything, a policy that had paid handsome dividends from time to time.

The Reverend Abraham J. Wright said, "The Lord be

praised! When that roll is called up yonder, the good Sister Lucy Penrod gonna *be* there!"

Lockington said, "At this rate, she may be there to *call* it. Reverend, I've been given to understand that you're familiar with the conservative element in these United States—I'm talking about extremist right-wing groups."

Reverend Wright said, "Yes, wall, y'see, brother, y'all gittin' rat back to where the possum pooped in the pea-patch! Thass ezackly how the anti-Christ is gonna look to this here whole gullible world—he gonna look conservative, he gonna look *rat-wing*, he gonna look good, brother, I mean *good*! He gonna look *so* good that the people gonna fall all over theyselves elevatin' him to the pinnacle of world govinment, because by that there time, the people gonna have had enough of this here liberal stuff, the Godlessness, the indecriminit sex, the drugs, the filthy movies, the lack of respeck for the aged, and all these here Communist-inspired false—"

Lockington cut in on him. "Reverend, tell me, have you ever heard of an organization known as 'LAON'?"

Wright squinted at Lockington. "'LAON'? Whassit all about?"

"'LAON' stands for 'Law and Order Now.' It's a radical faction, possibly given to violence, or so I've been told."

Wright frowned, opening a desk drawer to produce a sheaf of papers, thumbing his way slowly through it, then repeating the process before glancing up, shaking his head. "Ain't no such outfit listed here, brother."

"Well, it's probably very small—"

"Don't make no never-mind how small it is—this here 'LAON' could be holdin' its conventions in a *phone booth*, and it'd still be on this here list! Y'see, I happens to be a student of such affairs on account thass where the anti-Christ gonna come from! He gonna pop outten the ranks of one of these here far-right movements, and I gonna be layin' in the tall weeds fer that rascal! Brother, y'all talkin' to the man what gonna alter the course of Biblical prophecy, you juss stick aroun' an' watch!"

Lockington studied the Reverend Abraham J. Wright. Behind the thick-lensed spectacles his eyes glittered, and there was spittle foam on his lower lip. Lockington said, "Well, thank you for your time and patience, Reverend."

"That gonna be twenty-five dollars, brother—the standard consultation fee," Wright said.

Lockington shrugged, taking out his wallet to drop a twenty and a five on the desk-top.

"Brother, I got a special package offer what oughta int'rest y'all—fer another twenty-five you git one of these here Wright Ministries sweatshirts, red, blue or black, and y'all git yer soul saved at the same time! I gonna put y'all on that high road to Heaven, shoutin', 'Glory, Hallelujah, to the Lamb of Calvary!'"

Lockington got to his feet. He said, "Another time, perhaps." He went out, stepping over the prostrate body of the good Sister Lucy Penrod. He drove back to Grand Avenue, turning east, listening to the tune he was humming, identifying it from his childhood church-going days. It would have made one helluva polka, Lockington thought.

40

Stunned and on short notice, Lockington hadn't tried to locate her relatives. He'd simply claimed her body and made the best arrangements he'd been able to afford. There'd been a funeral service of a sort, conducted in a sleet storm by a preacher of a sort. Two mourners had stood at graveside—Lacey Lockington and Duke Denny. Denny had seen his ex-partner through the gut-wrenching ordeal, at his side every bitter inch of the way. Lockington had never gotten around to introducing Julie Masters to Denny, but he'd spoken often of her, and Duke had told him that he'd felt like he'd known her personally, so vividly had Lockington sketched the woman, her likes and dislikes, her needs, her idiosyncrasies, her hopes for the future that was to be cut so short as to amount to hardly any future at all.

They'd trudged through the cemetery in February's slashing wind and Duke had said, "Want a drink, partner?"

Lockington had shaken his head. "Maybe next time, Duke—I gotta get my world glued back together. Thanks, anyway—thanks for everything."

Denny had squeezed Lockington's arm. He'd said, "We'll get this *bastard, Lacey—whoever he is, wherever he is, he'll surface one of these days, and we'll nail him! Did Julie ever mention anybody—an ex-boy friend, maybe?"*

"Just a guy named Herzog—he was somewhere in her past— prominent once, but that was over."

"Are you sure *it was over?"*

"Positive."

"Why are you *positive?"*

"Because she told me so."

Denny had said, "I can't argue with that, partner. Look, if you come across anything—if you get a lead, I'll help you run it down."

"I know that, Duke." Lockington had turned away to hide the last of his tears. He'd driven slowly to his empty Barry Avenue apartment, leaving a bit of himself to be lowered into a hole in the ground.

41

Erika Elwood had been a client of Classic Investigations for approximately eighteen hours. She'd remained unassassinated and she'd been a ring-tailed tornado in bed, neither development being so much as remotely connected to Lockington's acceptance of her case. In the first place, there'd been no call to defend her, and in the second place, Erika Elwood's sexual proficiency could have been born only of arduous practice, beginning back about the time Erika had turned fourteen, Lockington figured. At the moment, Lacey Lockington rated as very little more than an easily-seduced plug-ugly bodyguard, but situations change, and in Chicago they change abruptly.

He reached his apartment shortly before noon. He checked his mailbox, discarded a circular having to do with Texas ruby red grapefruit, showered, changed clothing, and attempted to phone Duke Denny in Cleveland. Jack Slifka answered on the second ring, and Lockington said, "Hello, Jack, this is Lockington."

"Lockington?"

"Lacey Lockington in Chicago—we've gone this route before."

"Gotcha—you're the guy who's watching the store while Duke's here in Cleveland, right."

"Right."

"And you wanta talk to Duke, right?"

"You're on a roll, Jack."

"Gotcha, Lockington! Well, old Duke's downtown at his lawyer's office—it got something to do with money."

"There ain't no other reason to be in a lawyer's office, is there?"

"Gotcha! Hey, you're one sharp article, Lockington!"

"I was given the distinct impression that Duke was going to get that matter straightened out yesterday afternoon."

"Yeah, and Duke was given the distinct impression that you were gonna be someplace where he could call you last night!"

"He tried?"

"Hell, yes, a couple dozen times—at some tavern and at your apartment!"

"Yeah, well, sorry—something came up—something I should discuss with Duke."

"Gotcha! I'll have him call you the minute he comes in. You're at the office?"

"Will be, in an hour, give or take—I'm out to lunch."

"Gotcha! Be a good boy, Lockington."

Lockington hung up, grinning. He rather liked Jack Slifka. Jack would probably be a good man to get drunk with.

He slipped his .38 police special into its shoulder holster, dropped them into a brown paper bag, tucked them into the back seat of the Pontiac, and wheeled south to Belmont Avenue, east to the Outer Drive, then south along the lakefront. Lake Michigan was royal blue, whitecapped, sparkling in the sun, probably Chicago's last decent possession, and Chicago was poisoning it at a twenty-four-hour-per-day clip. He tooled the Catalina into North Michigan Avenue, checking building numbers out of the corner of his eye. If you want to find out what's happening in a hotel or condominium, go to the hired help, the maids, the janitors. 814 North Michigan Avenue was swank—under-the-building parking, canopied entrance, uniformed doorman, balconies second-floor to top, beautifully landscaped, the whole shot, and the rent would be staggering—more than likely the reason for Erika Elwood's bailing out to take a small house in the western boondocks. She was probably making a husky buck grinding out the Stella Starbright column—fifty, maybe sixty grand a year, Lockington figured, but why spend half of it just to live on the Gold Coast? Prestige is not edible.

He swung the raggedy-assed Pontiac up the ramp and down into the underground garage, there to be confronted by the parking attendant, a fat woman clad in brown uniform and visored cap, who threw crossed arms in front of her face, a defensive gesture peculiar to those receiving visitations of demons. She screeched, "Hold it, *hold* it, God damn it to hell, *HOLD* it!"

Lockington had stopped at first glimpse of her. He poked his head through the window. "He said, "Ma'am, don't holler like that—I *am* holding it!"

She came snorting around the left front fender of the car like a mama rhino around a fever tree, panting, pointing an accusing finger at Lockington. "You fool, you nearly ran me down—my God, you were driving fifty miles an hour!"

"Ma'am, this vehicle won't *go* fifty miles an hour."

Her hands went to her hips, western gunslinger style. "And what's more, you don't even *live* here!"

Lockington nodded. "*I* know that. How did *you* know that?"

"Simple! No tenant of this building would get caught dead in that stack of scrap iron! There ain't no visitors' parking in the garage, so take it on the duffy, mister!"

"Okay, but one question, please. Has anyone come around asking about Erika Elwood?"

"Erika Elwood—the newspaper writer?"

"You got it."

"She moved—must be a month now."

"Would the doorman be available?"

"For *what*? He don't speak English—he's from Taiwan." Lockington shrugged resignedly. He'd drawn a blank, but nothing ventured, nothing gained. The attendant was studying him with narrowed eyes. She hissed, "Wait a minute—wait a *minute*!" She placed her hands on the roof of the old Catalina, lowering her head to the level of Lockington's, her voice to the level of a funeral director's. She said, "You're a goddam *detective,* ain't you?"

Lockington said, "No, I'm a discus thrower."

"Don't pull my leg, you rascal—this junk heap is just a *front*—you probably got a Mercedes at home! I know the signs, junior—I read all them detective books—got one right here!" From her jacket pocket she whipped a paperback copy of *Lust is the Reaper* by Judd Hamelwicz, holding it up for Lockington's approval. She said, "Helluva yarn, so far!" Her credentials having been presented, she whispered, "You city, county, state, Federal, or private?"

Lockington whispered, "Private—private as hell."

She whispered, "No point in my asking your name, is there?"

Lockington whispered, "None that comes readily to mind."

She whispered, "You're incognito, of course—nobody ever dresses that crummy unless they're incognito."

Lockington whispered, "Yes, incognito."

She whispered, "Why are we whispering?"

Lockington said, "Damned if I know."

"Whatcha working on—serial murders, jewel heist, blackmail?"

"Sorry, can't talk about it—not just yet."

"That makes it a national security thing—Chuck Carey couldn't talk about it, either."

"Chuck Carey?"

"In *Pentagon Hexagon*—third book in the series—when he smashed that terrorist gang—Chuck Carey, the real suave private investigator from New England."

Lockington said, "I used to know a guy named Carey, only he was from Massachusetts."

"I get the impression you ain't real suave."

"Used to be, before I caught the mumps."

"Say, if I hear or see anything that got to do with this Erika Elwood, I could give you a jingle. Is she dangerous?"

"She has her moments."

"My name's Ada Phelps."

"Mine's Lockington. At the moment I'm operating out of Classic Investigations on West Randolph—it's in the book."

It'd been a matter of casting his bread upon the waters. Besides that, he had to find a men's room. Within five minutes, preferably less.

42

He took the Pontiac into the garage, pulling to the guardrail between a black Cadillac convertible and a fire-engine-red Jaguar, one of those V-12 jobs that he'd read about. He backed out of the stall, cut sharply to avoid a baby blue Lincoln Town Car parked directly behind him, and zipped onto North Michigan Avenue, feeling the hair on the back of his neck prickling. He turned west on Chicago Avenue, stopping at a plush little bar called "Honolulu Harry's." He ordered a Martell's cognac, hit the lavatory, gulped the cognac on his way out, spurning the water wash. He threaded his way through Loop noonday traffic to the Randolph Street parking lot, hiking to the alley north of the agency, his head threatening to explode like a Fourth of July starburst, suddenly seeing things from an entirely different angle, a dozen possibilities swarming through his recently clogged mental passages, clamoring for attention like a litter of hungry puppies.

He slowed his hurried gait in the alley, climbing the

rickety wooden stairs to hammer on the steel rear door of the Polack's gun shop. In a few seconds it opened and the Polack said, "You again! Look, Lacey, this ain't no public fucking thoroughfare!"

Lockington brushed him to one side, stepping in. He said, "You happen to have a Repentino-Morté Black Mamba Mark III?"

The Polack said, "How many you want?"

"One should suffice."

"You got four-hundred-ninety-five dollars plus tax?"

Lockington said, "I got a check book."

"So do a whole bunch of con artists."

"I could show you my balance page."

"What's your balance?"

"One-thousand-seven dollars and change."

The Polack shrugged. "Any sonafabitch who got only a grand just got to be an honest man." He slammed the steel door, locking it, heading for the counter.

Lockington said, "You got a small machinist's file?"

"For a sawbuck, sure, I got a small machinist's file. What you want with a goddam machinist's file?"

"I'm gonna file notches in the handle of my brand-new Repentino-Morté Black Mamba Mark III."

"What for? You ain't shot nobody with it yet."

"The day is young."

The Polack grinned, plunking a slender, oblong mahogany box on the glass counter top, popping a brass latch, flipping the lid. The Repentino-Morté glittered coldly on its bed of red velvet, a rhapsody in blue steel. The Polack shoved an Illinois firearms form at him. "You're a cop—just sign it and I'll fill it in later."

Lockington found his ballpoint and signed it.

The Polack said, "You want me to load this thing?"

Lockington said, "Why not? It don't make no noise if it ain't loaded."

The Polack ejected the clip and got busy. He said, "What happened—you wear your .38 out?"

"Naw, I left it in the car—too much trouble to go back and get it."

43

Lockington came down the vestibule stairway from the gunshop, entering the agency office to place the Repentino-Morté box on the desk. Moose Katzenbach was seated in the client's chair, glancing up, folding his copy of the Chicago *Morning Sentinel.* He said, "I just finished reading *Stella on State Street.* Guess what?"

"Guessing what is for suckers."

"Well, Stella Starbright says that the Salvation Army is a neo-Nazi organization with plans that would make your fucking blood run cold."

Lockington said, "Jesus, I wonder who cranked *that* one up."

Moose said, "What's in the pretty box?"

"Either a five-hundred-dollar insurance policy, or a five-hundred-dollar mistake."

Moose opened the box and his eyes bulged. "Holy Christ, it's a Black Mamba, ain't it? Five hundred fish—wish I could afford one!"

Lockington said, "The feeling's mutual. Did Grayson have fifty bucks' worth?"

"I don't know if it's worth fifty, but you were looking for a parallel and you just got one."

Lockington sprawled in the swivel chair, putting a match to a crumpled Marlboro. He said, "Hit me easy, I got a bad case of bursitis."

"Eleanor Fisher and Connie Carruthers were adopted kids."

Lockington nodded. He said, "It's worth fifty."

Moose dragged out his dilapidated paper notebook. "Father unknown in both cases."

Lockington said, "Same mother."

"Yeah, same mother—woman named Mabel Hammerschmidt. You already knew that?"

"I didn't know her name was Mabel Hammerschmidt."

"'Mabel Hammerschmidt' don't mean nothing to me."

"No, because that was probably her real name."

"Well, sure, what *else?* You think maybe she had *two* names?"

"If she's who she *could* be, she could have had a dozen names."

"Yeah, and if she's who she *could* be, *one* of 'em might be Rebecca of fucking Sunnybrook Farm! What's *that* supposed to mean—'If she's who she *could* be'?"

The phone rang and Lockington said, "That'll be Duke, probably." It wasn't Duke, it was a woman. She said, "Classic Investigations?"

Lockington said, "Yes, ma'am, may I be of service?"

"Say, are you the guy what was here at 814 North Michigan Avenue half an hour ago?"

"Yes, ma'am."

"Well, Mr. Lockington, this is Ada Phelps."

"Yes, Ada. Do you have something of interest?"

"Yeah—you're being tailed!"

"Is that right?"

"You bet! I ran up the ramp to wave so-long, and there was this car parked down the block, headed south. The moment you hit the street, it came outta the chute, peeling rubber! It closed in tight behind you! You didn't *see* it?"

"If I did, I forgot it."

"Uh–huh, well, you see, I read all these private detective novels, and I'm hep—I know the *signs*!"

"Yes, you may have mentioned that. Man or woman driver?"

"Man—I didn't get a good look at him, but he was in a new white Buick Regal. You turned west on Chicago Avenue, right?"

"Yep."

"Well, he was right on your bumper, and I got his *license number*!"

"Good girl!" He was hoping that Ada Phelps wouldn't become a problem, at the moment there wasn't room for a 200 pound groupie, but he'd humor her and clear the line for Duke's call. He jotted the license number she gave him on the desk pad, thanked her, promised to take her to dinner one of these evenings, and hung up, continuing to scribble, tearing the sheet from the pad, pushing it across the desk to Moose, following it with five ten-dollar bills. He said, "Have Grayson run these through the grinder."

"When?"

"*Yesterday*—there may be a crack in the kettle! And for

kicks, check out that license number. Incidentally, Buck Curtin's still out there."

"Think he'll fuck up the detail?"

"Probably not—it's me he's keeping tabs on."

"Okay if I grab a sandwich?"

"Make it on the fly—you better stay out of that Greek joint across the street—it may be in a bind with the Health Department."

44

Lockington opened his Thursday afternoon think session by throwing LAON out of the ball game. LAON, if there *was* such an outfit, came across as a group of foaming-at-the-mouth crusaders, and LAON would have killed and bragged about it, because if there is anything a foaming-at-the-mouth crusader can stand a lot of, it's attention. And if Chicago's media had ignored the story, LAON would have passed out handbills or thrown leaflets from a blimp. It hadn't happened. Somebody was pulling Erika Elwood's lovely leg.

It was Lockington's first brush with anything resembling a serial murders case but, inexperienced as he was in such matters, he knew that there are just two types of chain killers—those that have motives, and those that don't, and he knew that the trick to apprehending either lies in being able to determine which is which. The Stella Starbright murders weren't of the thrill kill variety—they reeked of motive. On the average, premeditated murder motives amount to three—revenge, lust, and a yen for profit. So, if it was revenge, what was being avenged? And do you square an old grievance with a big city newspaper by killing its ex-columnists and its chief attorney? More than likely, you plant a bomb in its press room. Lockington crossed revenge from the motive list.

The lust angle was porous. Had Eleanor Fisher and Connie Carruthers jilted the same man? Erika Elwood had intimated that Gordon Fisher was ambisextrous—did that indicate that one of Fisher's pansy suitors had eliminated Fisher's wife and a woman with whom he may have passed the time of day, then knocked off Fisher for good measure? Lockington shook his head. No way. Lust was out.

The motive was *money*—it *had* to be. Somewhere, somebody entertained serious designs on Max Jarvis's fifty million dollar bank account, and—the telephone rang, scrambling Lockington's thoughts. He glanced at his watch. The time was 1:55. The voice on the other end of the line was familiar.

"Dammit, Lacey, where the hell were you last night? I tried to call you clear up until midnight!"

"Well, Duke, I was at the residence of our new client."

"*That* late?"

"And then some."

"So you managed to get in touch with Fisher."

"No, Fisher needs more than Classic Investigations. Fisher's dead."

"*Dead?*"

"If you trust coroners. He got blown away in an Evanston motel room."

"But, why—who—what the hell?"

"Would you believe that Buck Curtin is looking for

the same answers?"

"Curtin got you tagged for the Fisher business?"

"Curtin got me tagged for everything but the fucking Boxer Rebellion, and he ain't all that sure about the Boxer Rebellion."

Denny's sigh drifted over the line. He said, "Well, don't sweat it—that's just one less shyster, and you got an alibi— you *do,* don't you?"

"Yeah—our new client."

"Which is who?"

"Which is Erika Elwood."

Denny chuckled. "*Sure,* she is. By the way, who's Stella Starbright picking on now?"

"The Salvation Army, they tell me."

"Why not—who else is left? Seriously, partner, who are we working for?"

"Seriously—Erika Elwood—at five-hundred per day. You're to bill the *Sentinel.*"

"I'll be *damned!* Enlighten me!"

"I'm her bodyguard."

"Protecting her from what?"

"LAON, presumably."

"LAON *exists?*"

"I doubt it, but she's convinced."

"LAON got Fisher?"

"She thinks it did—Fisher was a Commie lawyer handling the legal affairs of a radically liberal news publication, which might have made him eligible."

"Yeah, could be. What do your duties amount to?"

"I pick her up at the Sentinel Building, drive her home, spend the night, drive her back to work in the—"

"Wait a minute—spend the *night?*"

"Yep."

"Hot *damn!* You see her butterfly tattoo?"

"She don't *got* no butterfly tattoo."

Denny laughed boisterously. "Way to *go,* Lacey!"

Over the wire, Lockington heard a clock chime twice. He winced, and filed that into the recesses of his crowded memory. Denny was saying, "Where should I call you this evening—or *should* I?"

"Uhh-h-h, under the circumstances, maybe you shouldn't. If anything pops, I'll call *you*—how's *that?*"

A smile crept into Denny's voice. "Well, you can *try,* but they're throwing a polka party at the corner gin mill tonight, and the pickings are mighty good in Cleveland, partner!" The line went dead and Lockington folded his arms on the desk, resting his chin on them, the position lending him the appearance of an aging jungle cat. The speed of foot had faded, but the hunter's gleam was bright in the narrowed eyes.

He took Erika Elwood's Repentino-Morté from his jacket pocket, cocking it, studying the expensive weapon, whistling tunelessly. He'd neglected to ask Duke Denny how he'd made out at the lawyer's office.

45

At 3:30 the agency office was stuffy and Lockington dragged a dusty electric fan from a closet shelf, placing it on a desk corner, plugging it in, throwing the switch. It didn't work. Lockington unplugged the device, lowered it gently to the floor, stepped back, and kicked it across the room. He retrieved it to repeat the ritual. It still didn't work. He shrugged a fatalistic shrug. Lockington's fatalistic shrugs differed slightly from his philosophic shrugs, but *so* slightly as to have been undetectable to all save veteran philosophers.

He sauntered to the vestibule, peering out. Lieutenant Buck Curtin was seated at the wheel of a black Ford sedan. Lockington's smile was thin. A silent battle in a war of nerves. He watched amazed as Curtin lit a cigarette. It was the very first time he'd seen Curtin light one of his own cigarettes. Lockington ambled back to the desk, getting there in time to pick up the telephone on its first ring. Moose Katzenbach said, "Whaddaya say, Nostradamus?"

Lockington said, "Watch your fucking language."

Moose said, "You got hold of something, Lacey—two more cookie cutter cases—both kids adopted—no father of record."

"Both Mabel Hammerschmidt's?"

"Right—four for four. Old Mabel must have been been having babies and *selling* 'em."

"In a sense, yes. Anything on that license number?"

"Yeah, white Buick Regal, owned by Traveler's Car Rental on Touhy Avenue in Park Ridge."

Lockington nodded. He said, "Rented by a guy named Herzog?"

There was a lengthy silence before Moose Katzenbach said, "Hey, look, Lacey, if you already know these goddam things, why blow a bunch of money and run my wheels off?"

"I don't *know* 'em, Moose—I'm just guessing."

"Uh-huh, well, if I could guess like that, I'd be at Arlington Park."

"Moose, with the kind of money that's involved in this mess, you could *buy* Arlington Park."

"So, it's going on four o'clock. Where do I go from here?"

"Get back to Grayson and—"

"I *can't* get back to Grayson—he left early—doctor's appointment."

"He got the clap?"

"I'm a sonofabitch—Lacey, you're really a *genius*!"

"Okay, knock it off for the day. Come by City Hall first thing in the morning. I'm still looking for something on Fisher and I'll want to know if a guy named Herzog got himself married lately."

"Fisher came up blank. How far back is 'lately'?"

"Within the last year."

"Hell, I forgot to get Herzog's first name from Traveler's Car Rental!"

"Doesn't matter. How many Herzogs can there be?"

"Maybe a million—the Mexicans are overrunning the country!"

"'Herzog' isn't Mex, it's German." Lockington hung up. It was 3:42. He put on his hat, locked the office, and went up the vestibule steps to the Polack's gun shop. He said, "Gotta use your back door again."

The Polack said, "Piss on you, Lacey—I got better things to do than let you in and outta that fucking back door!"

Lockington slapped him on the shoulder. They'd always gotten along in roughhouse fashion. "Last time, Stash— Scout's honor!"

The Polack scowled, taking out his keys. He said, "'Scout's honor,' huh? Hey, did you read the Stella Starbright column yesterday morning? Stella says them Boy Scouts ain't all they're cracked up to be! She says they're probably involved in drug trafficking." He unlocked the door, swinging it open. He said, "A guy on my block got a kid who's a Boy Scout—I better call him—maybe he don't know."

Lockington shook his head. He snapped, "No time for that! Call the *F.B.I.*!"

46

He'd swung the Pontiac sharply into the parking lot of The Viking Restaurant on Roosevelt Road in Winfield. She'd spun to stare at him. "Are we being followed?"

"I don't think so."

"Then what's wrong?"

"Nothing, yet."

"Then why are we stopping here?"

"Late bulletin. I'm buying dinner."

She'd telegraphed her acceptance, her hands going to her hair, the certain gesture of a woman about to enter a public place. She'd said, "That'd be nice of you."

They'd taken a dim half-circular booth to the left of the entrance. He'd had five vodka martinis in rapid-fire order. She'd kept pace with that many old fashioneds. They'd spent a nearly silent hour, studying each other. Then she'd said, "Won't all those martinis dull your reflexes?"

He'd said, "Something wrong with dull reflexes?"

"Well, no—but if anything were to happen tonight—

LAON, or whoever—"

"Nothing's going to happen tonight—LAON or *any*body."

"You're sure of that?"

"Positive."

"Why?"

"Because it's going to happen later, if it happens at all."

"'If it happens at all'? I don't follow."

"Is there easy access to Max Jarvis—I mean, can people just walk into his office and talk to him?"

"They can request an audience, but it's like getting in to see the Pope."

"Does he have a bodyguard?"

"Two."

"Good ones?"

"Ex-Green Berets, I understand—they look tough, if that's what you mean."

"That's what I mean. Then he's probably okay."

"Max is in danger?"

"Let me put it this way—as long as Jarvis is okay, *you're* okay."

"Why is that?"

"Long story."

"Will you have your own gun soon?"

He'd tapped his shoulder holster. "I have it now—picked it up today. Why do you ask?"

"Nothing, except that you're probably a better shot with your own gun than with mine."

"Not necessarily—most of 'em shoot where you point 'em."

She'd shuddered a delicate little shudder. "Oh, golly,

it's hard to believe that all this has happened in such a short time."

"What's 'a short time'?"

"Well, what's it been—a *week*?"

"No, this show has been on the road longer than a week. It dates back to February, probably beyond that."

"*Really*—that *long*? Lacey, I'm *afraid*!"

"So am I."

"I don't believe that—you seem so very much in *control*."

"I *am* in control—that's my problem."

"You're worried about *me*?"

"No, not about you—not at all."

"That's encouraging, but—you're afraid—of whom—of *what*?"

"Of how it's going to end."

"*Will* it end?"

"Yes, soon—*very* soon."

She'd lapsed into silence. So had Lockington. They'd had green salads and hot roast beef sandwiches and fries, exchanging occasional glances, nothing more. They'd driven to her house after dark. When she'd locked the door behind them, he'd sat on the big leather couch, placing her Repentino-Morté on the coffee table. He'd said, "You'd better put that thing away."

She'd picked up the superb 9mm pistol, transporting it carefully into her bedroom. In a few moments, she'd called to him. "Would you come in here?"

He'd left the couch and gone in there. She'd been naked, her back to him, turning down the bed. Without looking at him, she'd said, "Uhh–h–h, look, Lacey, we've had dinner, there are no dishes to wash, we're already drunk enough, and

I'm so Goddamned hot I may blow a gasket! Turn out the lights, please."

Lockington had turned out the lights, feeling a sudden melancholy. We never knowingly do anything for the last time in our lives without experiencing sadness. He'd read that somewhere. He'd sat on the edge of the bed, and she'd swarmed over him with the awesome white-tipped frenzy of a Solomon Islands hurricane. A sense of imminent danger will do that to some women. So will a sense of imminent wealth.

47

Moose Katzenbach came into the Classic Investigations office at 9:54 A.M. Lockington said, "Whatcha got?"

Moose said, "Plenty, but it'll have to wait. Curtin just parked out front and he was getting out of the car!"

From the doorway, Lieutenant Buck Curtin said, "Well, *well*, if it ain't the vanishing Lacey Lockington and Omar, the fucking tentmaker!"

Lockington said, "What—"

Curtin said, "Sit down and be quiet!"

Lockington said, "I ain't standing up."

"That simplifies it—now all you gotta do is be quiet!" He jerked one of Lockington's Marlboros from the pack on the desk, lighting it with one of Lockington's matches. He said, "For your information, that old back door stunt ain't gonna work no more!"

Moose said, "We don't got no back door."

Curtin said, "Don't start up with me, fatso! Now, shall we get down to brass tacks?"

Lockington said, "You better ask Moose—I ain't allowed to talk."

Moose said, "It's okay by me—I got nothing better to do."

Curtin said, "All right, I've just been notified that Mr. Max Jarvis is missing. So is his Rolls Royce automobile."

Moose said, "Which way did they go?"

Curtin said, "Straight up. Somebody stashed about twenty pounds of TNT under the front seat."

Moose said, "Next time, Jarvis better look under the seat."

Curtin said, "It knocked out windows in fucking Toledo!"

Moose said, "I got an aunt in Toledo."

Curtin said, "So, boys, if you'll put on your hats, we'll truck on down to 26th and California, there to discuss certain matters considered pertinent to Max Jarvis getting blowed clear the hell to Covington, Kentucky."

Moose said, "I know a guy lives in Covington."

Curtin said, "Drop your cocks and grab your socks—you're off to see the wizard."

Lockington said, "Are we under arrest?"

Moose said, "Covington's just across the river from Cincinnati."

Curtin said, "C'mon, c'mon, let's *go!*"

Lockington said, "Curtin, sit down and listen to me!"

Curtin said, "I'll listen to you in the interrogation room at 26th and California."

Lockington said, "If we're under arrest you gotta read us our rights."

Moose said, "That Covington's sure a swinging town."

Curtin's face was the color of a five-alarm fire. He said,

"Okay, on your *feet*!"

Lockington said, "You ain't told us if we're under arrest."

Curtin roared, "Yes, you sonofabitch, you're under *arrest*!" His voice had risen a full octave.

Lockington said, "Let's hear the charges."

Curtin clawed for his shoulder holster and Lockington threw up his hands. He got to his feet, giving Moose a meaningful look. He said, "Well, you can't argue with an officer of the law." He slouched from behind the desk. He said, "Except when he won't listen." He busted Buck Curtin very hard on the point of his clefted chin. Curtin's knees buckled and he sagged slowly, settling to the floor like Godzilla going down in Tokyo Bay. Lockington said, "Get his gun, Moose, and we'll prop him up in the swivel chair."

Curtin came out of it slowly, twitching, a slender ribbon of bloody saliva trickling from a corner of his mouth, his eyes returning to focus, becoming twin beads of smoking malevolence. He rasped, "You cocksuckers are gonna do big fucking time for *this*!"

Lockington hovered over Curtin, leaning forward to clamp a hand on the detective's shoulder. Very softly, he said, "Hey, Bucko, *I'm* gonna talk, and *you're* gonna *listen*!"

48

When she'd gotten into the car she'd said, "You've heard about Max, of course." Lockington had nodded, and there'd been no further mention of the matter. The sunset of August 30 flamed beyond the western horizon, giving Lockington the impression that hell had just boiled over. He knew that it *hadn't*, of course, but he knew that it *would*, and damned quickly. He drove through thinning conversation, turning north toward St. Charles on Route 25, rather than 31. Erika Elwood was frowning. She said, "Why the switch?"

Lockington said, "I could use a drink."

"There's a pleasant coincidence—so could I."

"Right about now, I'll bet you *could*."

"And what does *that* boil down to?"

"It comes under the heading of pointed remarks."

"Obviously. Care to explain it?"

"Over a drink."

"I'll appreciate that."

"I doubt it."

He nosed the dilapidated Pontiac into the parking lot of The Wigwam on North Avenue in downtown St. Charles. The evening was sultry and the stench of rotten algae boiled up from the sluggish Fox River to blend with diesel smoke from the never-ending chain of trucks snorting up the Route 64 hill. Lockington saw the Fox River as a second-class swamp, and St. Charles as an overrated, noisy, filthy little town. They went into the Wigwam, a dim, cool, sprawling place decorated with plastic tomahawks, novelty shop arrows, and shabby reproductions of oil paintings depicting Indians riding spotted ponies in pursuit of buffalo, doing war dances, shooting it out with blue-clad soldiers, and conducting any number of Indian-like activities. There'd been Indians along the Fox River a long time ago and they'd liked it no better than Lockington, apparently. They'd moved on. There were a few people at the bar but the dining area was deserted save for an elderly, birdlike woman at the piano who was playing it well enough for Lockington to identify "Only a Rose." They took a table in a remote corner of the room, Erika studying Lockington, toying nervously with the flouncy pink bow at the throat of her provocatively sheer white blouse. She was edgy, she'd been bumped off center. Lockington waved the menus away, ordering a double Martell's cognac. Erika asked for a Tom Collins and when they'd been served, she said, "There's something altogether different about you this evening, I can *feel* it—a sudden mood shift, I'd say."

He took a slug of his Martell's, rolling it briefly in his mouth in the manner of those who genuinely appreciate strong drink. "You're probably right."

"Which brings us back to your pointed remark."

Lockington said, "Yes, I'd like to speak with you regarding your husband."

49

Her head snapped up, her eyes wide, her mouth open. She gasped, "My—my *what*?"

Lockington smiled mild approval. He said, "Not bad, but no Oscar. Your husband flies two flags—he was born 'Dennis Herzog' in Cleveland, Ohio. He changed his name—in Cleveland, probably—legally, I'd imagine. In Chicago, he's known as 'Duke Denny', most of the time. 'Herzog' is the German word for 'Duke', but you know that. He's killed half-a-dozen people, and you know that, too."

Erika Elwood was sitting erect, outrage personified. She said, "My *God*, what on *earth* are you *talking* about?"

"I'm talking about one of the more efficient assassins of our time, and I had every intention of killing the sonofabitch until my mood shift, as you've termed it. It may not last long—mood shifts come, and mood shifts go."

She reached to touch Lockington's hand, squinting at him. "Lacey, are you all *right*—what the hell kind of tangent *is* this?" The response had underlined bewilderment, but there'd been no bite in its delivery. Her back was to the wall—she was parrying without thrusting.

Lockington banged his forearms flat on the table, hunching forward, speaking rapidly, tersely. "Okay, sweetie, let's scratch the peek-a-boo routine—there are three different scripts for tonight's grand finalé, and you're familiar with one of 'em. The script that you know, the one that you helped write, goes like this—you and I drive out to your house this evening and when we go in, who is sitting there but Duke Denny, brandishing your Repentino-Morté 9mm pistol. Duke shoots me, ostensibly an intruding vengeance-crazy ex-cop who's there to eliminate the last of the Stella Starbrights. This accomplished, Duke stuffs my .38 police special into my dead hand, and you call the cops—oh, Dear God in Heaven, your husband has just shot a marauder who was attempting to murder you! Then you two bastards stroll hand-in-hand into the sunset with Max Jarvis's fifty million clams. Not a terribly bad effort, you understand, but too transparent to get off the ground."

Erika was nibbling half-heartedly on the limp orange slice she'd plucked from the rim of her glass. She said, "Maybe you should get into religion, or group sex, or *something*." The barb was dull, her voice was flat, her train was off the rails, but when the smoke had cleared, she'd still have one move left, one *only* but it'd be brilliant, it'd look like a checkmate, and a tactician of Erika Elwood's caliber would be certain to sniff it out—Lockington was betting all the marbles on that. He listened to the piano. The old lady at the keyboard was engaged in a free-for-all with "The Riff Song" and the Riffs were getting the best of it.

In a few moments he said, "Duke has rewritten the

original script. His revised copy has him relieving me of my .38, plugging *you* with *my* gun, plugging *me* with *your* gun, placing my gun in my hand, and phoning the law to report that his wife has just been shot to death by a certain Lacey Lockington and that Lockington has been duly polished off. That way, you see, Lockington takes the rap for another murder, his seventh, and as your grieving widower and legal heir, Duke Denny pockets the fifty million dollars willed by Max Jarvis to his four daughters and their mother. Then Duke packs up and hauls ass for the Bahamas before they've finished singing 'Abide With Me' at your funeral or 'Down in Jungle Town' at mine. By the way, *that* won't fly, either."

She avoided his gaze, busying herself with an attempt to spear the elusive maraschino cherry in the opaque depths of her Tom Collins. Without looking up, she said, "Let's get this straight, shall we?"

Lockington said, "Don't you think it's as straight as we're likely to get it?"

"You're accusing me of participating in a plot to take your life, am I correct on that?"

"Lady, I'm not *accusing*, I'm merely stating *facts*—you've already cooperated in the murders of your mother, your three sisters, your ex-brother-in-law, and your father, so what's just one more? Jesus, woman, Lady Macbeth was a bush leaguer!"

She'd captured the maraschino cherry to snip it from its stem with white teeth. She was meeting his eyes now, her voice level. "Look, before we go further, let's examine the third version of tonight's script. It'll be yours, I assume."

Lockington said, "Uh—huh, all mine—well, prior to my mood shift, I'd figured things to develop in this fashion—

Duke gets my gun, aims it at you, pulls the trigger, and the damned thing doesn't go off. With that, he's blown the whole package so far as you're concerned, so with all bridges down and no way to get back, he thinks that he'll cook up a new yarn before he calls the police—possibly something about me breaking in and getting hold of your gun and him grappling with me, and you getting hit before he manages to shoot me. Then he ups with your Repentino-Morté and jerks the trigger and *again* nothing happens, which is because I've filed the firing pins of *both* guns flush to their hammer facings. Now we come to the very best part."

"The part where you walk on water?"

"No, the part where I kill Duke Denny."

"With *what*? You're fresh out of guns, remember?"

"I've neglected to mention that there's another Repentino-Morté behind the cushions of your leather couch. I stashed it there yesterday evening."

Her reply came a split second late and this pleased Lockington—the wheels were turning. She said, "However, since your mood shift, you don't want to kill Duke Denny right?"

"Let's say that I'm awaiting developments."

Her sudden smile illuminated their corner of the room. "All right, Lacey, you win! There was nothing personal in this—I'm sure you understand." She'd been highly instrumental in the cold-blooded massacre of her entire immediate family and she was handling it as she'd have handled being a day late with her rent payment—sorry, but something trivial came up.

Lockington said, "Why, of course—it was free enterprise that made America great."

"Is there a possibility that we can do business?"

"Not on paper."

Her face was expressionless, she was a trooper. With fifty more Erika Elwoods and a few rowboats, Lockington would have attacked the Spanish Armada. She was saying, "Lacey, which of us do you want the most?"

"Dead, you mean."

"Yes, dead."

Lockington ground the butt of his cigarette into their ashtray. "From a bright woman, a stupid question."

"It's Duke—it *has* to be *Duke* because of Julie Masters!" There was her proposition—a trade—Judas for Brutus.

Lockington put the torch to the fuse. "No affidavits."

She gave him a tight, knowing smile, nodding curtly, licking her lips, standing, smoothing her skirt. She said, "When I come back from the little girls' room, I may give you one more script."

"That'd make four—nearly all of 'em."

"*Nearly* all? There are *five*?"

"There'd *have* to be."

"But only three of us *knew!* Who'd have authored a fifth script?"

Lockington winked at her. "I'd say it was a joint effort—Satan and Almighty God."

She returned his wink. "And their medium?"

"A neutral, I'd think—a party who's served neither."

She threw back her head, laughing the soaring laugh that Lockington liked. "Ah, the cryptic remarks of Lacey Lockington! You'll excuse me for a few moments?"

"Certainly." He watched Erika Elwood depart the dining room of The Wigwam, a river boat gambler with an ace up her sleeve, shooting for astronomical stakes. She'd seen her one remaining move and she'd make it without hesitation. She'd been a worthy opponent, intelligent, sophisticated, courageous, audacious, thoroughly treacherous, and if Lockington had been running the CIA, he'd have recruited her at any price. Then she'd have sold out to the KGB.

He sat through a lengthy medley of Romberg stuff, selections from *New Moon* and *The Student Prince*, before motioning to the waitress. He said, "Would you be so kind as to check the ladies' room? I seem to have lost track of my companion."

The waitress said, "Oh, sir, I'm sorry—I thought you *knew!* She left in a cab several minutes ago!"

Lockington said, "Thank you. May I have another double Martell's?"

50

He drove north on Route 31. Despite the dense greenery
fringing the Fox River, he could see no beauty in the area—
there was an inhospitable bleakness about it, it'd sucked up
too much of Chicago's atmosphere. Erika Elwood's front
door was wide open, her driveway was blocked—there
were two Kane County Police cars, an ambulance, and a St.
Charles paramedics van. There was a dark blue Ford sedan
parked on the lawn—coroner's office, possibly—coroners
seemed to have a heavy thing for dark blue. There were
ten or more men clustered around the front steps and
Lockington recognized two of them—Lieutenant Buck
Curtin and Moose Katzenbach. He eased the Pontiac to
a halt on the graveled shoulder in front of the little white
house and got out. Curtin and Katzenbach headed in
Lockington's direction, accompanied by a leathery, hawk-
faced, gray-haired fellow wearing blue denim jacket and
jeans, gray Stetson hat, and low cut Western-style boots.
Buck Curtin accelerated, reaching Lockington in advance of

the others. There was a prominent bluish bruise on the point of Curtin's chin. He said, "As a fucking strategist you'd make a fine towel boy in a Chinese whorehouse!"

The man in the gray Stetson nudged Curtin aside, shoving out his hand. He said, "They tell me that you're Lacey Lockington."

Lockington nodded, extricating his hand from a tiger-trap grip.

The man in the Stetson said, "Pleased to meet you, Lockington. I'm Joe Leslie, Kane County Chief of Detectives."

Lockington was surveying the scene. "Looks like trouble."

Curtin guffawed. "*Trouble?* Naw, no trouble here, Lockington—this is the monthly meeting of the fucking Kane County Audubon Society!"

Joe Leslie quieted Curtin with a withering stare. He said, "When Lieutenant Curtin contacted me this afternoon, I was under the distinct impression that this thing would go a trifle more smoothly than it went."

Lockington said, "Uhh-h-h, yes—well, you see—"

Curtin said, "Yeah, we see, all right—we see what—"

Leslie waved Curtin to silence. "You were Erika Elwood's bodyguard?"

Lockington said, "Briefly—after a fashion."

Leslie said, "All right, shall we run through the matter just once, for my edification?"

Lockington said, "Suits me. Does it suit Lieutenant Curtin?"

Leslie ignored the tag-on. He said, "My understanding of it was that you were to bring the lady home and that you stood a good chance of being confronted by her husband who'd probably have a gun, a 9mm Repentino-Morté pistol with its firing pin filed flat. Right?"

"Right."

"You were to be wired and we were to wait back in the woods, monitoring and taping the conversation in the event they implicated themselves in half-a-dozen unsolved murder cases—we were prepared to take the couple into custody. This jives with the plan you sketched to Lieutenant Curtin?"

"That's the way it should have worked."

Leslie said, "Your own gun's firing pin was to have been filed, this to preclude the possibility of the husband using it when he disarmed you."

Lockington took his .38 police special from its holster, handing it to Leslie. "It's been filed—check it."

Leslie said, "Later." He slipped the weapon into his hip pocket. "You'd hidden a back-up gun behind a cushion of her living room couch, this one in good working order. You figured to cover them?"

"If it got down to hardball, yes."

"The plan came apart at the seams when Erika Elwood arrived alone in a taxi."

"She'd given me the slip in St. Charles—we'd stopped at The Wigwam for a drink."

"How did she manage to do that?"

"Simply enough—she went to the ladies' room and didn't bother coming back."

Curtin said, "It took you forty-five fucking minutes to find out she'd taken off?"

Leslie said, "Cool it, Curtin—*I'm* asking the questions." His voice was soft, but his eyes were gray flint.

Lockington said, "What happened here?"

Curtin said, "What *happened* here—what the fuck *didn't*

happen here, you stupid—"

Leslie said, "Curtin, you aren't in Chicago, you're in Kane County. Now, I'm requesting your cooperation and, God damn it, I'm going to *get* it, one way or another!" He returned his attention to Lockington. "She opened close-range fire when his back was turned, apparently. She got the whole clip into him—shot him in the heel, the calf, the upper leg, the hip, twice in the ass, twice in the back—he took one frontal hit in the left shoulder, probably when he was flat on the deck, getting one round off—he put it through her navel. Both were dead by the time we got the door knocked down."

Lockington made no comment.

Leslie said, "The firing pin of his gun had been filed, but not thoroughly—a trace of a stub remained—probably not enough projection to detonate a rim fire cartridge, but considerably more than enough to pop a fulminate of mercury cap."

Lockington said, "So I blew it."

Leslie was studying him with canny eyes, a smile twitching a corner of his mouth. He said, "Y'know, Lockington, I rather doubt that I'll ever be certain of that."

Curtin said, "If the second heater was hidden, how'd she manage to locate it five seconds after she went into the house?"

Lockington said, "That quickly?"

Leslie nodded. "There was gunfire almost immediately following her arrival."

Lockington said, "I guess she just lucked out."

Curtin stomped toward Lockington, hollering, "She just lucked out, *shit!* You *told* her where it was, you sonofabitch—

you set it up—you had it figured from scratch—you *wanted* a shootout!"

Leslie stepped into Curtin's path. He said, "It's *over,* Curtin—you're spinning your wheels!"

Curtin snapped, "They're *my* wheels, ain't they?"

Leslie said, "Don't push your luck."

Curtin puffed up like a pouter pigeon. He said, "Fuck you, you one-cylinder, barnyard shitkicker!"

Leslie cupped his hands to his mouth. He yelled, "Hey, Sam!"

A heftily-built young man left the gathering at the front steps, coming at a gallop. He said, "Yes, sir!"

Leslie said, "The coroner about through in there?"

Sam said, "Yes, sir—he's waiting for the photographer— they're gonna stop for a few beers."

"Okay, then you can run Lieutenant Curtin down to Geneva and lock his ass up."

Curtin grabbed Leslie by the front of his denim jacket. "On what *charge,* you tin star rube cock—"

Leslie set himself and nailed Curtin with a whistling right uppercut. Curtin staggered into the arms of Moose Katzenbach who caught him, picked him up, and dropped him face-down on the roadside gravel.

Sam said, "Yes, sir, but what *is* the charge, sir?"

Leslie glanced at Lockington. "Give me a charge, for Christ's sake!"

Lockington said, "How's 'chronic diarrhea of the mouth'?"

Leslie said, "You catch that, Sam?"

Sam said, "Yes, sir, but I can't spell 'diarrhea'."

There was a weariness in Joe Leslie's voice. He said, "Use the dictionary in my desk—bottom drawer."

51

Moose Katzenbach broke the Route 31 silence. He said, "There ain't no LAON?"

Lockington said, "LAON was a gimmick designed to mess up my thinking, and it *did*. What time did Duke show this afternoon?"

"Shortly after three. We'd been in the woods behind the house since about two—Joe Leslie knows the area—he brought us in on foot from a side road."

"How did Duke get there?"

"Came in a cab—he probably ditched that rented Buick in St. Charles."

A yellow full moon was topping the hills beyond the slimy muck of the Fox River. Moose said, "Any idea why Duke changed his name from Herzog to Denny?"

"He didn't trash 'Herzog', he used both names. There were certain advantages, two valid driver's licenses, for instance. He was 'Herzog' to one woman, 'Denny' to the next. Duke was a slippery guy."

They were rattling eastbound through Streamwood when Moose growled, "Well, it was her best shot at the whole fifty million—they'd needed each other to get that far down the pike, then I guess it became a case of 'what have you done for me lately?' Hell, since when ain't twenty-five million been enough?"

"Since there's been *fifty* million."

Lockington could sense the big man's struggle to herd recent events into understandable order. After a while Moose said, "Y'know, Lacey, if you'd given that firing pin a couple more strokes, she'd have dropped Duke, he wouldn't have fired a shot, and she'd have been on top of the world!"

Lockington nodded. "She'd have walked free on a self-defense plea—the gun in Duke's hand was her ticket to anywhere."

"Yeah, but, dammit, how do you claim self-defense when you've shot the other guy in the *back*?"

"Joe Leslie said that he took one in the left shoulder from the front, probably the last round in her clip, but it *could* have been the *first*, her response to being threatened with a gun, and how would they prove differently? Duke was right-handed—if he'd been shot in the *right* shoulder, he'd have dropped his gun and there'd have been an element of doubt, but as it worked out, there'd have been none."

Moose said, "She'd have claimed that she'd blacked out, not realizing that she was still blazing away—the blind panic thing."

Lockington said, "Erika Elwood was an excellent actress—she'd have sold that package to any jury in the country."

"*If* they'd bothered to indict her."

"Which is doubtful."

"I wonder why she tore him up like that—it was almost like she *enjoyed* it, thinking that he couldn't shoot back."

"If that's what she thought, it cost her. Duke was a lead-pipe cinch to get *one* in—he was a damned good hand with a gun."

"But why would she *think* that?"

"How do we know that she *did*?"

"What about that firing pin, Lacey?"

Lockington lit a cigarette, pitching the match through his open window, ushering in a long period of silence.

Moose didn't chase the subject. Instead he said, "She must have known that Duke intended to kill her."

"Apparently."

"How would she know?"

Lockington shrugged. "Female intuition, maybe."

Moose shifted his bulk on the sagging front seat of the Pontiac. He said, "What kicked this business off in the first place?"

"Fifty million dollars."

"Yeah, but where did it actually *begin*?"

"God knows. I'd say that it started with Duke Denny who may have struck up a drinking buddy relationship with Gordon Fisher, possibly on the Gold Coast. Fisher had big bucks, Duke pretended to be up in the chips, and the Gold Coast attracts both types, the genuines and the phonies. Somewhere along the line, Fisher could have hoisted a few too many and let it slip that his ex-wife was the daughter of Max Jarvis and that she, her mother, and her sisters would hit the jackpot when Jarvis died."

"And who would know better than Fisher? He was the

Sentinel's attorney and he'd drawn up the will! You think he identified the other beneficiaries by name?"

Lockington shook his head. "Probably not, but Duke had been a police detective, he knew the tracer's tricks, and he had Bugs Grayson and the City Hall computers at his disposal—chances are he took much the same course that we've taken. Duke was a man dedicated to hitting the heavy lick, the one that'd put him on Easy Street. This was a long shot, but it represented a chance to score big. He located the ladies in question and he went to work. When Duke Denny was in overdrive, the average female was at a decided disadvantage!"

"You're saying that he romanced *all* of 'em with an eye toward marrying one."

"Exactly. Marry one and eliminate the others."

"He made it with their mother, the old stripper?"

Lockington grinned. "Why not? She'd have appreciated the attentions of a younger man. Duke was *thorough*."

"Yeah, but, Jesus Christ, she must have been a thousand years old!"

"Uh-huh, but for fifty million it could be managed, don't you think?"

"So he got acquainted with 'em, charmed 'em into bed, and sorted 'em out."

"They were easy lays—Julie Masters was a lost lamb, confused, a snap for a guy with Duke's persuasive powers—Eleanor Fisher was a hot-crotched divorcee, so was Connie Carruthers. A few repeat performances and he had 'em sized up. He settled on Erika Elwood—she was the prettiest, the sexiest, the weakest in a few respects but the strongest overall, certainly the greediest. Duke poured on the coal, marrying her in January. He felt her out—did she know that five people stood between them and fifty million dollars? Erika Elwood knew a good thing when she saw one—Erika went along."

"She actually dropped the boom on her own *family*?"

"That wouldn't have been particularly difficult for Erika—she'd never known these people as relatives, and it wouldn't have made a great deal of difference if she *had*. The bottom line was fifty million bucks and Erika wasn't the type to get sidetracked by sentiment."

"Julie Masters was the first in line?"

"Yeah, Duke got it into Julie early, and when she'd moved in with me, he continued to see her—not often, but once *too* often."

"They'd set you up as their fall guy right from the beginning?"

"No, their campaign was already underway when they realized that I'd make an excellent red herring. I shot Sapphire Joe Solano and Stella Starbright did a column on that. The Timothy Gozzen incident helped, and when that thing with the two Mexican switchblade artists got me suspended, I'd become a coincidental bonus, a guy convincingly portrayed as a screw-loose renegade likely to go off the high board with no urging."

"Okay, but why did they need you, anyway? Nobody suspected either one of 'em—they could have taken the money and lammed."

"I was the plug, Moose—a dead Lacey Lockington would have sealed off the past, there'd have been no further investigations of the murders. The law would've jumped at the chance to clear the books. Framing a corpse is easy—it'd have worked."

They were at Elmhurst Road and North Avenue, waiting for a green traffic signal. Moose said, "What put you onto Duke—where did he slip up?"

"Well, the clincher came when I stumbled onto his black Cadillac convertible parked in the underground garage at 814 North Michigan Avenue where he lived in Erika Elwood's condo, but there were other little blunders. He called, ostensibly from Cleveland, on the afternoon following the death of the Carruthers girl, and he mentioned that his Cleveland attorney would be closing his office in three hours."

"All right, what about it?"

"Duke called at two, lawyers close shop at five, there's a one hour time differential between Chicago and Cleveland, it was *three* o'clock in Cleveland, and a Cleveland attorney would have been closing his office in *two* hours, *not* three. Then he called yesterday, and during our conversation I distinctly heard a clock chime *Chicago* time. I ain't no Ellery Queen, but I can do simple arithmetic."

"Then he never *was* in Cleveland—not at *all?*"

"I don't think so. He probably packed a suitcase and left his apartment like he was going on a trip. He moved into Erika Elwood's apartment and he did Connie Carruthers, Gordon Fisher, and Jarvis from there."

The traffic signal flickered to green and Lockington eased the Pontiac into the intersection, braking abruptly to avoid a southbound Omni that had ignored the red light. A fat woman, Lockington thought. Moose said, "How did you pinpoint tonight as fireworks night?"

"With Max Jarvis out of the way, I represented the last

barricade. Erika Elwood had maneuvered me into exactly the right position for the *coup de grâce*, the plan appeared to be working flawlessly—Duke had momentum. I knew how he thought, he believed in striking while the iron was hot—tonight *had* to be the night!"

"Straighten me out on something. Why did he hit Gordon Fisher? Fisher couldn't have figured into the Jarvis will, not when he was divorced from Jarvis's dead daughter."

"Gordon Fisher was no numbskull. He recalled telling Duke of the Jarvis will conditions and if he didn't know that Duke and Erika Elwood were married, he certainly knew that they were close companions. He put two and two together, and if he didn't come up with four, he had a sure three-and-a-half. He came to Classic Investigations to question Duke Denny and he bumped into you. I made mention of the Fisher contact to Duke. That was a mistake—it got Fisher murdered."

Moose said, "They couldn't possibly have hung all of those killings on you."

"If I was alive, no—but I wouldn't have *been* alive, and dead men have no alibis."

"What about this Cleveland character who was covering for Duke?"

"Jack Slifka. Slifka kept Duke informed, and he lied for him, but I think Jack's okay. Slifka probably thought that he was helping Duke with some sort of innocent practical joke."

Moose stretched and yawned. "Well, I gotta say one thing for old Max Jarvis—he took good care of his own. But how come Julie Masters didn't get a crack at that Stella Starbright column?"

"She'd probably received a job offer from the *Sentinel*,

but Julie was geared differently, her ambition was to write a novel. Julie was a dreamer—hardly practical enough to settle into the everyday grind of a newspaper column."

They were in Chicago and the moon was high, its glow dulled by city night-smog. Moose Katzenbach said, "Uhh–h–h, Lacey, one more question, if it's any of my business."

"Shoot."

"How was Erika Elwood in bed?"

Lockington thought it over. Then he said, "Like fifty million dollars."

52

It was a typical Friday night at the Shamrock Pub when Lacey Lockington walked in at 11:45. He sagged onto a seat at the end of the bar, just in time to see Jennifer Hallahan fall head-first from her barstool. Mush O'Brien said, "The usual?"

Lockington nodded, watching Rip Rafferty knock Tom Conroy on his ass. Lockington said, "Full moon tonight."

Mush O'Brien said, "Yeah, and all them werewolves ain't out in the woods."

There was a light touch on Lockington's shoulder. Edna Garson stood beside him, studying him with smoky-blue eyes. She said, "Let's go to bed."

Lockington said, "But I just got here."

Edna said, "So did I. Let's go to bed anyway."

Mike McBride threw a chair through the television screen. Lockington said, "You want a drink?"

Edna said, "No, I want to go to bed."

Mamie Horton got sick on the floor. Mush O'Brien covered his eyes with his hands. He said, "Oh, Great and

Flaming Omnipotent God Almighty!"

Edna Garson said, "Locky, have you ever seen a woman go up in flames?"

Lockington said, "Not to the best of my recollection."

Rosie O'Toole was whacking Hank Desmond over the head with a beer bottle. Edna said, "Well, if we ain't in bed by midnight, *you* are in for a brand-new experience!"

The bar phone was ringing and Mush O'Brien grabbed it, speaking briefly before handing it to Lockington. He said, "For you."

Lockington took it and growled, "Yeah?"

Moose Katzenbach said, "Hey, Lacey, are you watching television at the Shamrock?"

Lockington said, "No, the television set's out of order."

Moose said, "Big fire downtown!"

Lockington glanced at his watch. It was 11:54. He said, "In just six minutes there may be one at the Shamrock."

Moose said, "The Chicago Morning Sentinel Building's burning and they can't save it—she's going to the ground!"

Lockington said, "I'll be damned!"

Moose said, "WGN got a mobile unit on the scene and it just announced that a radical group is claiming responsibility—outfit identifying itself as 'LAON'."

Lockington didn't say anything.

Moose said, "Lacey, you get that?"

Lockington still didn't say anything.

Moose said, "Lacey? You there, Lacey?"

Lockington said, "Yeah, I'm here, Moose. How did the Cubs do?"

"They're in the sixth at San Diego—losing 5–1."

Lockington said, "Okay, Moose, have a nice weekend."

He returned the phone to Mush O'Brien.

Clancy O'Doul slugged Dave Flanagan, driving him through a plate glass window. Approaching police sirens wailed from the east. Daisy O'Dugan kicked Studs Cassidy in the groin. A vast fatigue was settling over Lacey Lockington. He took Edna Garson by the arm, peering at his watch. He said, "Can we make it to your place in five minutes?"

DEATH WORE GLOVES

When Sister Rosetta's niece goes missing, the nun (whose favorite poison is anything bottle-bound and boozy) hires shifty P.I. Tut Willow to find dear Gladys. But as Tut pulls back the curtain on Gladys' checkered past, he also finds that someone doesn't want her found, and soon bodies begin to pile up. Is Sister Rosetta, lured by a twisted sense of family loyalty, behind the deaths of those out to harm her niece, or are Tut and Gladys just pawns in a much darker game?

Full of laugh-out-loud comedy and the darkest of intrigue, the author of *Death Wore Gloves* draws together femme fatales, a not-so-saintly nun, and a gumshoe willing to do anything to help an old flame.

KIRBY'S LAST CIRCUS

When the CIA chooses Birch Kirby, a mediocre detective with a personal life even less thrilling than his professional one, no one is more surprised by the selection than Birch himself. But the Agency needs someone for a secret mission, and Birch may be just the clown for the job. Going undercover as a circus performer, he travels to Grizzly Gulch to investigate the source of daily, un-decodeable secret messages that are being transmitted to the KGB. Birch interacts with wildly colorful characters while stumbling through performances as well as his assignment. With the clock ticking, Birch must hurry to take a right step toward bringing the curtain down on this very important case.

THE LACEY LOCKINGTON SERIES

THE DEVEREAX FILE

Former cop, now private investigator, Lacey Lockington gets lured into a case of something less smooth than his usual tipple: the death of his old drinking buddy and ex-CIA agent Rufe Devereaux. No sooner does he start his investigation than he finds himself chased by the Mafia, hunted by the CIA, stalked by a politician-turned-evangelist out to kill him and "helped" by the sultry Natasha, a KGB agent who always knows more than she lets on. Sucked into the dangerous world of international espionage, Lacey knows he is in way over his head. What started as a search for the truth behind his friend's death turns into a whirlwind tour that leads Lacey from the gritty bars of Chicago to Miami's cocaine-filled underbelly and culminates in an explosive ending that must be read to be believed!

THE FEDOROVICH FILE

The Cold War heats up when trouble comes knocking on the door of ex-cop turned Private Eye Lacey Lockington. Lacey is hot on the trail of Alexi Fedorovich after the high-ranking general publishes a controversial exposé detailing that Glasnost/Perestroika is a hoax. Federovich goes into hiding in the last place he suspects someone will look for him—somewhere in Youngstown, Ohio.

For someone who's pretty much seen and done it all, Lacey's unnerved when he starts dealing with Russian spies, Federal Agents, a man who doesn't want to be found, and an increasing body count of all his leads. Will Lacey, along with former KGB agent and live-in lover Natasha, get to the bottom of it all before Fedorovich finds himself on the wrong end of a firing squad?

THE CHANCE PURDUE SERIES

THE DADA CAPER

Chance Purdue may be better at a lot of things than he is at detecting, but he's the only man for the job when the FBI comes looking for someone to take on the Soviet-inspired DADA conspiracy.

Plus, he needs a paycheck. Chance gets off to a rough start as he's led on a merry chase through Chicago's underbelly and drawn into a case of deception that can only be solved with the help of a mysterious femme fatale who's as beautiful as she is cunning.

THE REGGIS ARMS CAPER

Try as he may, Chance Purdue can't seem to escape the world of private investigation. The now tavern owner returns to action to protect Princess Sonia of Kaleski, who claims to be the wife of an old Army buddy. Convinced he'll get to the bottom of things at his Army battalion's reunion, Chance indulges in the entertainment while leaving the more serious detective work to his new colleague, the scintillating Brandy Alexander. For Chance, the case provides more fun than intrigue, and yet its solution is a surprise for everyone involved.

THE STRANGER CITY CAPER

A quick and easy buck sounds good to Private Investigator Chance Purdue. But the paycheck seems to be a bit harder to earn when the job entails more than just looking into the a minor league baseball team in southern Illinois. His new client, the gangster Cool Lips Chericola, is definitely leaving out details. Enter Brandy Alexander, whose unexpected appearance in Stranger City, Illinois complicates things. Then throw in the Bobby Crackers' Blitzkrieg for Christ religious crusade, and you've got a super-charged powderkeg of a caper, with Chance holding both the match and the barrel.

THE ABU WAHAB CAPER

What happens when Chicago detective Chance Purdue is hired to protect a gambler with a target on his head? For starters, all hell breaks loose…

"Bet-a-Bunch" Dugan is being hunted by International DADA (Destroy America, Destroy America) conspirators, a terrorist organization out for control of the world's oil market. Dugan needs more than a little luck to walk away unscathed. He needs a Chance, and though he knows that half of Purdue's reputation is that of a guy you are aching to punch, the other half is that he's a dogged, if occasionally doomed, investigator.

No matter where Purdue's leads take him, though, he always seems to be one step behind DADA. As a hapless Chance watches DADA's deadly scheme move forward, a siren named Brandy Alexander enters the picture and things finally fall into place, or so Chance hopes…

THE RADISH RIVER CAPER

Private Investigator Chance Purdue and Brandy Alexander work in tandem on a case that finds them traveling to the Illinois town of Radish River. The CIA continues to need help putting a stop to the DADA (Destroy America, Destroy America) Conspiracy, a terrorist organization whose latest plot is completely under wraps, except that it promises immense destruction. Things prove difficult for Chance and Brandy as they do what they can to remain focused on the task at hand. But it's hard when distractions from football-playing gorillas, chariot races, copious booze—and especially each other—weave in and out of their lives and keep this case on the back burner.